TREACHERY AND TRIUMPH

AN ANTHOLOGY OF WORLD WAR II STORIES

Edited by Jeremy Mouser

PNEUMA SPRINGS PUBLISHING UK

First Published in 2015 by:
Pneuma Springs Publishing

Treachery and Triumph – An Anthology of World War II Stories

ISBN13: 9781782283959

British Library Cataloguing in Publication Data. A catalogue record for this book is available from the British Library.

Pneuma Springs Publishing
A Subsidiary of Pneuma Springs Ltd.
7 Grooviest Road, Dartford Kent, DA1 5JD.
E: admin@pneumasprings.co.uk
W: www.pneumasprings.co.uk

This is a work of fiction. Names, characters, places and incidents are either products of the author's imagination or are used fictitiously. Any resemblance to actual events or locales or persons, living or dead, save those clearly in the public domain, is purely coincidental.

War is treachery and hatred, the muddling of incompetent generals, the torture and killing and sickness and tiredness, until at last it was over and nothing has changed except for new weariness and new hatreds':

Col. Lanser in John STEINBECK, *The Moon is Down* (1942),

chap. 2, Heinemann p. 25.

Acknowledgement

Thanks to all the anthology contributors for being a joy to work with.

Alone we can do so little;

Together we can do so much

- ***Helen Keller***

CONTENTS

Cometh the Enemy
Karl Brockmann

The Bakelite telephone lets out its high-pitched ring for the umpteenth time before anyone answers it. A tall adjutant eventually saunters over; lifting the receiver he speaks in a slightly irritated voice:

'Ja, Divisional HQ. How can I help?' The voice at the other end relays the message, and the blood can be seen to drain from the adjutant's face. In not such a lofty voice as before, he assures the caller that he will pass the message on immediately and almost sprints through the corridors of the vast building to deliver the bad news.

On the Normandy coastline, the bad news is already a reality. On 6 June 1944, an armada of vessels in the English Channel inches closer towards the fortified beaches. Huge shells from the warships roar overhead and explode with devastating effect amid the defending German forces in the towns and villages, which occupy the land next to the shoreline. The defending troops have been expecting this attack at some point, but at which stretch of coastline has been unconfirmed until now. Communications are frenetic with orders and counter-orders as men rush into position to defend their stations along the 'Atlantic Wall'.

A young lieutenant peers into the supply-room of his bunker and feels his neck redden and his chest tighten as he realises that the bunker will have enough ammunition to fend off such a large force for no more than a matter of hours and not days, as he has been instructed to do at various command meetings held over the previous months. Turning the handle on the side of his black telephone he contacts the next bunker along:

'Otto, it's Klaus here: do you have any spare ammunition that we can have? We are looking seriously short if we are expected to hold off that lot.' An almost hysterical laugh - the reply he gets - is not what he needs to hear.

'Are you joking, my friend? I have even less than you! When Field Marshall Rommel inspected these bunkers a few months ago, I heard him say our defences are too stretched out with nowhere near enough supplies for us to do our job properly.' Returning the hand-piece to its cradle, Klaus once again peers through his binoculars at the growing menace which is heading his way.

As the morning unfolds, it becomes apparent that the Allied forces are trying to establish five bridgeheads along the French coastline in an attempt to deliver over 155,000 initial troops, complete with armoured vehicles, on to French soil. The smell of spent ammunition fills the interior of the bunker as the MG42s burn their way through another ammo-box of bullets at an unbelievable rate. The men on the receiving end down on the beach take the full force and lie shattered and bleeding all around. The Allies have managed to get close enough to disgorge their landing craft of men, only to be annihilated before making any headway at all through the tangle of barbed wire and tank-traps which are strategically placed all along the shore line.

'Keep the fire rate up, men!' shouts our young lieutenant as he toils to deliver his MG crews sufficient supplies to carry out the orders he has just instructed them to do. Outside, the bullets and missiles from the Allies pepper the exterior of the concrete bunker, chipping and blowing great chunks out of the superstructure which, despite all of the attention it is receiving, still stands firm. The sea-water is a shocking sight, with hundreds of dead and dying soldiers polluting the water with their blood, which gives the waves a deep burgundy colour as they roll up on to the sandy beach. Another wave of landing-craft attempt to land, and, as the front of these vessels drop down exposing the men inside, the defending gunner's fire into these boats giving the occupants no chance of ever making it to dry land. One such craft also takes a direct hit from a hand held Panzerschreck which blows some of the occupants apart, scattering body parts into the water.

Despite the causalities, the Allied attack continues, as, once the whole thing started, it would be pure madness to try to retreat back across the Channel. As each minute passes, more and more men manage to get ashore before digging themselves into the sand to avoid the murderous fire from the cliff-tops above. Mortar rounds are also causing havoc with the attacking men who are literally at the mercy of these shells which explode between them, sending hot shrapnel in all directions. One young American soldier leaps forwards after cutting through the barbed wire in front of him, he fires his rifle as he runs up the beach towards the German defences but crumples into a heap holding his midriff, as a nearby MG catches him with a deadly burst of fire sending him sprawling on to the sandy floor beneath his feet. Racked by pain, he screams out for a medic, as he does his best to contain his internal organs from slipping out between his blood-drenched hands. A medic nearby who hears his screams rushes to his aid tearing at the packaging which surrounds a field dressing as he runs. As the medic reaches his prone comrade, he realises that he is going to need a little more than just a lint padded dressing to save this man!

With frantic but expert hands, the medic attempts to stem the massive blood loss which the injured soldier is suffering by tearing open another dressing with his teeth, before trying to wrap it around the young soldier's torso. Just as he manages to do so, a mortar round lands directly on top of them, blowing both men to pieces and leaving a charred blackened hole behind with remnants of what used to be two people. A little higher above the beach, things are not going any better for the defending German bunkers, despite the comfort of the thick walls around them. Heavy shelling has breached the outside wall of the lieutenant's bunker, causing a fire which all men are attending in a desperate attempt to extinguish the blaze. The whistle of the heavy naval shells scream above their heads before making the ground shudder as they explode with titanic effect.

Two MG gunners are forced to leave the fire-fighting to continue with the massacre of the young men landing on the beach below them. With barrels glowing almost white hot and with no time for the regulation changes, their weapons are in danger of jamming.

'Lieutenant, more ammunition,' pleads one of the men over his shoulder, just as his latest burst of concentrated fire hits one of the enemy soldiers sprinting up the beach across his face, separating the top of his head complete with helmet from the rest of his body. Twitching for a few moments in the sand this latest victim is soon trampled upon by his fellow comrades as they do anything to avoid the swarm of German fire which flashes between them in a dazzling display of tracer fire.

***

Two fresh ammo-boxes are dumped between the MG42s which plough their way through the contents in no time at all, causing death and destruction down at the water's edge. Our lieutenant quickly counts how much ammunition remains and calculates in his head that they will be completely spent within the next hour! He pulls his tunic sleeve up to reveal his watch, just before 10am. They engaged the enemy around 6.30 that morning and will no longer be in a position to fight on past 11am. 'So much for the orders that all bunkers should have at least three days of ammunition to fend off the enemy,' he thinks to himself. His private thoughts are shaken from him as the ground beneath his feet shudders violently, causing him to be thrown first one way then the other, as the bunker, manned by his friend Otto, takes a direct hit from one of the massive naval guns in the Channel. It disappears in a huge fire-ball, which leaves it a total wreck with no chance of anyone inside surviving.

Unable to resist the chance to check that anyone may have survived the blast, our lieutenant runs up the concrete steps at the back of his bunker and peers over the edge of the defences. What he sees makes him wish he hadn't done so! There, a short distance away, burning brightly, is what is left of Otto's complex, completely destroyed with two bodies enveloped in orange flames now scattered out in the open among the smouldering smashed concrete. Just inches from where he is stood, a Stahlhelm rolls past with the top peeled back leaving jagged edges from the force of the blast which had obviously blown it from its owner. As it comes to rest, he can see the name Voltz painted on the inside of the rim amid the dripping gore which is the only thing remaining of the head of the soldier who was wearing it.

As he runs back inside, the scene which meets him is chaotic, as one of the gunners has an eye injury from a shard of concrete which has struck him courtesy of heavy Allied fire concentrated around their viewing slits. As his loader helps him away, Klaus mans the MG and attempts to keep the fire rate up, concentrating his aim towards a group of men so terrified that they flock together for comfort, not daring to move as individuals for fear of being cut to pieces. This makes for an easy target, as Klaus pulls the trigger and cannot help but hit the green and khaki mass which is soon splattered with dark red blood, it sprays into the air as each bullet buries itself into the flesh of the attacking soldiers. Running just behind this group of men is a flame-thrower team of three, attempting to get close enough to fire its evil jet of liquid into one of the concrete bunkers. Swinging the MG around to make it an easier shot, Klaus alerts his men to the danger:

'Achtung! Flammenwerfer!' The other gunner also closes in on the flame-thrower crew and between them send a hail of lead in their direction, which instantly ignites the tank of deadly fluid and explodes, engulfing all three men and condemning them to an agonising death in the sand.

Regardless of this success by the MG crews, more and more Allied soldiers bravely spill on to the beach from landing craft to be processed in this outrageous turmoil of death, which destroys them one by one without mercy, as they attempt to push forwards toward their goal of establishing a bridgehead, in order to land urgent supplies vital for the invasion and the thrust into France and beyond. Men slip and fall over the smashed remnants of their fellow countrymen who are splattered across the beach, almost unrecognisable as human beings due to their massive injuries sustained from the merciless fire from above.

***

Further out to sea, the Allies attempt to launch heavy armour towards the beach, by using floating tanks ingeniously developed to be able to make their way towards dry land under their own power. But in the rougher-than-expected conditions, many if not all of these are condemned to a watery grave within a few moments of leaving the safety of the vessels which carry them. The weather is overcast and dreary, and, with the added battle which rages all around, the sky hangs heavy with smoke which darkens the atmosphere further into an almost grey haze - transformed every now and then as another landing craft takes a direct hit blowing it to smithereens or when another German bunker begins to burn from the shelling.

Box after box of ammunition is emptied until there is hardly anything left to fight with, until in the end all of the supplies are spent, leaving Klaus and his men totally helpless against the wave of American soldiers which still attempt to push forwards.

'Alle Männer zurück!' he shouts, ordering all of his men to withdraw and flee the bunker, via the concrete steps towards the rear of the structure. Outside, the air makes it difficult to breathe owing to the smell of cordite and burning smoke which seems to be everywhere. Pausing for a moment only to rip the leather ammunition pouches from four dead Kameraden nearby, the men continue to run towards where their Zundapp motorcycles and Kettenkrad are parked nearby under a small group of trees. As they look each way, it is plain to see the Americans have forced their way up toward the cliff-tops and are now gaining the upper hand. With the limited rounds at their disposal, our group of seven men begin to muster themselves into a unit which begins to fire back towards the enemy, as well as using stick-grenades which were stored with their vehicles. Slightly stunned by the neat and precisely aimed fire, the Americans take cover near the bunker, unsure of the strength of men attacking them. One man peers over the edge of the steps only to catch a 7.92mm round straight between his eyes which at this relatively close range blows the back of his head off, splattering his comrades taking cover behind him in the pink and red gore complete with white pieces of bone.

Spitting this matter back out of his mouth, an American sergeant who was shouting orders at the time feverishly wipes his face on his sleeve trying to rid himself of the young man's brains, before another well-aimed bullet catches him in the throat, causing a fountain of blood to jet into the air as he too tumbles backwards, dead before reaching the floor.

'Keep it up, boys! We have them pinned down,' shouts Klaus to his men, who are all enjoying having the upper hand in this mini-conflict. Bundling groups of three stick-grenades together for a more devastating explosion, our group prepare themselves to leap forward to attack the sheltering Allied infantry, who appear to have no enthusiasm to venture any further forwards into the murderous fire coming in the opposite direction.

A moment before, Klaus orders his men to follow him in the charge forwards. A British war-ship in the Channel fires one of its last mighty naval shells towards the coast. Klaus manages to shout the order, 'Vorwärts!' just before he looks up on hearing the huge whistle as the enormous projectile lands amidst them, vaporising each man in the massive blast. In his final moments, Klaus realises what is about to happen. In his mind he sees the battle as if it were a still photograph; he also wonders in a split second what death will feel like, hoping for it to be quick. He need not have worried, for as these thoughts were still in his mind, he along with his six Kameraden had simply vanished off the face of the earth.

***

Even though this small duel has come to an end, the battle continues to rage all along the French shoreline with Allied troops from various countries being butchered by the poorly equipped and in most cases unprepared German troops, manning the bunkers along this so called Atlantic Wall. Out in the Channel, several fast-moving German E-boats decide to keep their distance from the huge invasion fleet, unlike months earlier when they stumbled across 'Operation Tiger' - the dry-run training exercise off the Devon coast arranged by the Allies. On that day, they fired their deck-mounted torpedoes towards the Allied fleet, sinking two of the vessels as well as costing the lives of over 900 American soldiers whilst wounding a further 200 in the process! But today there will be no repeat of that victory. Today is shaping up to a very different outcome, as slowly but surely the ammunition shortage and the only partially trained troops available to the German forces slowly succumb to the greater Allied pressure.

'What do you mean, no one has informed the Führer? We need to get mobile rather than sitting here on our backsides!' rages SS Major König as soon as he hears the news of the Allied invasion in his location just west of Paris. 'Get me Divisional HQ before the enemy has a chance to walk unopposed all the way to Berlin!' As König pulls maps out of a draw and spreads them across his desk, the young soldier nearest to him with trembling hands attempts to carry out the order, praying that the call will be answered as soon as possible. A few moments later:

'Sir, I have them for you,' he says with some relief in his voice, happy that König will not subject him to the full force of his anger if he hadn't managed to get through.

'What are we doing about this damn situation then?' questions König into the receiver. Some minutes pass as the heated conversation flows back and forth. Finally, with a resounding crash, König slams the telephone down with such force it shatters the Bakelite casing which houses it! Turning around almost at bursting point, he addresses a lone figure standing to attention as rigid as a statue at the far end of the room.

'Sandig, get our Abteilung ready and any of our men on leave back with immediate effect!' Without showing any emotion whatsoever, a short

'Consider it done, Herr Major', is the immediate response, before Sandig turns on his heel and out of the room to prepare the battalion to move out to engage the Allied invasion.

Love, Loss and War

Annie Coyle Martin

Liam Kelly had what was considered a good job in the creamery in Ballynanog and had married his sweetheart Rose a year ago; they settled in a cottage at the edge of the village. His father had died five years earlier, and it was left to Liam's brother, Sean, to stay home and look after the farm. In truth, there was little to do; the land, forty acres, was let to a neighbouring farmer except for an acre plot by the Kelly cottage, where their cow grazed, and a half-acre where they grew vegetables. There was a hen-house where his mother raised chickens (and sold the eggs). In spring and autumn Sean worked for a local farmer. But at twenty-two years of age Sean felt his life had no purpose.

On 4 September 1939, a Sunday evening, Sean walked up the lane from his home, the wind from the lake below parting and blowing his black hair, the day starting to fade into evening. The lane slanted upward, and he looked with sad eyes at the grey stone walls - what hard men had piled stone on stone, building them to contain the satisfying patchwork of fields? Some fields still had standing sheaves of oats and wheat, others cocks of harvested hay that threw shadows from the west-moving sun. Farther away, there were fields with raw furrows where the farmers had dug out the potato trenches, while others had green grass where cattle and sheep grazed. Soon the farmers would cart away the hay, oats and wheat, leaving the fields bare. Sean was headed for his friend Mark O'Shea's house at the top of the lane. He needed to talk to Mark: he would understand Sean's ambition, his determination to do something useful, to change his life. The world was passing him by.

Four days earlier, Hitler, the German Führer, had invaded Poland, and France and Britain had demanded that the Germans withdraw. The Germans having not done so, yesterday Neville Chamberlain, Prime Minister of Britain, declared that Britain was at war with Germany. Sean was very impressed by the speed with which he had acted. That day's *Irish Independent* newspaper seemed to indicate a war was already under way, and the BBC program on the battery wireless confirmed it.

Sean was tired of his life, bored with life in Ballynanog. Sometimes he thought about emigrating to America, but that was so far away, and the cost of travelling there was way beyond anything he could afford. Besides, his mother would not want him to leave, and neither would his girlfriend Kathleen. But what was the point of living in this out-of-the-way place, where one day faded into the next and nothing ever happened?

When Sean reached Mark's place, he found him sitting on the front step of his house, smoking. His mother would not allow him to smoke indoors. 'Grand evening,' Mark greeted him, moving over to make room for Sean on the step. He offered Sean a cigarette, and the two friends sat enjoying the soft air of early evening and their cigarettes, clouds of smoke blowing away over their heads.

'What do you think about this war that's coming, Mark?'

'It's nothing to do with us lad, nothing at all.'

'You're wrong there, I don't agree with you on that. That bastard Hitler will go after Ireland, he'll invade us unless he's stopped. We should be part of the effort to stop him. Think of how he would overrun this country. It didn't take long for Chamberlain to act, to state his position.'

'Sean, you're daft, talking rubbish.'

'I don't know about that. We're just a stone's-throw from England, and, if that fellow invades England, we're next. And the wireless said this morning that English planes have started dropping leaflets over Germany.'

'For what?'

'So the German people would revolt, would stop Hitler.'

'Do you think that will happen?' Mark asked.

'I don't think so. I've been listening on the wireless to Ed Murrow, and he says that London is getting ready for war: all Germans or Austrians over sixteen must report to the police. He said 600 people were rounded up. Looks like war to me, Mark.'

'I don't believe that. From what I read about Hitler, he's an eejit, a total clown, never finished school, and he's not even German.'

'What's that got to do with it? He's getting people worked up for war. I've a good mind to enlist, Mark.'

'In what? The British army? You're mad!'

'Well, what the dickens am I doing around here? A bit of work now and then, and the rest of the time listening to the wireless or reading the paper.'

'You don't join the British army because you're fed up at home or because you walked on a wandering sod. Besides, I'm sure de Valera will ban it, he hates the Brits. And what about Kathleen?'

'Kathleen always goes along with what I say.'

'Don't be too sure about that. This is a different matter altogether, Sean.'

'Last evening we went to the pictures, and Pathé news was about the Germans in Poland, it sounded as if they had overrun the whole country.'

'I'm not so sure about that. I've heard tell that half of Pathé news is dodgy - some of it made up.'

'How could it be? It's film, it's photographs.'

The conversation was getting tense, so Mark, always the peace-maker said,

'So what's on at the cinema?'

'*Boy's Town*. About the founding of an orphanage for boys. Mickey Rooney was fantastic in it, and Kathleen loved it. And we went to her place after, and her mother gave us tea and jam sponge.'

'Sure, with a nice life like this, why bother with this nonsense of enlisting with the Brits? Sure, what I read, the war is just a local thing, a row between Germany and Poland. I heard them say in the pub that the Brits just declared war to make the German people stop Hitler from pulling them into a war.'

'Fat chance of that, Mark. And the Brits are smart: they cancelled the annuities last year. They're looking for a way to be sure they have a strong Ireland at their back if they have to go to war.'

'What are those annuities, anyway?'

'Ireland's payments of our share of the British debt.'

'Oh, I see. But if you go on with this nonsense about enlisting, the person who will suffer is Kathleen.' But Sean was feeling his life floating away; his choices, always few, were narrowing even more every day, and he said,

'Kathleen will stand by me, no matter what.'

Nothing would change while he was at the war. The tree to one side of Mark's house seemed not to have aged in the years they had sat there; it would be there when he came back. Now its leaves were beginning to turn. By the time they had fallen he would, he just knew, be doing his share against the Germans, doing his bit, as the Brits expressed it. He felt excited, exhilarated: he would be doing something worthwhile at last. And he would return with some money and marry Kathleen.

Kathleen was spending the evening with her mother, Cassie, who was always lonely on Sunday evenings. She was a widow, and two of her four daughters had emigrated to England, as many Irish girls did. Her third daughter had married a small farmer. They lived six miles away in the little town of Redhills. After their evening meal, she and Kathleen sat outside in the fading light, and Kathleen told her about her week working in McGee's store, weighing out sugar, flour and tea, converting the huge chest of tea and the big bags of flour and sugar into small bags suitable for sale to the customers in the following week, and sometimes helping customers, and standing at the cash.

'I'm glad you have a job here, Kathleen,' her mother said.

'Me too. I wouldn't want to have to leave to find work somewhere else.'

'I wouldn't want you to leave either,' her mother said so earnestly that Kathleen decided she would never leave the village. She had Sean, and she had her job.

***

On Monday evening, Sean stopped at the village pub for a pint, and Andy Galligan was expounding on joining the British Army.

'How the heck will you do that?' another drinker asked.

'Well, I hear if you go to the Legion you can get a pass to cross the border to the North and join there.'

'And how does a man do that?

'Well, on our side, the border guards don't care a damn who crosses, it's lads coming the other way they stop - Brits that don't want to enlist.'

'Are you thinking of crossing, Andy?'

'Not really, Sean.'

'Maybe I will.'

'De Valera is against it. They say you will be blacklisted, called a deserter, if you cross over.'

'I'm sick of this town. No work, just the odd job when the farmers need a hand in the spring and in the harvest. Last winter I spent three months on the dole. At least in the army I'd get well-paid and, when I come back, myself and Kathleen will be able to think about getting married.'

'Maybe the army won't take you.'

'You're joking. They'll take anyone they get if this is anything like the last time.'

'That was different: we were under England's heel that time.'

And so the days of summer slid away, and Sean continued thinking about and investigating how he might cross the border. He did not share his plans with Kathleen, but they spent the September and early October evenings walking the lanes, watching the leaves turn, in the distance the autumn sunset golden and at dusk flocks of birds dark against the sky. Sometimes, having a pint in the pub, they talked about when they might marry. Money was their main concern. Sean felt that, if he spent six months or a year in the army, he would save enough to give them a start. Although they could, he was sure, live with his mother, they wanted their own place. Everyone said the war would not last more than a year. The thought that he might be killed or even injured never crossed his mind. Time passed, Sean still thinking about joining up – enlisting - and Kathleen adamant he would not, that it was a reckless idea, and, while Sean did not argue with her or challenge her opinion, he still considered enlisting, as many others were doing.

Everything changed the following August when, on 26, a Monday, German planes dropped four bombs in the small town of Campile, in County Wexford, killing three people at the Shelbourne Co-operative. Then, on the second day of January 1941, Terenure in South Dublin was bombed. The Irish people began to be angry with de Valera, and their anger was further increased when, on Saturday 31 May 1941, German bombers struck the North Strand, killing twenty-eight people. The Irish people, enraged and shocked, believed Germany was warning Ireland not to join England in the war. The number of Irish joining the British army multiplied, despite enlistment being strictly forbidden. And it changed Kathleen's opinion of Sean's plan to enlist in the army. She began, reluctantly, to see his point of view.

Without telling anyone what he was planning, Sean went one morning on the bus to Swalinbar and at the British Legion office was provided with a 'Letter Of Introduction' which he would use to cross the border into Northern Ireland. He was also given the address of the British Army Recruiting Office on Clifton Street in Belfast.

The following Wednesday, when Kathleen had a half-day off, they visited the local photographer and had a picture taken, because Kathleen had said she wanted a photograph of them together, to keep, if he carried through with his plan to enlist, although she hoped and prayed he wouldn't. The photograph would be developed and ready the next day. Sean paid for it, and Kathleen said she would pick it up at her midday break. That evening, when he told Mark about the photograph, Mark said,

'Kathleen is a beautiful girl, the prettiest in the town and a hard worker too. I don't know how you can bear to leave her. You know she has the sweetest nature, Sean.'

'I know, Mark, but I feel I must do my bit, especially since that bombing.'

'You can't change what happened.'

'I'll be back, Mark, don't worry. And sure you'll keep an eye on Kathleen when I'm gone, make sure she is OK, and she has her mother, and her job.'

'Sean, I'll see she wants for nothing, but I wish you weren't going.'

'I'm going, lad. My mind's made up.'

When Kathleen picked up the photograph, she was delighted with it. She and Sean looked so happy together, she leaning against Sean, he with his arm over her shoulder. She got a frame for it and showed it to Sean, hoping Sean would reconsider enlisting, and to her mother, and then kept it on her bedside table.

The Irish policy of neutrality continued with a few exceptions. These included permitting the use of the Donegal corridor to Allied aircraft, and a number of sites for collecting detailed Atlantic weather reports. However, Irishmen fighting in the British army were still considered deserters. But many did not support de Valera, the prime minister, nor had they voted for him, and they continued to enlist.

***

Sean planned to leave at the end of September. On the last weekend of September, Kathleen's mother decided to take the bus to Redhills to spend the weekend with Una, her daughter, who lived there with her family. McGee's grocery closed from six on Saturday till nine on Monday. Kathleen, taking advantage of her mother's absence, invited Sean for a meal on Saturday evening.

They had ham and cucumber sandwiches, cream scones with jam and afterwards sat listening to the BBC Home and Forces programme and enjoying some Pimm's. Kathleen, who loved Sean so deeply and was so sad he was leaving, sad that she might never see him again, suggested he should stay the night, and all night long they lay in each other's arms. They slept and woke and made love and slept again. In the morning, when he kissed her goodbye, she wept, and he comforted her.

'I'll be back, darling,' he said, 'and we'll have a lovely wedding. And you have your family here, and I know you'll be OK, and, as I told you, Mark, who is such a good friend, will look out for you. And my brother Liam will too.' They kissed goodbye, Kathleen weeping and Sean sad but determined to go. She watched him through her tears cycle down the lane till he disappeared from her sight. Her lover had joined the Irishmen who fought in the war and by the war's end were thought to number over 50,000. They would be called deserters, blacklisted by the Irish government and denied work when they returned. When Sean left, Kathleen dried her tears and with a sad heart set about the household chores. When her mother returned from her visit to Redhills, Kathleen told her Sean had left to enlist in the British army.

'Well, that's that,' her mother said. 'He's not the only one: there are lads in Redhills taking the same road.'

***

Three days later, Kathleen received a letter from Sean expressing his love and telling her he had enlisted in Belfast and was on his way to England to join his regiment. She went about her work in McGee's grocery, sad, missing Sean, waiting for news from him, but no letter came. Her friend Sheila, who also worked in McGee's, said, as they sat eating their lunch in the room at the back of the store, 'Cheer up, girl, the war will be over before you know it.'

Three weeks later, Kathleen began to worry she might be pregnant. She remembered Sean's last night at home, that night they spent together when they made love so passionately. Could she be? A short time later she was sure and terrified. What could she do? Where could she get help? Her mother, noticing her tired face, asked what was wrong, and Kathleen said she wasn't sleeping well and that she was tired. Her mother said she needed more exercise and fresh air. But Kathleen knew well how an unmarried pregnant woman was a disgrace in the village, treated with contempt and sent to the home for unmarried mothers run by nuns and there forced to work in the laundries the homes ran and to give up her child. She worried, unable to sleep, constantly thinking about it and the staff at work staring at her pale face.

One evening, desperate, almost overcome with tears, she walked up the lane to Mark's house: he would help her, and Sean had said he would. She knocked, and Mark answered the door.

'Oh, Kathleen, Kathleen,' he said, beginning to draw her inside. 'Come in, come in.'

'No, Mark, no.' Seeing how distressed she was, he stepped out and closed the door, and they walked farther up the lane into the woods, and he led her to a bank and they sat down.

'Please don't cry, Kathleen.'

'I'm in such trouble Mark, I wish I were dead.'

'Now, Kathleen, don't say that. Sean will be back.'

'I'm pregnant.' Mark stared at her and then said,

'My God! When?'

'In about eight or seven and a half months.'

'Oh, dear God! Does Sean know? Did you write to him?'

'No, I have no address.'

'Maybe we can try the address where he enlisted in Belfast.'

'I never thought of that. I'll go home and write now.' Kathleen dried her tears.

'Do, Kathleen, and remember I'm here for you, I'll look after you, even if I have to marry you myself. Now come back to my place and we'll have a cup of tea. My mother is gone to visit her sister, but I'll make tea for the two of us.'

That evening, Kathleen wrote to Sean at the address of the British Army Recruiting office on Clinton Street in Belfast, where he enlisted, and posted it the following day. The letter was returned, and pasted on it was a printed note saying the addressee had passed through the office and was now a member of the armed forces. When Kathleen showed the returned letter to Mark, he said,

'Time is getting on. Let's marry, Kath, there is no other way. We'll go to the church on Saturday and see Father Mulligan. We'll tell him the story and ask him to marry us as soon as he can.'

When they met Father Mulligan, they told him Kathleen was carrying Mark's child. He took a stern view of the matter but, to avoid scandal, agreed to dispense with the reading of the bans. A marriage was arranged for two weeks' time. Then they went to see Sean's mother, and tearfully Kathleen told her the story. His mother was shocked, then sad, but said she would not like the village to know Sean had sinned, so she asked Kathleen to keep the baby's parentage secret. Mark told his mother he was the father of Kathleen's child and that they had seen Father Mulligan, and she said, 'Well, you had better hurry up and marry.'

Two weeks later, they were married, Mark's sister and her husband standing witness. After a family lunch in the village hotel, they left for a week's holiday in Bundoran, a small seaside village. While they were away, Sean's mother received a telegram telling her Sean was MIA, missing in action. Later, she received a letter indicating he was killed in the Western Desert.

***

Kathleen, when she heard, was sad but thankful she had married Mark, and they settled into life on the farm, and, when Kathleen delivered her baby just seven months later, to her joy it was a girl. They called her Agnes, after Mark's mother. They had a busy life on the farm and, in 1945, just as the war ended, Kathleen was delivered of a boy whom they called Sean. Reflecting on her life, Kathleen felt she was fortunate, despite losing her first love. She was content to be alongside Mark and her two children.

Mark died in 1990 but Kathleen survived until 2000. After the funeral, her children, Agnes and Sean, emptied the house before it went on the market. Agnes was sorting through her mother's wardrobe when she found a photograph, its glass cracked, wrapped in tissue paper and stuffed in a shoe box. It was her mother, looking about twenty years old, standing with a handsome young man, he with his arm around her shoulder. She showed it to Sean; neither of them had any idea who the man was, never suspecting he was Agnes's father. Kathleen looked so happy in the photograph, and so much like Agnes's own daughter, Carmel, that Agnes kept the photo. She had it framed and put on the piano in her front room.

Thirteen years later, Agnes's husband returned from work as she was tidying the front room. He told her that the bill he had drafted was to become law. The Justice Minister, Allan Shatter, would formalise the pardon he previously granted to the Irishmen who fought against the Nazis. Agnes picked up the old photo to dust it and said to her husband, "Sure don't they deserve it? But never mind anyway, it's nothing to do with us." She put the photo back on the piano and they went through to the kitchen for their tea.

The Gosford Ghost

Julius Falconer

This is a true story. Only its contents are made up.

On 12 April 1941, the National Emergency Committee issued the following notice:

> The intensity of the recent air attacks on Coventry, involving the deeply lamented loss of so many lives, has created a situation of difficulty, and the National Emergency Committee, in consultation with the Regional Commissioner, have decided that the only course will be for everybody to be buried in the communal grave at London Road Cemetery.

This is the story of one of these citizens. Or perhaps it isn't. You'll see what I mean in a bit. It was told to me by an ancient gentleman as we sat on a bench in Gosford Green – within spitting distance of where Bolingbroke duke of Hereford (later Henry IV) and Mowbray duke of Norfolk met to decide their differences, before being exiled by Richard II in 1398. And quite close to Dame Ellen Terry's natal house. ('Gosford'? I seem to remember being told as a child that the name indicated a ford shallow enough for geese to be driven across on their way to market - but when I was a nipper there were not many geese to be seen in Coventry, I can tell you!) I had strolled out to take the air, and, as I sauntered through the park, the old gentleman, whom I had never clapped eyes on before, to my knowledge, called me over.

'Here, young man,' he said, 'I can't eat all this. You have some. You look as if you could use it, too,' and he handed me a generous wedge of Black Forest gâteau. Well, I didn't refuse – of course, I didn't - and in no time at all we were chatting away as if we'd known each other all our lives; that is, he chatted while I listened. His name, he told me, was Aubrey, and he'd been born not a stone's throw from that very spot, in Grafton Street.

As old men will, he began to reminisce: not much to look forward to - except the grave, I suppose - but lots to look back on, and memories will enliven many a dull hour. Before long he was talking about the war - understandable in a city which suffered so badly 1939-1945, with a heavy loss of life and the destruction of so many mediaeval buildings, including its noble cathedral (although it had been a 'cathedral' only since 1918). The city fathers have never managed to recapture the spirit of the mediaeval city that Tennyson knew - but that's another story. The tale Aubrey told me, though, was more a ghost story than a war story, and I reproduce it here for your entertainment. He assured me it was true, every last word.

'Yes,' he said in the course of his reminiscences, 'see that roundabout?' and he pointed back to the main road. 'Site of the old White Lion Hotel,' he said. 'Bombed out in 1941, of course, like so much else round here. The main blitz five months earlier didn't do much damage hereabouts - smashed the centre up, good and proper. You see, the Germans didn't rightly know where the armaments factories were: just dropped hundreds and hundreds of bombs on the centre and hoped for the best. They came back the following year - and that's when the White Lion went down - or rather up: an incendiary device, it was. There's a story about that pub - well, it starts at the pub - that might interest you.' He rubbed his chin and, after a pause, carried on, taking my acquiescence for granted, no doubt. 'A young chap worked there: Guy Holbrook. Lived just round the corner, with his dad. Worked every evening at the pub, seven nights a week: blokes had to, you see, so many had been called up. His dad was a doctor, one of the few left behind to aid the war effort back home, where the need really was just as great as at the front: same illnesses and complaints as always and very few doctors. Hadn't had a day or night off in two years, until he was all but burnt out. But it's Guy I want to tell you about. Didn't know him personally, but I knew plenty of people who did.' The sun had come out at last, and the park showed up at its best, with the fresh colours of a late spring. One or two mothers were walking their toddlers, and proud grandparents steered push-chairs and strollers along the gently curving paths. There was nothing to disturb the peace of a very civilised scene.

'Guy and his father,' Aubrey went on, 'lived round the corner, above a row of shops.' He pointed at a piece of road. 'A flat, it was, on the third floor. The doctor's house and surgery were on the other side of town, in Holyhead Road, but the doctor was having work done on the house - all took much longer in those days, with so many men away at the front or in military training - and had moved into this flat temporarily, until the work was done. Guy had had to move out, too, of course, and he'd got himself this evening job at the local pub. Well, on the night of the 8/9 April, 1941, the bombers came - and how! No less than 230 of them, which dropped hundreds of tons of high explosives and 25,000 incendiary devices. Hundreds of people were killed, hundreds more injured. The buildings lost to posterity included Christ Church - although the spire's still with us, as you know - King Henry VIII school, where Guy had been a pupil, the Coventry and Warwickshire hospital and the medieval St Mary's Hall - not destroyed completely, but badly damaged. I remember the night well, grotesquely illuminated by fires wherever you looked, the scream of the bombers, people's panic, the crash of crumbling buildings. A nightmare.

'There weren't enough air-raid shelters, of course - not for everyone - and people took cover where they could. Well, I'm not quite accurate there. There was a shelter, a trench shelter, but it had received a direct hit the previous autumn, and people tended to avoid it! Anyway, it was impossible to tell where the next bomb was going to fall, where the next house would go up in flames. No place was surer than any other, and even cellars weren't safe - if you had one, that is. I remember my wife and me sheltering under the piano for part of the night! Guy had not long finished for the evening, and he and the landlord were sitting in the bar with a quiet pint ready to clear up a bit. Then the raid started. Just a few minutes' warning as the sirens blared out. Then it was pandemonium. Were you better in a building or outside? There was no knowing. Before the landlord and Guy had thought about what action to take, the pub was in flames. Guy made for the door, which was probably sensible, but when he got outside he realised that the landlord hadn't made it. What could have held him up?

He went back inside. The place was in darkness and full of smoke, and the fire roared in his ears. Lying flat on the ground, he crawled back into the bar, hoping that the ceiling wouldn't collapse on top of him. He found the landlord hunched up where he'd fallen, with a bar-stool on top of him and a bad gash in his leg. Grabbing him under the arm-pits, he manoeuvred him along the floor even as the ceiling began to cave in. A piece of burning timber struck him on the back, and he could feel his clothes burning. Not panicking, he carried on pulling the landlord out of the collapsing building, willing himself on despite the noise, the darkness and the increasing heat. Reaching the outside, he pulled on into the road, heaving his unconscious burden to safety. Unfortunately, at that moment, when success seemed assured, a gas-cylinder in the house next-door exploded, and bricks flew out in all directions, one of them striking Guy a fatal blow on the head.

'In that same raid, although of course he didn't know it straight away, the doctor's surgery and house were destroyed. It was only after the doctor had threaded his way on foot across the stricken city on the following day, dismayed at the damage, the reek of burning in his nostrils, bewildered citizens wandering around in search of relatives, or premises, or some assurance that the world hadn't ended, that he discovered the sad truth that his own house was gone. With his son dead and the surgery flattened, worn out with the effort of maintaining medical care in a city full of wounded, Dr Holbrook moved away to make a fresh start if he could. I've never heard of him again, to this day, but if ever I saw a man at the end of his resources, a prey to the deepest despair, that man was Dr Holbrook. Shattered, he was, physically, mentally and spiritually. The shadow of a man.

'However, the world goes on. You young people should thank Providence you never had to live through such times. Perhaps you do thank Providence – except I don't suppose most of you even believe in any such person any more.' The old man gave a meditative pause, devoted, I supposed, to the shortcomings of the younger generations not directly affected by the events of 1939-45. Aubrey was, I guessed, in his eighties, but to my mind spry enough despite his grizzled countenance. His clothes were not expensive but clean and neat. I put him down as a retired teacher, or perhaps a practitioner of some profession like psychotherapy. He quickly resumed. 'The Holbrooks' flat was taken on by an elderly couple whose own house had gone in the blitz. The last air-raid hit Coventry sixteen months later, the Stoke Heath area of the city: not too far from where we are now, but far enough to cause no more damage here. Things settled down again, although the war still had three years to run, and Coventry remained flat-out - if you'll excuse the phrase - producing aeroplanes, aeroengines, aeroparts and weapons.

'About a year after they'd moved in, the elderly couple in the old doctor's flat began to experience phenomena which struck them as intriguing rather than alarming. Every night, about the time of the day when the White Lion went on fire the year before, they'd hear footsteps in the corridor outside their flat, ringing clearly on the bare floorboards and stopping at their door. I should perhaps explain, young man, that the building was on three floors. The ground floor was occupied by a shop – a grocer's, I think it was – or do I mean a hairdresser's? My memory's not quite what it was. The middle floor was empty, but was furnished – sparsely- as living accommodation. The couple lived on the top floor, with views to the south over the green and the park. Of course, when the noises started, the old man opened the door to see what was going on, but he never saw anything, and, with time, the couple grew so accustomed to the footsteps that they took no more notice.

'*They* didn't take any more notice, but someone else did: an employee of the *Coventry Standard*, whose mother knew the couple. He heard the story from his mother and became curious. He mentioned the matter to his editor, who thought something might be made of it. Now you mustn't run away with the idea that, as the war wore on, we'd become blasé and frivolous. Oh, no, the daily grind continued relentlessly – but that made it even more important to provide ourselves with outlets, amusements, moments of relaxation. You never listened to ITMA, of course – probably never even heard of it, I daresay - but it was radio programmes like that, and films at the cinema, and of course all the usual things like bingo, eating out, concerts - where you could find them - and so on which helped to keep us human. Well, the editor of the *Standard*, pursuing his idea that the matter might make a few good column-inches, thought it would make sense to harness the assistance of a local ghost-hunter, Stilcombe by name, who used to give talks on ghosts to the WI and clubs interested in the paranormal - that sort of thing. He'd also published a few books, I think. Anyway, Stilcombe, then in his seventies, was delighted to be involved and suggested a *modus operandi*. The team of investigators should consist of three people, he said: a journalist to sit with the couple in their flat, experience what they did and write up the story; Stilcombe himself, as the 'expert' - although he didn't style himself an expert at all; and a photographer armed with an infra-red camera. Well, I don't think it was an infra-red camera as we know it today: they hadn't been invented then, I don't think. But it was a camera with infra-red-sensitive film - or something like that.

'Well, on the night chosen for the experiment, the three men assembled in the road as the shop on the ground floor was closing. It happened to be 8 April 1945 - just a month before VE Day - although none of them realised its significance - I mean, it hadn't been deliberately chosen as the anniversary of Guy' death. It wouldn't have made any difference, anyway, I don't suppose. After the grocer - or hairdresser - had departed, the team of intrepid investigators entered the premises and, with the permission of all concerned, made a thorough inspection: doors and windows, cupboards, recesses, drawers and so on. They were not going to leave any room for tricks, unexpected noises, bumps in the night or interference with their work. They joined the couple on the top floor, had tea and then whiled away the time until later in the evening, when it was time to take up their posts.

'Just let me tell you another quick story which comes to mind.' He smiled at me, his eyes alight with amusement after the emotion of reliving the grim war years. 'A man was invited by a friend to spend the night in a haunted room in his country house - by way of a challenge. The man, whose name was Fosdyke, happily accepted and turned up on the agreed day, full of good spirits and in a state of high anticipation. After a leisurely dinner – there were other guests as well – the party repaired to the drawing-room for bridge and cigars. The evening came to an end, and everybody retired to bed. Fosdyke took possession of the alleged haunted chamber and prepared himself for the night ahead. He exchanged his day-clothes for pyjamas, dressing-gown and slippers and went along to the bath-room, which was on the other side of the corridor, leaving his wig and his teeth in the bedroom – you'll excuse me these details, I'm sure, young man. He performed his ablutions and other necessary functions and returned to his bedroom – only to discover, to his annoyance and dismay, that he'd left the key to the Yale lock inside. There could be no question of rousing his hosts at that hour of night: bald and toothless? not to be contemplated! Of course, he didn't realise that he'd have to at some stage, if he was ever to rejoin his clothes. For the moment he could think only of getting under cover. He tentatively tried a few doors on the landing, until he found an unlocked and empty room, in which he made himself as comfortable as he could and was soon fast asleep.

'The following morning, he managed to attract the attention of a passing servant, explained his dilemma and obtained a duplicate key. Thankfully he rushed to get inside and found the room exactly as he had left it – except that his wig had turned as white as snow in the night!' Aubrey chuckled inordinately at this – which I took to be a joke rather than a serious attempt to add to the world's stock of spectral appearances. I chuckled with him, naturally.

'So, back to Stilcombe and the *Coventry Standard.*' He smiled capaciously, glad, I supposed, to have an audience – so receptive an audience, too! He went on: 'The journalist sat with his hosts in their flat, agog to hear whatever might transpire. Stilcombe and the photographer settled down outside their door, looking down the corridor to the head of the stairs which came up from the floor below. It was very dark, of course, even though full black-out was no longer in force as the German war-machine weakened.

Stilcombe told his companion to take photographs when he felt Stilcombe's hand on his shoulder, whether he himself saw anything or not. In due course, steady footsteps were heard coming along the corridor on the floor below and mounting the stairs, with deliberation and unhurriedly, as if it were a matter of routine. However, instead of proceeding along the corridor towards them, as the elderly couple had suggested they would, they stopped at the head of the stairs. Stilcombe saw the figure of a young man. Blood was pouring out of a wound in the man's head - or had perhaps congealed, Stilcombe couldn't be sure. The figure paused, slowly beckoned, then, deliberately and slowly turning round without speaking, went back down the stairs. His back-view seemed to show blisters and singed flesh and the remnants of a shirt burnt off his back: and then - silence; nothing. All this time, Stilcombe had been tapping the photographer on the shoulder, and a number of photographs were taken.

'To the horror and ghoulish entertainment of its readers, the *Standard* printed these photos in the following day's edition, along with a sensationalised account of the adventure. The editor explained to his readers that some of the photos were too dark or blurred beyond recognition, but he hoped that the three reproduced, of the initial appearance, of the gesture of beckoning and of the head and shoulders disappearing back down the stairs, would convince them that they had been party to a spectral phenomenon of no mean importance. I saw the photos myself.' The narrator looked at me, as if daring me to challenge his story. I wasn't in the frame of mind to challenge it. I couldn't work out a tactful response anyway, and I certainly shouldn't have wished to cause the old man offence by appearing sceptical. As the Holy Book says, 'Stand up in the presence of the aged, show respect for the elderly and revere your God.' As I was framing a suitable comment, he went on.

'There are two sequels to this little tale,' he said. 'The first is that from that day the noises ceased. The couple were never troubled by footsteps again.' He stopped for so long at this point that I thought he'd lost the thread of his discourse. I prompted him:

'And the second sequel?'

'Ah, well,' he ventured, 'that's even more mysterious. The momentous daily news of the crumbling of the German forces, the multiple surrenders on the western front and the eastern front, the retreat of the German army from Finland, the establishment of camps for the thousands of prisoners, the death of Mussolini and so forth occupied us throughout the rest of April and into May. Finally VE Day erupted, and we went wild with delight. We could hardly believe it, after nearly six terrible years of war, destruction, rationing, loss, bereavement and troubled sleep. Towards the end of May, Stilcombe thought he would examine the photographs more closely than he had done. He wondered whether the spectre could have been faked in any way, although so few people knew beforehand of the investigation that it was hard to imagine who could have been responsible. Anyway, one day he went along to the newspaper offices in town, having phoned the editor in advance to warn him of his visit. He was warmly received, and the editor had been courteous enough to look out the file which contained the photos, both negatives and positives. Stilcombe took the file and sat down at a desk, ready to take his time in a close examination. He looked carefully, but there could be no doubt about it: the figure had disappeared from the negatives.' Aubrey paused knowingly, to let his final statement sink in.

I have my own theories about ghosts. Will you bear with me a minute, gentle reader? We always see them as revenants: dead people who return to this life, at least in a way which permits the living to experience them somehow, through any of the five senses. The dead belong to the past, but they choose to appear in our present. Since such theories are fraught with difficulties, I have begun to wonder whether we shouldn't reverse the order: perhaps 'ghosts' appear when we, from our present, reach back into the past. Take Jung's 'collective unconscious' – more commonly known today, I understand, as 'autonomous psyche' or 'objective psyche'. Put it this way. Along with genetic material, we inherit from our parents all sorts of other features, including – perhaps – some of their memories lodged in their unconscious. Why not? Their memories will naturally include not only their own history but that of other people who have told them theirs. Under particular stimuli, of time or place, we tap into this reservoir of collective memories and relive the past. Like all memories, inherited ones are random and inexplicable. Why do I easily remember trivial details from my own life but have difficulty in recalling important facts? The same would apply to memories retrieved from the collective unconscious. I haven't worked out all the details of this little theory yet, but do you think I might be on the right lines?

Even through the miasma of my own heady thoughts, I sensed movement from the person on the bench beside me. Aubrey was getting to his feet with a bit of effort.

'Well, it's been good to talk to you, young man,' he assured me. 'I always enjoy a bit of a chat. I'm off for my daily snooze now: when you get to my age, you know, early afternoon's rather a low point in the day. I haven't bored you, have I? We old folks can rabbit on a bit, that's for sure, but I thought that that little tale would interest you. Don't often get a chance these days to tell it to a stranger. By the way, you haven't told me your name: we might meet again, you never know.' I had the grace to hesitate before replying.

'It's Guy,' I said: 'Guy Holbrook.'

Treachery
Peter Good

1

William Silcox stood six feet tall, his skin tanned from his life in Kenya. He was standing on the veranda of his house in Nyeri, Kenya, situated some 110 miles (about a two-hour drive) north of Kenya's capital Nairobi, on the main Nairobi to Addis Ababa road, in the country's fertile central highlands. Nyeri, of course, was also known to be the place where Lord Baden-Powell, the founder of the scout movement, settled with his wife. He was known to have written, 'The nearer to Nyeri, the nearer to bliss', and William could easily understand why Baden-Powell had written those words, for it had just gone six o'clock, and the sun had already risen, casting its rays in ever-changing colours over the land before him, which was a coffee plantation. Over to the north-east was majestic Mount Kenya, an imposing extinct volcano lying astride the equator. It was the highest mountain in the country and the second highest in Africa, after Mount Kilimanjaro.

William lit his pipe and, puffing, got it alight and recalled how, after serving in WWI, those stationed at the base here in Kenya who had £1000 in assets were offered a free 1000 acres to set up coffee plantations, the goal being to speed up modernisation and economic growth in Kenya. Of course, it did require expensive machinery and obtaining a stable labour-force, all of which he, with his wife Rosemary and their only daughter Sandra, soon set up. He let out a sigh as he sat himself down on the wicker chair on the veranda, just as his wife, her skin also tanned from her life in Kenya, followed by their daughter, again tanned, with long blonde hair and an hour-glass figure, came in with a freshly percolated pot of coffee and sat down with him. This was their daily routine. They were all used to it by now, getting up this early, and they all enjoyed the early rising of the sun, its rays changing from red, to orange, then to golden as it lit up Mount Kenya and their coffee plantation here in Nyeri. After finishing their coffees, they retired to the dining-room, where their breakfast awaited them. Having completed their breakfast, William would be off to the plantation for yet another busy day, whilst Rosemary busied herself with homely duties, and Sandra got herself ready for the short drive into Nyeri Town, where she worked as a teller at the local Standard Bank.

Ten miles to the east of William Silcox's coffee plantation was the large dairy farm of Otto De Bruin. Otto was a thin tall craggy-faced man tanned from living in Africa. His wife Noreen too was tanned, as was their son Evold, who stood six feet tall and had already built up a reputation of the love-all-marry-none type. Evold had also, because of his academic prowess, taken and passed the qualifications to be an accountant and was registered as such for his father's farm. The De Bruins had come to Kenya from El Leh in Ethiopia in 1920. No one in Nyeri ever knew what they had been doing in Ethiopia, and they themselves never spoke about their life there. They had bought the area on which their dairy-farm now stood. It was an ideal spot for dairy-farming: the fertile volcanic soils, together with high rainfall, ensured a high-quality nutritious pasture throughout the year. Otto had purchased and brought in the Friesian herd of black and white cattle which originated in the Netherlands.

The life of a dairy-farmer is not an easy one: to get the required yield there has to be careful planning. The farmer has to plan ahead to ensure that his herd is in milk at the right time. Not all cows in the herd give milk all the time. There is a large proportion of cows which are not in milk, because they are between the end of lactation and their next calving. The cows produce milk when they calve, and this calving takes nine months after successful mating.

Otto and his local African labour-force had managed to keep track and ensure that all ran as smoothly as possible. During the years that they had been in Nyeri, either Otto or his son Evold, would do monthly business trips back to El Leh, so much so that the border-staff at Moyale would look forward to their visits, and they arranged it so that the De Bruins were never unduly detained at the border-crossing, even though they did wonder why, in the past few months, Evold had done nearly three times his usual visits. They presumed that he must have a lady-friend that he had left behind in El Leh, but it was purely the border-staff's private thinking, and none of them would dare ask him outright. But they all thought how nice it was that he was able to get away from his accountancy duties so regularly.

Brian Hargraves was an Inspector in the Kenya Police Force, stationed at Nyeri. He was 5ft 10ins tall, obviously tanned from his police career in Kenya. His wife Kathleen had been born in Kenya. Their son Tim, a keen sportsman whose muscles rippled under his tanned skin, stood six feet tall. He worked for the Public Works Department, his main duties being the construction of culverts (structures to allow water to flow under a road) along the main Nairobi- Addis Ababa road, from Nyeri to Moyale, a market-town on the border of Ethiopia and Kenya.

Henry Moody was a short plump man with balding hair and known to all in Nyeri for his sense of humour. He was the owner of the Nyeri Hotel. His wife Elizabeth was a large homely woman, and her reputation for serving the most delicious meals was shared by all in Nyeri. Their daughter Susan stood 5ft 6ins. With red hair and known to take after her father, she was full of fun and was the receptionist at the hotel.

If you were travelling from Nairobi, the capital of Kenya, going north towards Moyale on the Nairobi- Addis Ababa road at that time, you would have had to pass through the small town of Nyeri, which anyone passing through would consider a quaint tidy and friendly town, the township having been neatly laid out. Owing to the fertile soil and high rainfall, trees and neatly mown lawns surrounded the shops, giving the town a distinctive atmosphere that would immediately envelope any traveller, and, if you happened to stay over at the Hotel, you would recall for years afterwards the many fine dishes that had been served and enjoyed during your stay.

2

Evold had spent another boring week as the accountant for his father's farm, and, as Saturday drew to its close, he rode up to the main farm-house on his jet-black stallion, its long black mane bouncing round its neck and its long black tail swishing from side to side. As Evold approached the main arched entrance to the farm-house, he dismounted, and the groom who had been waiting for his arrival stepped out and, taking the reins, gently led the stallion to its stable, where he would unsaddle, then brush and clean the animal before opening the stable-door, and the stallion would walk over the newly cut straw to where its meal and water were situated. The groom would then close and lock the stable-door and proceed to his other chores. Evold went up to his room, where he undressed, went to the bathroom and stepped into the shower. Once showered and dried, he wandered back to the bedroom, and there, neatly laid out on his bed, were his clothes for that evening, which he quickly donned, and then headed to the lounge, where by this time his father Otto, having also bathed, was standing at the bar, with his mother Noreen by his side. The drinks for all three had been made ready by the barman, an African, smartly clothed in a white trousers, shirt and jacket. The three of them gathered their drinks, thanking the barman, and walked over to sit at their favourite places, Otto and Noreen on the settee and Evold in the armchair. They would be facing the veranda and watching through the open doors the setting of the sun, its rays turning from a red to a deeper red, till it looked as though the sky were on fire. They toasted the end of another week, and Otto, turning towards Evold, said,

'Well, my boy, what plans for this evening?' Evold turned from watching the sunset and, looking over at his parents, said,

'Well, I thought I would pop down to the hotel and have a few drinks with Tim - as usual.' He paused then continued: 'I told the cook this morning not to prepare anything for me tonight, that I would eat at the hotel.' He raised his glass and drained the last of his drink before rising, walking over to the settee and tenderly kissing his mother on the cheek. Then, turning his head, he kissed his father on the head, saying, 'If you're still up, I'll see you later ... If not, I bid you a pleasant night,' and with that he left the house and walked to the garage, where he jumped into the old Bedford truck. He switched it on and, as he pressed the starter, the engine barked into life. He slowly reversed out of the garage and drove off into town.

Tim Hargraves and his gang of labourers had been working on a culvert some ten miles from Nyeri, and, when it had been completed, Tim got into his Chevrolet truck, the labourers jumped into the back, and they all trundled off towards Nyeri. Tim dropped off all the labourers at the Nyeri compound and then drove off towards the Nyeri police station, where he lived with his parents. He parked up, and, as he did so, his father, Inspector Brian Hargraves, came out of the police station main entrance.

'Hiya, Tim,' he called out, and Tim replied,

'Hi, dad,' as he got out of his truck, closing the door behind him, and they fell in side by side as they walked the short distance to the police house where they lived. As they approached the door, Tim held back so that his father could enter first, and there, waiting inside, was his mother. She smiled and nodded at Tim and then, addressing Brian, said,

'All done for tonight?' and Brian replied,

'Yes, just handed over to Sergeant Ndoma, so all is done,' and he gave his wife a kiss and headed for the veranda, with his wife Kathleen following. He knew that she would have had a brandy and ice already waiting for him, and, as he sat down in his armchair, she duly handed over his drink, whilst taking her orange-juice and sitting down on the wicker chair next to him.

Tim appeared after a little while, having showered and dressed, and he came in and sat down with them, as they too watched the sun set over the distant hills. As they did so, the house-boy appeared, and said,

'Excuse me: dinner is served,' and turning walked back into the house as Brian, Kathleen and Tim stood up and followed him to the dining-room where the meal had been set for them. They had sat down and started eating when Brian turned to Tim and said,

'Usual for tonight, then?' and Tim replied,

'Yeah, meeting Sandra, Evold and Susan at the hotel for a few drinks,' and, with that, continued eating his dinner. When he had finished, he got up and, leaning over, gave his mother a kiss on the cheek, saying, 'See you later,' and with that he strolled out to where his car was parked and, getting in, started the engine and, engaging first gear, drove off towards the hotel.

When Tim got to the Nyeri Hotel, he found that Susan Moody was still at reception. He climbed the stairs and popped over to her desk.

'Hello, Susan, you still hard at it?' he said in a teasing way. Susan looked up.

'Hi, Tim … yeah, still waiting for the evening receptionist to arrive. You'll find Sandra and Evold out on the side veranda … I'll join you as soon as I can.' Tim thanked her, walked to the bar, ordered a beer, which was poured into a frosted glass from the fridge, and walked out to the side veranda. He found Sandra and Evold sitting at a table having a drink and making general talk. Sandra looked up as Tim approached.

'Hi, Tim,' she said sweetly, and Tim crossed over to her, gave her a kiss to which she responded immediately and, as he broke away, caught the instant look of hostility on Evold's face. This was not unsuspected, as Evold and Tim had, a few months earlier, come to blows over Sandra, and Tim had managed to catch Evold with a right cross that sent him tumbling to the ground. Afterwards, Evold had agreed that he would not try and entice Sandra away again, but he could not help harbouring a dislike for Tim. After all, Tim had always been Sandra's favoured even in sport. Tim had always been the better batsman and better bowler than Evold, and deep inside this hatred was bubbling. Shortly after Tim had sat down, when Susan arrived, she raced up and sat down on Evold's lap and turning gave him a kiss.

'Well, loverman, here I am at last,' she cooed. It was public knowledge that the two of them had been dating, ever since the incident involving Tim and Sandra.

'Ah, about time!' Evold replied in a joking tone, and she smiled at him and remained seated on his lap.

As the evening went on, Evold as always suggested playing darts, to which they all agreed. He was very happy, as this was one field at which he was much better than Tim. As expected, during the evening Evold won three of the four games that they played, which put him in a better mood.

Just before closing-time, the stout figure of Henry Moody ambled over to them. Reaching them, Henry said,

'Hey, guys and gals, glad I got you before you all left, just wanted to remind you that tomorrow afternoon we're going to be having a barbecue, so hope you'll all be here.' As he looked at them, they each responded with,

'Yes, Henry, you can count on us being here, wouldn't miss it,' and then Evold and Tim chipped in with,

'Sure, the folks will be along too,' to which Henry responded:

'Oh, good, that would be lovely. Well, see you all then.' Then turning to his daughter, he said, 'Don't be too late in, poppet.' He wished them good night and headed into the hotel. They all finished their drinks and made their way back to their vehicles - except Susan, who just had to walk into the hotel - and then they all went their respective ways.

The following day went quickly by. In the afternoon, sure enough, Tim, together with his parents Brian and Kathleen, Sandra and her parents William and Rosemary all arrived at about the same time at the hotel. They exchanged pleasantries and were just starting up the stairs when Evold with his parents Otto and Noreen also arrived, and, joining them, they walked out to the side garden. There they found Henry Moody supervising the cooking staff, who had already got on large amounts of meats and sausages, whilst over to the side Elizabeth Moody was directing her staff, who were laying out all the salads and home-made bread buns, together with her favourite home-made sauces. At the end of the tables were the plates, knives and forks. At another table there was an array of puddings to tempt anyone with a sweet tooth. As soon as the meats were cooked, Henry gave the come-and-get-it call, which had them all getting up and, forming a line, having taken a plate each, they proceeded to help themselves firstly to the meat selection and then to the salads and bread selection, before returning to their seats.

As they were all about to start eating, the barman, Jim Hazlett, came running out, wielding a radio in his right hand. Following him was one of the African staff, with a 12-volt battery. As he was connecting the radio up, he said,

'Please hush: this is awful! Listen: war has been declared!' As a hush came over all those present, the radio burst into life, crackling badly, but the announcer's voice was distinctly heard to say that a state of war existed between the British Empire and the Nazi State of Germany. All present gave a gasp and looked round at each other. The shock of what they had heard this Sunday 3 September 1939 had taken all the fun out of the gathering. Tim was the first to speak.

'Well, I know what I must do.' He paused for a while whilst all heads turned to face him, and he continued: 'I'll be off first thing Monday to join the King's African Rifles.' Sandra took an intake of breath.

'Oh, Tim, darling, are you sure?' she said, and, although you could hear the fright in her voice, you could also detect how proud she was of him. Tim looked at her and said,

'Yes, sweetheart, it's something I feel I should do.' There were cries of 'Well done ... Good on you, my boy,' from most of those there. In the midst of it all, the De Bruins finished eating, said their good-byes and left the hotel heading home. Evold, took Susan with him to his truck, and, kissing her goodnight, he too left.

3

True to his word, the following morning Tim went to Gil Gil, which is situated between the towns of Naivasha and Nakuru on the main road from Nairobi. Because of his civilian work on culverts, the King's African Rifles recruited Tim and had him on their engineering staff. He was given a basic induction, reduced to just three months, after which he was promoted to sergeant. Because of his understanding and local knowledge, plus the fact that he could also speak not only fluent Swahili (the local African language) but also fluent German (which he had undertaken privately), his talent was recognized, and he was soon promoted to lieutenant in command of his own platoon of Askaris (African Members of the King's African Rifles).

As Kenya bordered on Italian East Africa to the north, at the start of the war it was feared that the much larger Italian army would advance into Kenya, and the King's African Rifles (KAR) would be responsible for the defence of the whole British-occupied East Africa.

Of course, his parents were very proud of him, as was Sandra, though she still harboured dread that he might be involved in serious combat, and the thought of losing him always brought tears to her eyes. Fortunately, because of his residing at Nyeri, not far from the main camp, he was allowed to continue residing there. The King's African Rifles Commandant, General Michael Anderson, knew that, if needed, Tim could be easily reached and would be back in camp in a relatively short time. This being the case, Tim was able to continue seeing Sandra, and they were able to continue their gatherings at the hotel, and Sandra loved the fact that Tim was always in uniform (just in case he would suddenly be required): she thought he looked so dashing.

It was at one of their regular get-togethers at the hotel, in March of 1940, when Tim, Sandra, Evold and Susan were having their usual drinks and darts, that Tim turned to Evold and said,

'Hey, Evold, with the increasing call-up of all those considered eligible for service within the armed services that's going on, have they caught up with you yet?' He paused for a moment then continued, 'If so, have you considered which armed service you'd like to join?' He paused again then quickly added, 'You know, I could get you into the KAR at Gil Gil. Hey, it would be nice for us both to be together. What d'you say ?' Sandra and Susan both looked at Evold, waiting for his response, but were quite unprepared for his answer. Evold averted his glance and said,

'Oh, I've been excused from joining, on the grounds of my being a farmer.' Turning, he went to the dart-board, retrieved his darts and said, 'Your go, Susan.' They all just looked at one another, let the subject go and continued their game, but Tim was not so easily convinced. He knew that Evold was not a farmer, just an accountant on his father's farm and as such would not have been excused call-up. He made a mental note to check the facts and returned to the game.

The following day, whilst at the Gil Gil camp, he made enquiries and was soon shown the copy of records showing that Evold had indeed been exempted as a farmer (farming was considered an essential service) and had produced a letter from his father Otto, swearing on oath that Evold was a farmer and saying that, without him, the farm could not function. Being the patriotic person he was, Tim was quite taken aback by the obvious untruth that Evold's father had told in order to have his son exempted, and he made a note of it mentally, in case an occasion to use it should ever arise.

4

A month later, whilst they were all having their usual drinks together, Tim announced that the following afternoon he and his platoon were going on patrol that would take them to Marsabit looking for any evidence that might show that the enemy Italian forces had encroached on Kenyan territory and tampered with any of the culverts along the road. It was feared that the much larger Italian Army might advance into Kenya as it had done into British Somaliland and that the KAR would be responsible for the defence of the whole of British-occupied East Africa. Sandra immediately voiced concern:

'Oh, Tim, sweetheart, you will be most careful, wont you?' Tim reassured her that he would be. Evold cut in:

'Well, surely, you don't think that the Italian forces would already have entered Kenya?' Tim said,

'No, but we cannot take any chances: it's vital that this road be kept open,' and with that they all settled down and enjoyed the rest of the evening.

The following day, just after noon, Tim and his platoon left Gil Gil and headed to Nyeri, and then they proceeded up the road towards Marsabit. At each culvert crossing they came to, they stopped short of it and carefully made their way round the culvert from each side, Tim taking half of the platoon and his sergeant Solomon taking the others with him. They would advance carefully, checking and rechecking the ground round the culvert for any signs of tampering, and, only once they were convinced that it was safe, would they return to their truck and proceed up to the next culvert. This continued until they neared Marsabit. It was just about 4pm as they were once again circling a culvert when they heard the sound of aircraft. It was very cloudy that afternoon, and they could see nothing untoward, but the sound got louder and louder, till suddenly two Italian Caproni bombers came out of the clouds and started their dive towards where they all lay, each side of the culvert. Tim shouted, 'Take cover!' and then they could hear the bombs falling as they crouched down along the sides of the dry river-bed. The bombs fell on the side where Sergeant Solomon and his troops were crouched down, the blasts lifting up huge particles of earth and dust mingled with limbs of those Askaris that had been caught up in the explosions. It was only after the dust had settled that Tim and his Askaris rushed over to where Sergeant Solomon and what was left of his troops lay. Sergeant Solomon was bleeding from where shrapnel from the bombs had struck his left arm, but already the medical aide was busy bandaging up his wounds.

'You OK, Solomon?' Tim enquired, and Solomon replied,

'Yes, sir, but not so my Askaris.' Tim followed Solomon's gaze, and there lay the remains of about twelve Askaris littered over the bomb-crater. Tim called his Askaris and said,

'Please collect all the remains we can, put them in the tarpaulin, so we can take them back with us,' and, calling over his radio-man, told him to send a message back to Gil Gil camp, detailing what had happened and informing them that the patrol were coming back right away. Tim could not help but wonder how on earth those bombers could have known that they would be on that stretch of road. They got back to Gil Gil just after 6pm, and Tim went and reported to General Anderson. After the debriefing, he went home.

That night, whilst Evold, Sandra and Susan were sitting on the veranda, on Tim's arrival Sandra could tell that something was up. She rose and walked to meet him.

'Tim,' she said, 'are you all right? What's the matter?' Tim took her in his arms and stood cuddling her for what seemed an eternity before he slowly told her what had happened. Sandra let out a loud,

'Oh, no, Tim! How terrible! Oh, darling, so glad *you're* safe!' This had Evold and Susan turning in their chairs to look at them. As they slowly walked back to the table and sat down, Sandra could not keep it quiet:

'Tim was attacked today. Italian bombers. A dozen of his Askaris killed!' she cried, and Tim calmed her down. Susan and Evold just looked on, and Tim said,

'Yeah, it's true.' He paused then continued: 'We were just examining a culvert when they appeared. The worrying question is: how did they know we would be on that particular road?' They continued with general chit-chat, but Tim had noticed something in Evold's face when he mentioned about their being concerned about how the Italian bombers knew where they had been, and he retained that in his mind.

On the evening of Tuesday 11 June 1940, as they were all having their usual drink and darts game, Tim, turning to Sandra, said,

'Oh, by the way, sweetheart, thought you should know that I will be leaving tomorrow for the fort at Wajir [which was the Southern Rhodesian air base]: not too sure for how long.' He paused again, noticing that Evold had suddenly stopped talking to Susan and was paying particular attention to what Tim had been telling Sandra. Sandra said,

'Oh, Tim, hope it won't be too long, I'll miss you terribly. Please take great care,' as she squeezed his hand. Tim, seeing tears forming in her eyes, said quickly,

'Of course I will, darling. Now come on, let's see whether we can for once beat Evold and Susan at darts.' No sooner had he said that, Evold stood up, and said,

'Sorry, one and all, I can't stay on tonight: got to leave in a short while ... have to go to El Leh for dad early tomorrow.' Susan said,

'Oh, no, not again, Evold. I do so worry when you cross into Ethiopia. It's where the Italian army is, and it was just a few days before Tim's outfit was bombed that your dad was there.' She trailed off as Evold seemed to push her hand from his. He said a hasty good-bye to them all and left; but what he had said again left its mark in Tim's memory.

On the evening of Wednesday 12 June 1940, Tim and his platoon, together with the 1/6th Battalion of the King's African Rifles, arrived at the Fort at Wajir. Early the following morning, Thursday 13 June 1940, three Italian Caproni bombers appeared and bombed the Southern Rhodesian air-base. The Rhodesian aircraft were still warming up and preparing to take off on a dawn patrol. The Capronis bombed the fort, the landing ground and nearby housing. The KAR, then garrisoning the fort, lost four killed and eleven wounded; two Rhodesian aircraft were badly damaged; and the biggest blow was that a large dump of aviation fuel was set on fire. At dawn the following Monday, 17 June, the Rhodesians struck back and supported a successful raid by the 1/6th Battalion of the KAR (which included Tim's engineer platoon) on the Italian desert outpost of El Wak. (It is interesting to note that twenty-eight-year-old Nigel Gray Leakey, a sergeant in the 1/6th Battalion King's African Rifles, was awarded the regiment's first and only Victoria Cross - sadly posthumously - in recognition of his bravery on 19 May 1941 when, in the face of withering fire, he leapt on top of an enemy tank, wrenched open the turret and shot all the crew except the driver, whom he forced to drive the tank to cover. Then, along with three others, he tried to repeat this with another tank, but, just as he opened the turret, he was killed. But the confusion and loss of armour Leakey caused was critical to the Italian defeat in the battle at Kolito.)

It was on 21 June when Tim and his Platoon returned to Gil Gil. After debriefing, Tim was glad to be able to drive home to Nyeri. Arriving home he was gleefully welcomed by his mother and father. Later, as Tim and his father Brian were chatting over a cold beer, Tim mentioned the strange fact that, both on the culvert bombing and on the attack at Wajir, either Otto De Bruin or his son had made what they called a business visit to El Leh. Brian, being an inspector in the Kenya police force, said,

'That does seem quite a coincidence. Tell you what, my sergeant Ndoma has done three years in the Criminal Investigation Department, as an undercover man. Next time you know you are going somewhere, tell me well in advance, and I'll get Ndoma to carry out some checks. He was actually born in Ethiopia, and his parents oddly enough live just a few miles outside El Leh.' Tim said he would do so but then excused himself, saying,

'Sorry, dad, have to go and meet Sandra now!' He walked out, got into his car and drove off towards Nyeri.

Tim picked Sandra up from her parents' house, then drove to the hotel. After parking his car, he and Sandra walked up the steps and saw that Susan had only just finished handing over reception. Evold was standing nearby, so Tim called out,

'Hi, there, Susan, Evold!' They both turned at the sound of his voice and waving called back,

'Hello, Tim, Sandra,' and, as Tim and Sandra caught up with them, they walked into the bar. After ordering their drinks and some sandwiches, they walked over to tables nearer the dartboard, where they all sat down. They chatted on mundane matters till Evold said,

'Well, since you're back, fancy another beating at darts, Tim?' Tim immediately wondered why Evold had said, 'since you're back', as if he were surprised that Tim had made it back. The darts game commenced and ended as usual with Evold and Susan winning - yet again.

5

It was two weeks later that Tim, returning from duties at Gil Gil, met his father in the latter's office at the police station. After sitting down, Tim proceeded to tell his father that he had let General Anderson know what strange coincidences had occurred and that they had agreed to make it known that the following week his platoon was going to be checking the culverts on the stretch of road between Wajir and Ramu and that they would be camping down at the old now-vacated Public Works Department camp just two miles south of Ramu. Tim went on to say that at the border post at Ramu the senior immigration officer, Bill Shankey, who was known to Tim, had been advised of the story that was going to be circulated and asked him to inform them if there were any consequences - which he agreed to do. They also asked that he light the fire in the PWD camp ground, and have a few shirts on a bush, as if drying, and a few cycles propped up against the wall. Brian immediately said,

'Great, I'll get Ndoma to leave tomorrow to visit his parents at El Leh, with specific instructions to keep a look-out for either Otto or Evold.' And so the trap was set.

That evening, as Evold, Susan, Sandra and Tim were playing their usual darts game, Tim called Sandra over after her throw. He was standing with the poster, 'Your Country Needs You', on the one side and the poster, 'Walls Have Ears', on the other, and for a moment he thought how apt that was: here he was, telling a tale to trap a traitor, as he told Sandra in a whisper where he would be going next week. Just as Tim had hoped, Sandra, taken aback, said loudly,

'Oh, no, Tim, not two weeks at Ramu! That's right on the border. Oh, darling, you will take great care? Gosh, I remember the one occasion that I went with you, and we stayed at that PWD Camp, so I'll sit and picture us back then, before all this terrible war blew up.' She entwined her arms round his neck and gave him a deep lingering kiss. Tim had been watching Evold particularly when Sandra was talking: how he had told Susan to hush, how his eyebrows rose when he heard what Sandra said, and imagined that, deep inside him, he was rejoicing as he thought about the Italian bombers strafing that defenceless camp, with Tim inside. This could at last be the end of Tim, and he would be free to date Sandra.

Ndoma had been with his parents in their home for two days when he informed them that he was going into El Leh to spend some time with his sister Mufasi. He bade his parents good-bye and walked down the well-worn dirt road that led into the town. His sister owned a shop specialising in clothes' repairs as well as selling new clothes. Her husband Kaleem assisted her in the clothes' sales part of the business. Neither of them could believe their eyes when Ndoma walked into the shop. Mufasi stopped sewing and rushed up and cuddled him, explaining how lovely it was to see him after such a long time. (She always complained about the latter part, as she would have dearly liked him to be working in El Leh.) Kaleem walked over, and the two of them exchanged a handshake as Kaleem asked Tim:

'Well, will you be staying for a while?' and Ndoma replied that it would be until he had concluded his mission. Mufasi let out a gasp, and Ndoma took his brother-in-law by his shoulders and led him to a darkened corner in the shop. Ndoma explained the main reason why he was in El Leh. As he did so, Kaleem interrupted him and said that strangely the last two times that either Otto or Evold De Bruin came to El Leh, neither of them took the time to visit the local cattle farmers. One of the farmers saw Evold in the street, did ask him why, but Evold said that he was too busy sorting out other affairs. Kaleem then went on to say that one of the farmers had spotted Evold down one of the side-streets, in a nook, and swore blind that the person that he was talking to was a local by the name of Mapeto a sergeant in the Italian army. (Many of the locals had joined the Italian Forces.) Mapeto was known to be an extremely cruel person, who had killed several of the locals with whom he had been friends before he joined the Italian army. The reason for the killing was that, unlike him, they were not rushing to join the Italian army! Ndoma too well knew Mapeto and had heard of some of the stories relating to the killings. Ndoma thanked Kaleem for all that information and stressed how important it was that this went no further. Not even his sister or his parents must know, as he did not want anyone to say anything that might alert Evold that they were on to him.

Three days later, Ndoma got word from one of the farmers that Evold was in town. Ndoma thanked him and asked where Evold was last seen, and, when told, he thanked him again and headed out into the town. He blended in with all the locals, many of whom he knew, so he was able to chat with them about everyday things, and that too helped his not standing out. It was whilst he was talking to one farmer that he suddenly spotted Evold on the other side of the street. His heart began to beat faster as he walked along chatting to the man by his side but all the time keeping a strict eye on where Evold was heading. After walking a couple of blocks, Ndoma noticed that Evold had suddenly been joined by one of the locals and that the two of them were in deep conversation. Ndoma quickened his step, and, when he was directly in line, his heart gave a skip as he noticed then that the person was in fact Mapeto. Ndoma immediately pulled down his fez (a flat-topped conical red hat with a black tassel) so that his face would not be easily recognized. As he did so, he noticed that Evold and Mapeto had taken the next side-street to the left. So he now had to cross over and be very wary how he proceeded. He stepped into the side-street and, taking out a cigarette, lit it whilst looking down the side-street, and, about half way down, he could plainly see that there was now a third person - and this person was in Italian army uniform. That was all Ndoma needed to see. He turned back and walked into the main street and on to his sister's shop. Reaching her shop, he went inside, greeted his sister and her husband, and, as he did so, he nodded to Kaleem to come over to a corner of the shop where there were not many locals shopping. As Kaleem reached him, Ndoma said,

'I've seen it all now with my own eyes. Your farmer friends were correct: he's meeting personnel from the Italian army.' He paused, then continued: 'My job here is done. I'm going to return to Nyeri right away. Please thank my sister for having put me up, and perhaps you can pass on my thanks to my parents too when you next see them.' Kaleem nodded, and the two men embraced, and then Ndoma was out into the street, heading for the bus-stop.

6

Brian Hargraves was sitting in his office at the Nyeri police station when there was a knock at the door.

'Come in!' Brian called out, and the door was opened, and in walked Sergeant Ndoma, smart as ever in his police uniform. He came to a halt in front of Brian's desk and snapped out a salute. Brian saluted him back. 'Ah, Ndoma, I wasn't expecting you back so soon. I can only presume that you have some good news.' Ndoma gave a smile and said,

'Good news indeed, sir.' Brian said.

'Right-o. Well, close the door, pull up a chair and sit down.' Ndoma did so. Once sitting, Ndoma went on to recall his following of Evold, whom Evold met and how Evold had been seen meeting Mapeto days before the KAR had been bombed when checking culverts, and also days before the Wajir base was bombed. Brian said,

'The bastard! Well, it'll be very interesting to hear the result of this last meeting. Thank you, Ndoma, you have indeed been of great service, and I will note this on your record of service.' Ndoma came smartly to his feet.

'Thank you, sir.' He saluted, about-turned and walked out of Brian's office. Brian picked up the phone and phoned through to KAR in Gil Gil. He spoke to General Anderson and asked whether he and Lieutenant Hargraves would be free for him to come in and see them. The general said that they would be, and Brian said that he would leave shortly. He replaced the phone, left his office, walked to his official police car, got in and, having started the engine, drove off towards Gil Gil.

Arriving at the KAR Camp in Gil Gil, he was stopped at the gate by an Askari, who asked what his business was at the camp, and, when told, the Askari went to the guard-room and phoned through to the commandant. Within a few minutes he re-appeared, approached Brian and said, 'Thank you, sir, the commandant is expecting you. When you pass the gate, continue down the road. The building you want is second from last on the left hand side,' and with that he went back to the guard-house and raised the barrier, and Brian was able to drive through.

Brian drove down the road until he reached the second from last building, pulled up at the kerb, parked and got out. As he walked to the building, it was guarded by two very smart KAR soldiers, who came to attention and saluted Brian. He saluted them back, and then the one Askari, reaching down, opened the door. Brian was able to gain entry. Inside, the room was well lit, which was just as well as all the windows had been blacked out. In the centre of the room was General Anderson's desk, and beside it was another table on which there was a large-scale map of Kenya. The general rose as Brian entered and walked over to shake his hand. Standing at the desk was Brian's son Tim. The general indicated Brian's seat, and then all three sat down. The general said,

'You told us you had some rather important information you wanted to share with us.' He paused as he lit his pipe, and Brian said,

'Yes, indeed, I know that my son Lieutenant Hargraves had you filled in on what I was doing. Well, my sergeant Ndoma arrived back this morning, and, to cut to the chase, he has confirmed that, days prior to the attack on the KAR at the culvert inspection, and also prior to the Wajir bombing, either Evold De Bruin or his father Otto was seen in El Leh speaking to an Italian army sergeant, a man named Mapeto. Then, two days ago, Evold was spotted by Sergeant Ndoma walking and talking to Mapeto. Ndoma was able to follow them down a side-street, where they met an Italian soldier in uniform. Unfortunately Ndoma was not able to see what rank he held without giving himself away. I can only presume that Evold De Bruin, had heard what was said at the hotel, about my son going to the old PWD camp near Ramu. Anyway, I've arranged for signs to be put at the camp to make it look as though it is in fact inhabited and am now waiting to hear whether the Italians will bomb this as well.' He paused and picked up the cold glass of lime-juice that was before him and took a large refreshing drink. He replaced the glass, and General Anderson said,

'Yes, your son did fill me in, and now this does seem to be something young Evold De Bruin is informing the Italians about: where the KAR are, but, more importantly, where the KAR under your son's command are.' Again he paused and took a few more puffs on his pipe before saying, 'Is there some sort of bad feeling between young De Bruin and your lieutenant?' He turned to face Tim. Tim looked his commandant straight in the eye and said,

'Yes, sadly, Evold has always had a soft spot for my girlfriend Sandra, and, although he is courting Susan Moody, he still has a hankering after Sandra.' Tim paused before going on to say, 'I can only suppose that he had hoped in the past two incidents that I may have been among those killed.' Before he could say any more, Brian cut in:

'Well, seems a hell of a thing, to be willing to betray your country, just to eliminate your love rival, so it'll be most interesting to hear the latest outcome.' All three round the table agreed, and General Anderson suggested that Tim should remain here in camp, keep out of sight and not contact anyone, just as it would have been if he had gone to the PWD camp. Once again all agreed, and Brian left and drove back to his office in Nyeri.

7

The days slowly passed till that morning, when the phone rang at the police station. The officer who took the call put the caller through to Inspector Brian Hargraves. Brian picked up the receiver and said,

'Hello, Inspector Hargraves, Nyeri Police.' The voice on the other end was that of the senior immigration officer at Ramu, Bill Shankey, who said,

'Good morning to you! Just wanted to let you know that your suspicions seemed correct: just after 6am this morning, four Italian bombers swooped down on the old vacated PWD camp and blasted it to bits: every shack was razed and left on fire, nothing was left standing.' He paused and then said, 'It was a damn good show. Thank goodness there was no one really there as, if they had been, they would have all perished.' Brian thanked him very much and hung up. Smiling to himself, he reached for the phone once more and again phoned through to General Anderson at the Gil Gil KAR camp. When he was put through, he said,

'Good morning, general, just had a call from Senior Immigration Office Bill Shankey at Ramu. You may be interested to know that at 0600 hours this morning, out of nowhere, four Italian bombers swooped down and blew the old vacant PWD camp to bits: absolutely nothing left standing.' As previously agreed, they were not going to make any broadcast of the attack - as yet. They were more than interested in the reaction that might come from Evold De Bruin. They would, of course, get a release for broadcast, should there not be any reaction from Evold: they were hoping that, in his excited state, he might reveal his treachery.

Earlier that same morning, Otto and Evold De Bruin left the main house and ambled towards the milking barn, as usual, except that in this instance they changed direction and went into the feed barn. Once they were inside, they climbed the wooden ladder to the loft. Once there, Otto retrieved the radio-receiver that was hidden there, on which they had been receiving messages as to how the information they were giving to the Italian army had been acted on. That day Evold was in a state of excitement greater than usual, as he was waiting to hear whether Tim had met his fate, opening the way for Evold to court Sandra. With bated breath, he waited to hear what had transpired at the PWD camp near Ramu. It did not take long before the receiver crackled into life, and the message came through loud and clear that the PWD camp near Ramu was observed to have been occupied - clothes, cycles and fires clearly seen - and that Italian bombers had swooped down and bombed all the buildings, utterly devastating the camp. There could have been no survivors. The message was repeated, just in case they had not heard it correctly, and ended by thanking the De Bruins once again for their valuable efforts in the war and hoping that they might long continue to furnish valuable reports in the future.

Evold was hardly able to control himself. He was so elated, he wanted to jump up and down and shout hooray, but Otto, sensing his son's reaction, caught him by his shoulder, and said,

'Now, son, don't be so exuberant: we don't want any of the African staff wondering what we're up to up here, listening to some unknown language reports, now do we?' To which Evold replied,

'No, papa, no, certainly not,' and he helped hide the radio-receiver once again. They climbed down the ladder, and this time Otto did go to watch the milking, but Evold continued back home.

Evold could not wait to go into town that afternoon; he could not wait to see Sandra's face when she found out that Tim had been killed. How he would console her and win her! Evold arrived at the hotel just before 5pm. He found both Sandra and Susan already seated by the dart-board, and, ordering a drink, Evold joined them. Sandra was quite taken by surprise when Evold, instead of sitting with Susan, pulled his chair round and sat beside Sandra. Susan had noticed this, and her quizzical face matched that of Sandra as they looked at each other. They shrugged their shoulders. Of course Sandra had been told what to expect that evening by Tim, and she was playing her part to perfection.

Meanwhile, Brian, General Anderson and Tim had themselves arrived at the hotel but kept themselves well hidden. Sandra immediately started to sing the praises of Tim and his bravery, adding how much they were looking forward to getting married, and this was Evold's breaking-point. With an evil chuckle he said,

'Oh, dearie me, Sandra. Too late: haven't you heard that he and his platoon were wiped out at the old PWD camp they were at near Ramu? Four Italian Bombers razed the place ... nothing left standing.' Sandra let out a gasp and, pretending to be in anguish, ran off towards the ladies' toilets, with Evold in hot pursuit, saying,

'Don't worry Sandra, I'm still here! You know I adore you. You can marry me instead, now that I'm rid of Tim at last.' He stopped short, realising what he had just said, as Tim, General Anderson and Inspector Hargraves appeared from inside the ladies' toilets.

'Oh, you mean you got rid of me, Evold?' Tim said. Evold just stared at Tim.

'No, it can't be! You said you'd be at that camp!' Again immediately he realised what he had said. Susan, who had been bringing up the rear, said,

'Evold, how could you, you despicable man?' and then cried, 'Oh, goody!' as Inspector Brian Hargraves clasped Evold, put his hands behind his back and handcuffed him.

'Evold De Bruin, I arrest you for treason,' and, with that, he and General Anderson escorted Evold to his police car, whilst Tim, holding Sandra in his arms, together consoled a tearful Susan.

At a later search of the De Bruin farm, the radio-receiver was found. Otto De Bruin was also charged. His poor wife Noreen, not knowing what had been taken place, was left, and she continued to run the farm and was one of the first to be invited to Tim and Sandra's wedding. Nyeri again settled down after the war. As Lord Baden-Powell had said, 'The nearer to Nyeri, the nearer to bliss'.

Le Fantôme du Maquis

Neal James

1

Alan Harrison turned from the window through which he had been staring for the last five minutes and looked at the young man sitting at the opposite side of his desk. He had been the governor of the North Sea Camp borstal since its opening in 1935, and John Naylor had been in and out of the institution on two occasions. Knocking out the contents of his pipe into an ashtray, he sighed and sat down.

'All right, Mr Brough,' he said. 'That'll be all; I'll call for you when Naylor and I are finished.'

'Sir.' The clipped reply was typical of an army NCO which was, in fact, what Brough had been until an honourable discharge at the age of forty-eight in 1934.

With the door now closed and privacy assured, Harrison opened the brown manila file on the desk before him. He read again the contents, slowly shaking his head at the familiar words. He closed it and looked into Naylor's eyes.

'What is it, John, that drives you back here time and again?'

'Don't know, sir,' Naylor replied, looking directly ahead.

John Naylor had one week left to serve at North Sea Camp, and then he would once more be free to return home and carry on with his life. That life had been one of juvenile delinquency since early childhood, and he had progressed through a range of institutions culminating in two visits to the borstal run by Alan Harrison.

He had been born in 1916 to a tannery worker in the Derbyshire village of Langley Mill. His father, Reginald, had served with the

British army and was killed at the Battle of Cambrai on 22 November 1917. Left to bring up their son alone, Emily Naylor worked tirelessly to put food on the table and keep a roof over their heads, but by the time John was seven he had become a troublesome youngster. Roaming the streets after school, he was a constant source of irritation to neighbours on Sedgwick Street initially, and then further afield as he grew older. When Emily died from pneumonia in 1926, John was sent to live with an aunt in Nottingham.

From the age of ten until his first incarceration at approved school, the youngster took to the city's streets, regularly missing school and finding amusement with a group of older boys in the Meadows area of his new home. Jean, his aunt, struggled hard to cope with the disruption of her formerly placid life but when, at the age of nineteen, he was sent to North Sea Camp for the second time, she made it clear that he was no longer welcome in her home.

'Look, lad,' Harrison said. 'You need to get your life sorted out. I don't want to see you back here in another few months. How old are you now? Twenty-one?'

'Twenty, sir,' John replied.

'Twenty,' the governor shook his head again. 'You do understand that if you carry on like this you'll probably end up in prison, don't you? Borstal can only take you up to twenty-three, and it's a much harder life inside.'

'Yes, sir.' Naylor stared at the floor, suddenly realising the seriousness of his situation.

'Have you considered joining the army? They'll give you training, and at least you'll have a home to go to now that Nottingham's no longer an option.'

'Sir?' Naylor looked up – he had never considered the lifeline that Harrison was holding out to him.

'Go and speak to Mr Brough, son. He was an RSM in the Northumberland Fusiliers; I'm sure if you ask him politely he'll point you in the right direction.'

'Yes, sir. Thank you, sir,' John replied, brightening suddenly.

'Well, this time next week you'll be free again, and I really don't want to see you back. You're much better than the rest of the lads in here.'

As good as his word, John Naylor spent an hour with an extremely surprised Arthur Brough and, at the end of that time, came away with not only the address of the recruiting office in Nottingham, but also the name of a former colleague in the army. One week later he left Nottingham, bound for the Northamptonshire Regiment in Wootton; from there he was sent for basic training in the Norfolk town of Thetford with a number of other new recruits.

Naylor prospered in the disciplined lifestyle which the army presented to him. He had always considered himself to be reasonably fit, but a regime of route marches, frequently in excess of twenty miles, and daily drill under the watchful eye of SM Barrowman, saw him quickly become one of the best recruits in his company. By the end of his ten-week stint at the Norfolk camp, he was looking forward to a brighter future in his new 'family'.

When the war clouds began to gather over Europe in 1938, John had been in the Northamptonshires for almost two years and, as a result of dedication to the task at hand, had risen to the rank of corporal. He looked at the new recruits coming through 'B' Company and smiled - had he really been that raw himself? When war was declared by Neville Chamberlain's government on 3 September 1939, he was amongst the first of the Northamptonshire Regiment to be sent to France as part of the British Expeditionary Force committed to driving the German invaders out of Poland. Nine months later, he was a member of the rear guard protecting the retreating British and French forces on the road to the beaches of Dunkirk where a flotilla of small boats was ferrying soldiers to larger ships offshore.

'Corporal Naylor!' The command came from Lieutenant Peters. 'Take a dozen of your best shots and pin the Jerries down at the end of the street.'

'Yes, sir,' John replied. Calling out a series of names, he led the way back along the rubble-strewn street and took up a position at the crossroads one hundred yards from the retreating members of 'B' Company. A steady toll was taken of the advancing German infantry, as a regular stream of sniper-fire from both sides of the ruined French street kept them pinned down and unable to make any headway. That scenario suddenly changed with the appearance of the tank summoned to clear the way.

'Fall back!' Naylor shouted. 'Two sections - one covering the other.'

With his group now retreating before the advancing armour, Naylor saw his chance. The tank commander, seeing the fleeing British troops, appeared above the turret for a better view of the street. Passing Naylor's position without a sideways glance, he was unaware of the danger into which he had allowed his crew to stray. John looked back up the street and, seeing no infantry, made his move. He stole in behind the vehicle; a burst of shell fire from the tank concealed his progress up the track guard, and, by the time the commander turned, it was too late. A crushing blow from Naylor's rifle butt sent him slumping back into the interior of the tank, and he was followed by a fistful of grenades dropped in behind him by the now fleeing British corporal. The four-second fuse gave Naylor just enough time to dive for cover as the tank exploded, killing all those on board and sending the first wave of advancing German infantrymen running for shelter amongst the ruins of the once-beautiful street. John took the opportunity to make good his escape, joining up with the rest of his company at the beach.

'What was all that, Naylor?' Lieutenant Peters asked. 'The rest of your men arrived here a while ago.'

'Just a bit of a lesson for the Jerries, sir,' John smiled. 'Where's the Bren?'

Moving back up the beach, Naylor set the machine-gun up to cover the end of the street now blocked by the burning tank. His only targets would be the German infantry inching past the searing heat of the wreckage - they were easy prey, and bought more time for those on the beach. He maintained his position for a full hour until ordered to withdraw by his commanding officer; he was one of the last to leave for the 'little ship' sent to rescue them.

Back home, and at regimental headquarters ten weeks after Operation Dynamo, he stood to attention before his battalion commander, Lieutenant-Colonel Dodsley. Dodsley had served in the Great War and had risen to his current rank by means of the same kind of action for which he was now about to reward Naylor.

'Corporal Naylor,' he barked. 'Your field promotion to sergeant, awarded by Lieutenant Peters, is confirmed and the regiment is proud at the recommendation of the award of the Military Cross in recognition of your acts of outstanding bravery in the face of the enemy at Dunkirk.' Naylor snapped to attention and saluted smartly. Once free from the ceremony, and after a round of handshakes from his fellow 'B' Company regulars, he was summoned to a side room by Lieutenant Peters who gave him a note.

'I've been ordered to give you this,' he said. Naylor frowned in puzzlement at reading the contents and looked up at his superior officer.

'I don't understand, sir. Am I being discharged?'

'All I know, sergeant, is that the man whose name is on that note has pulled some strings to get you seconded to his unit from the Northants. Can't tell you any more, but I'd get my skates on if I were you.'

Two days later, Sergeant John Naylor was in London's Baker Street, knocking on a plain door bearing the number on the note in his hand. He was greeted by the smiling face of an older man who opened it.

'Sergeant Naylor?' he asked. 'Please come in; we've been expecting you.' With the door now closed behind him, John Naylor was about to ask why he had been pulled out of his unit – he was beaten to the punch.

'My name is Ralph Morrison – welcome to the ranks of the SOE.'

2

'The what?' Naylor asked as he followed Morrison into a sparsely furnished office.

'SOE, Mr Naylor, stands for Special Operations Executive.' He waved to a chair on the other side of the desk where he was now sitting. 'Do please take a seat.'

'And what does it do?'

'The Special Operations Executive is a new organisation. It was officially formed by Hugh Dalton, the Minister of Economic Warfare on 22 July, to conduct espionage, sabotage, and reconnaissance in occupied Europe against the Axis powers and to aid local resistance movements.'

'Never heard of it.'

'Oh, few people are aware of SOE's existence, Mr Naylor.'

'It's *Sergeant* Naylor, Mr Morrison – I'm in the army.'

'No longer, I'm afraid.' Morrison smiled and sat back in his chair. 'You've been officially transferred to us under emergency powers - we are at war, you know.'

'Okay, what do want *me* for?' Naylor crossed his arms and sat back. Opening the top right-hand drawer of his desk, Morrison placed a file before himself and opened it. He smiled as he leafed through the pages, enjoying Naylor's irritation at a situation which was out of his control.

'I see that you've been in trouble quite a few times down the years.'

'How did you get those ... ?'

'We have our ways and means, even at this early stage in our development, and we need people like you.' He paused, briefly, to let the statement sink in. 'I understand that your last stay at the North Sea Camp was as a result of a shooting.'

'Pigeons.'

'You were sent to borstal for shooting pigeons? What did you use, a double-barrel shotgun?'

'An air-rifle - while they were in flight.'

'Impressive, but surely shooting pigeons shouldn't have earned you a place at North Sea Camp.'

'They were the local police sergeant's racing pigeons, and he wasn't very pleased about it.'

'Ah, yes, I see. That would explain it.' Morrison smiled again. 'You no doubt took that skill into the army with you, as I can see that your record on the firing range was exceptional whilst you were undergoing basic training.'

'Static targets are a piece of cake once you get used to the kick of a Lee Enfield; I never failed to hit the bull's-eye.'

'That's going to come in very handy where we'll be sending you after you've had some additional training. You'll have to go through a crash course in French and German, though. I'm afraid there's no way around that.'

'Not necessary.'

'I beg your pardon?' Morison looked up from the file where he had been reading of Naylor's exploits at Dunkirk.

'I'm fluent in both.'

'How so?'

'My mother was Swiss, and after she died my aunt couldn't cope with me all the time, so in the school holidays she sent me over to Switzerland to stay with her mother and father. They run a hotel just outside Interlaken in the Bernese Oberland. I picked up both languages pretty quickly – you can do that when you're very young.'

'Well, that's certainly going to help,' he said. 'You will, of course, cease to exist from this moment as John Naylor, and we'll furnish you with all of the paperwork and information to establish a new identity. You'll undergo a six-month training regime which will provide you with all of the skills and knowledge needed by an operative working behind enemy lines.'

'So, I'm to be a spy?' Naylor asked.

'No, that would take far too long,' said Morrison. 'The French are setting up a resistance movement – they're calling it the Maquis – and the task for you and others like you is to train them in acts of guerrilla warfare against the occupying forces.'

'How do I keep in touch with you?'

'You won't at the start; that would be far too dangerous. Supplies will come through a series of pre-arranged night-time drops, but essentially you're on your own once your briefing is completed.'

'Seems I have no choice in the matter.'

'Excellent!' beamed Morrison. 'The sooner we get started, the better.'

John Naylor's training was carried out at a secret base in Snowdonia. Summer quickly turned to autumn and winter, and conditions in the Welsh mountains soon made army life seem like a distant dream. He learned survival techniques, armed and unarmed combat, use of explosives, and sabotage. From a raw recruit back in 1936 he had become a hardened freedom fighter, prepared to kill without question and dispose of any evidence efficiently. He was also drafted into SOE's language program to train other recruits without his native abilities. By February 1941 he was ready and sitting once more in the Baker Street office where he had first met Ralph Morrison.

'We have your first assignment.' Morrison looked up from an identical file to the one he read from at their first meeting. This time, however, he slid it across the desk. 'You'll be dropped by parachute under cover of darkness outside the town of Abbeville in the French region of Picardy. There you will be met by members of the Maquis and taken to a place of safety; you will do as they say without question and their leader will brief you.'

'That would be ... ?'

'There are no names in that file except for your own. The Maquis will tell you all that you need to know at their end. For the moment, you have one week to memorise your new identity.' Morrison paused. 'You also have to understand that the Gestapo will certainly have operatives working in the same area - do I make myself clear?'

'Perfectly, but, if it's that dangerous, why not leave it to the French?'

'Because once the Nazis are defeated and de Gaulle returns to France in triumph, Britain will call in the debt which his country owes through people like you. Guerrilla warfare isn't an exercise in altruism – there's far more at stake than you could possibly imagine.'

'I assume that I can't take this file away from here.'

'Correct. You'll live here whilst you complete the preparation work, but once you hand that information back you'll have to remember every detail.'

'When do I leave for France?'

'Depending on the weather, and we need cloud-cover to conceal the aircraft's approach. It will be some time next week and will be carried out at a moment's notice, so be ready.'

The Westland Lysander crossed the English Channel on Thursday of the following week shortly after midnight. Its course failed to attract the attention of any German forces either on the ground or in the air, and a single parachute opened automatically as the sole passenger left the plane. John Naylor's descent was smooth and uneventful, and the training he received on the parachute equipment in Snowdonia gave him an almost soundless landing. Almost immediately, three figures appeared out of the tree cover to his left and he feared, initially, that his mission had been compromised. A French voice removed all of his doubts.

'Come with me, quickly,' it said. 'German patrols are common even at this time of night.' Their destination was a farmhouse two miles from the drop zone, and John was ushered in through the back door. The room was lit only by a log fire and candles - all of the windows were covered by thick curtains. An older man approached as they entered.

'Good evening, I am Pierre Clichy.' He stretched out a hand. 'You must be Gaston Dubois.'

'I am,' John replied, wondering whether the man also knew his true identity; he took the proffered hand and smiled.

3

The extent of the gaps in the knowledge of the Abbeville Maquis became apparent to John Naylor very quickly. A group of dedicated and enthusiastic patriots, their harassment of the occupying German forces had been limited, so far, too sporadic and largely ineffective raids on their stores. Nothing of any real value had been obtained beyond the odd item of small arms and other equipment. They lacked not only the raw materials to mount a serious assault on the Nazi war machine, but also the technical know-how to use those resources even if they had them. Using a range of prop materials, Naylor demonstrated how to plant, arm, and wire an explosive device to inflict maximum damage to a range of German facilities. He also trained the small team in methods of silent approach, camouflage, and a variety of ways of killing an enemy without leaving any evidence behind. In six weeks, he had around him a well-coached group of resistance fighters all of whom were prepared to lay down their lives for their country. The first real test came with information relating to the movement of a consignment of arms destined for the German front line. At a clandestine meeting the day before the arrival of the train, Naylor laid out the details of the plan which he had concocted.

'Timing is the key,' he said. 'We need to lay the explosives just before the scheduled arrival; too early and we risk discovery by German patrols, too quickly and we'll probably fail to set the devices properly. Stick to the training which I've given you, and we'll be fine. Any questions?' The ensuing silence gave Naylor some comfort, and preparations began for the laying of explosive charges along a section of the track three kilometres to the south-east of the town. Just after midnight on the day in question, the group of six were in position under cover of trees. Naylor looked at his watch. 'Okay, we split up into three groups and plant two sets of charges each,' he said. 'Make sure you lay them twenty metres apart so that we inflict maximum damage to the train.'

'What about anyone leaving it?' The question came from one of the two women in the group. Naylor had not really noticed her before, but as she stepped forward he held his breath; she stood five feet six, had black hair and a pale complexion. Beyond that, her features were denied to him by the darkness. Nevertheless, he felt an instant attraction which he shook off with some difficulty.

'I'll take care of that,' he replied. 'Pierre,' he turned to the older man who had greeted him on his arrival at the Abbeville farm, 'you man the plunger and wait for my signal.' Clichy nodded, and Naylor was glad of the diversion which the instruction had given him - there would be time to return to the subject of the young woman at a later stage. With an hour left before the arrival their target the group split up on their individual missions, returning forty-five minutes later with the cables connecting the detonators to the explosive charges which had been laid. Naylor stripped the wires and wound them around the plunger terminals as the rest of the group watched. He turned to Clichy.

'Pierre, as long as the plunger is down, we're safe. When I give you the first signal, pull it upwards to arm the connection, but wait for me to drop my hand to depress it fully, okay?'

'Of course, Gaston,' he replied. Naylor still found his new name and identity strange but nodded in return. His attention was drawn away by the sound of an approaching train in the distance behind the trees further down the line. 'Positions!' he said.

The munitions train was advancing at speed from Pont-Remy, and Naylor watched its approach through a set of binoculars which the Maquis had stolen on one of its earlier forays against the local German garrison. He raised his hand as it closed on their position and Clichy pulled the plunger up to its full height. A raised finger held the Frenchman's attention as John counted down to its arrival at the point where the explosives had been laid.

'Now!' He dropped his arm, and the plunger hit the box with a thud. For a moment nothing happened and Naylor thought that the detonators had all misfired. Then, with a thunderous roar, three of the wagons left the track in a flash of light; other connected trucks ignited as they came into contact with the heat generated by the first batches of explosive. Flames reached high into the sky and smoke poured into the night.

'Look!' Clichy pointed to the rear of the train where five figures, illuminated by the flames, were running from the guards' van at the rear. 'They're getting away!'

'Stay where you are!' Naylor hissed. Unshouldering his rifle, he leaned against the nearest tree and shouted out a command in what he hoped was a convincing German accent. 'Halt! Hände hoch!' In true Wehrmacht tradition, the five fleeing soldiers stopped in their tracks and looked around for the source of the command. It was the last thing they ever did. Naylor picked them off in rapid succession, and they fell where they had been standing. The silence following the explosions was deafening, and all eyes turned to Naylor in disbelief at what they had just witnessed.

'Go!' he shouted. 'Bring the bodies over here – we'll bury them in the woods. Take from them whatever you can – guns, grenades, knives; anything that we can use.' With the raid completed, and the train fast becoming nothing more than a smouldering wreck, the Maquis gathered up whatever kit they had taken from the dead soldiers and began to make their way back to the farmhouse three kilometres away. One of the group, a young man, walked alongside Naylor and pointed at the rifle.

'My name is Etienne. Your gun is a fine weapon; what is it?' Naylor unshouldered the weapon once more.

'A Lee Enfield Mark Four. It's been modified for use as a sniper rifle,' he replied.

'May I hold it?'

'No, it's not for anyone else to use.' Naylor tucked it under his arm.

'You are not a Frenchman,' Etienne, feeling snubbed, replied in the way that only one of his countrymen could; the sneer was not lost on John Naylor. 'Your accent is good; good enough to fool a German, but you would never pass for one of us around here.'

'Listen.' Naylor stopped and grabbed the younger man by the sleeve. 'As far as you're concerned I'm Gaston Dubois; do you understand?' Clichy, having heard part of the exchange, stopped and returned to their position. A flick of the head was enough to send Etienne ahead of the group.

'He's a young man full of zeal and with an intense hatred of anyone daring to take from him the things that he loves. The Germans are the focus of all of his loathing at present, but I fear that you may have inadvertently made an enemy of him. Take care to keep him within sight, Gaston.'

The group's return to the farmhouse was followed by the departure of three of the team to their homes in a neighbouring town. Some of Clichy's cell were carefully selected from outlying areas which the Germans would find hard to locate. Etienne and the young woman were the only other ones from the locality. In the light of the large kitchen, Naylor got his first clear look at the young woman he had seen in the darkness of the trees. She was several inches smaller than he was; her black hair cascaded down across her shoulders, and a pair of the brownest eyes he had ever seen flashed a smile at him from across the table.

'My name is Michelle,' she said, extending a hand which Naylor took. Turning it over he planted a brief kiss upon it in true French style.

'Enchanté, mademoiselle,' he replied in flawless French. Across the room, Etienne smouldered with rage at this insult. He had long considered that Michelle and he would reach an understanding, and now this foreigner dared to step into his territory. He left the farmhouse and slammed the door. Clichy glanced after him and shook his head; he left to fetch a bottle of wine from the cellar.

'Oh, ignore Etienne,' Michelle said with a shrug. 'He believes more than he can achieve. He and I grew up together, and now he thinks that I'll marry him. He's just a young man with a temper. You, however, are a mystery, Gaston Dubois.'

'I'm just a freedom fighter, the same as you and your group.'

'Perhaps, in your own way.' She came round the table and stood directly before him. 'But I sense something more, something deeper – you're a troubled soul, aren't you?'

'And how could you soothe my pain?' He reached out for her hand, but she pushed him gently away.

'Maybe when we know each other a little better I'll answer that question.' She smiled and nodded in the direction of the door. 'For the moment, my father returns with a celebratory drink.' The three of them drank a bottle of the finest red wine Naylor had ever tasted, and an hour later John made his way to the outbuildings where the group had stored the weapons taken from the dead Germans; they would need to be concealed from any passing patrols. He rested his rifle against the wall and began to examine the weaponry which had been gathered. He turned swiftly at the soft footfall which betrayed Etienne's presence but was not quick enough to prevent the young man from seizing the Lee Enfield.

'Now let's see how brave you are, Englishman,' he sneered. 'Oh, yes, I worked that out for myself very quickly. We don't need your kind here, and Michelle is mine. Such a pity that you were foolish enough to look at her in the way that you did. I'll tell everyone that I heard the shot as I was leaving after checking and hiding the German guns. You have to be so careful with dangerous rifles like these.'

4

'Put the gun down, Etienne, before someone gets hurt.' Naylor spoke softly to the young man, holding his gaze.

'What's the matter, Englishman? Are you afraid now that I have control?' Naylor's eye was drawn to the barn door which had slowly begun to open, and he held his breath as the figure of Pierre Clichy moved silently to the left. The older man was too far from Etienne to attempt to disarm him and went, instead, for a direct approach.

'What's going on here?' The words sent a jolt through Etienne Gaubert, and he turned sharply to face the farmer, stepping backwards to bring both men into his arc of fire. A tense stand-off ensued as all three weighed up their options.

'What are you thinking of, you fool!' whispered Clichy. 'This man is our comrade; he risks his life in a fight which is not his own.'

'We don't need the English, Pierre,' he replied. 'They ran away at Dunkirk instead of standing and fighting.'

'And if they had, how many do you think would be left to carry on against the Nazis? They left to fight another day – over 300,000 escaped instead of being slaughtered. This man is here to help us in our struggle.'

'No! You're wrong.' Etienne raised the rifle, pointing at the older man. 'You will share his fate!' Naylor, reaching behind his back whilst the young Frenchman was ranting at the farmer, pulled out his knife from the sheath attached to his belt. Etienne never saw the blade as it whistled across the barn, burying itself in his right arm just below the shoulder. Screaming in pain, he dropped the rifle, his right hand clutching at the knife in his arm. John picked up the rifle and grabbed Etienne, pulling him across the floor to a pile of straw.

'Pierre!' he said. 'I need a needle and some thread to stitch this wound and any anaesthetic that you have.'

'Anaesthetic? We're at war, Gaston; that's impossible.'

'In that case, I'll have to resort to another method.' He looked down at Etienne. 'Sorry, young man.' Raising the rifle, he brought the butt down at the back of Etienne's head, and he passed out. 'I'll staunch the blood while you get the needle and thread.' With the blood flow stopped and the knife wound stitched, Naylor lay the young man back on the straw. Clichy shook his head at what had happened.

'That could have gone very badly for us all,' he said.

'You have no idea,' replied Naylor. 'He was lucky - a German would now be lying dead with that knife sticking out of his throat. What are you going to do with him?'

'He won't remain here after what he's done,' the farmer said. 'We can't have members of the group fighting amongst themselves. He's a good man, but full of his own importance - he thinks he can take on the entire Wehrmacht single-handed. We'll get him out of the area as soon as possible. He has family in Poitiers; he'll be safe there.'

John Naylor's budding relationship with Michelle Clichy developed over the course of the following eighteen months as the Maquis caused significant disruption to the German war effort in northern France. To the French he had become known as *Le Fantôme*, but by the end of 1943 the garrison commander, at his wits end, was replaced by Walter Altendorf, Standartenführer in the Waffen-SS. He was a brutal man who saw no advantage in maintaining any kind of relationship with the French 'peasantry', and treated them with all the disdain of an aristocrat, which is what he was. His appointment signalled a halt to the activities of the Abbeville Maquis, and Naylor's recall to London came soon afterwards.

'Don't worry,' he said to a tearful Michelle, 'I will return. When all of this is over, I'm coming back to you.'

Two days later he was back in Baker Street sitting opposite Ralph Morrison in the very same office where his career as a saboteur had begun. The room looked just the same - faded wallpaper, yellowing white paint on the skirting boards and window-frames, and curtains which had clearly seen much better days. After the homely warmth of the rural French countryside, the atmosphere in the building was depressingly drab.

'Ralph,' Naylor said. 'Where's the fire? The recall came a bit out of the blue.'

'You've done as much as you can in the Maquis - with the SS now breathing down their necks we felt it best to pull you out. Anyway, there's a much more important matter that we need to address. Ever seen this man's photograph before?' He slid a black and white image across the desk, and John picked it up.

'No,' he said after a cursory glance. 'Who is he?'

'Take a closer look; you'll be expected to recognise him on sight.' Morrison lit his pipe, waved away a cloud of bluish smoke and continued. 'His name is Claus von Stauffenberg; he's a colonel in the Wehrmacht and also the Chief of Staff for the Commander-in-Chief of the home army.'

'Very interesting - what's that got to do with me?'

'The Germans are losing the war,' Morrison said. 'The retreat from Moscow and the defeat at Stalingrad have them on the back foot for the first time in mainland Europe. It's come to us through contacts in Germany that several of their high-ranking army officers are hatching a plot to have Hitler killed along with his entire general staff. They'll then take over command of the army and sue for peace with the western Allies.'

'Before the Russians reach the border,' Naylor finished the sentence. 'They're scared to death, aren't they?'

'Like you wouldn't believe. The idea is to keep as much of Germany intact as possible and line up with Britain and America whilst they have the chance.'

'Okay, so what's their plan?'

'Hitler is holding a meeting with all of his top brass on 20 July at the Wolf's Lair, his East Prussian headquarters. It seems von Stauffenberg may have drawn the short straw in planting a bomb at the meeting. With any luck the entire Nazi hierarchy will be taken out in one fell swoop.'

'Sorry, I don't understand,' Naylor frowned. 'What's my part in all of this?'

'The SS and the Gestapo have eyes and ears all over the place – it's the only reason Hitler's survived so long. SOE need someone over there to ensure that von Stauffenberg gets to the Wolf's Lair alive.'

'You want me to be his bodyguard?'

'More than that. SOE will provide you with all of the paperwork and equipment to enable you to cut right through the ranks of the Wehrmacht that surround the Colonel, and take down anyone who comes within a mile of harming him. Come with me, and I'll show what we have in mind.' Moving further into the depths of the building, Naylor was ushered into a large back room where a number of people were occupied at a variety of tasks. Morrison led him to a corner where an older man stood making final adjustments to a collection of clothing on a tailor's dummy.

'This is Gerald,' said Morrison. 'We've borrowed him from an exclusive Savile Row gentleman's outfitters.'

'I'm astounded,' Naylor said, shaking hands with the man. 'Is it authentic?'

'Of course,' Gerald replied. 'All the materials come from the same source, and the buttons and insignia have been copied from original patterns. I doubt whether anyone where you're going will be able to pick you out from a real officer.' Back in the office, Morrison laid out the plans for the mission and equipped Naylor with everything that would be needed to complete the task.

'The thing to remember is attitude,' he said. 'Act the part and, in that uniform, no-one in the Wehrmacht will even look at your face. Remember - arrogance is the key and confidence will get you exactly where you'll need to be. Good luck!'

5

The silent parachute descent placed John Naylor two miles to the north-west of the town of Olsztyn in occupied Poland, six miles short of the Wolf's Lair at Rastenberg. He had been told that von Stauffenberg would be in the town briefly before moving on to the headquarters where the Führer was scheduled to meet his general staff. Quickly donning the uniform supplied by SOE, he made his way carefully into the Polish town. Stepping unseen into the main street, he flagged down a passing army staff car and directed it to von Stauffenberg's headquarters.

'Wait here!' he snapped to the driver. Marching up the steps he entered the building, raising a hand in the accepted manner as he passed through the reception area filled with Wehrmacht troops. He stopped in the centre of the room.

'You!' he pointed at a random individual. 'Take me to von Stauffenberg immediately!' The omission of the colonel's rank was never questioned, and he followed the guard up a flight of steps to a room on the first floor. He entered without knocking and dismissed the man.

'Who the hell ... ?' the colonel began, suddenly silent as the effect of the black Waffen-SS uniform stilled any protest.

'Can we be overheard?' Naylor asked.

'No, but who are you?'

'An Englishman sent to ensure the success of your mission at the Wolf's Lair. Once you're inside the perimeter, your life will be in considerable danger. My orders are to ensure your safety, and once there you're free to do whatever it is that your group has planned.'

Over the course of half an hour, Naylor went over the details of his mission with the German officer, and he left the building in the same staff-car which had brought him there a short time earlier. Stepping out of the vehicle at the place where he had commandeered it, he dismissed the driver in true Waffen-SS style and strutted away. Once certain that he could no longer be seen, Naylor headed across country to the spot where he had concealed his parachute and clothing. Burying the SS uniform, he headed for Rastenberg and the compound containing Hitler's bunker.

Though security at the Wolf's Lair was tight, all Naylor's SOE training came to the fore as he evaded detection and entered the woodland surrounding the complex. Out of sight of any guard posts, he quickly assessed the route which von Stauffenberg's car would follow on its way to the meeting. A bend, hidden from the main access road, was the spot which *he* would have chosen for an ambush, and a lone figure, unaware of his silent approach, was already in position awaiting the arrival of the Wehrmacht colonel. Naylor settled down to wait, unshouldering his sniper rifle in readiness. The staff car rolled slowly up the drive - only von Stauffenberg and the driver were inside. Suddenly the figure, dressed in Wehrmacht uniform, stepped out and held up a hand. A demand for identification was made and, arguing strongly, the colonel stepped out of the vehicle to confront his inquisitor. The machine-gun slipped smoothly into the assassin's hands and von Stauffenberg stepped back. The driver, seeing the gun, began to exit the car. A burst of automatic fire threw him back into his seat and the weapon now turned on the colonel.

Naylor's reaction was fast - much faster than the assassin's. A single shot dropped the killer where he stood, and John raced to the shocked figure of von Stauffenberg.

'Quickly,' he said. 'Drag the body into the undergrowth while I change uniforms with your driver. You can't turn up on foot!'

'What will you do?'

'My mission is to get you to the Wolf's Lair,' Naylor said. 'Beyond that, you're on your own.' Moments later they were back in the car and drawing up outside Hitler's headquarters; the last Naylor saw of the German officer was as he passed through a guard point at the main door. Moving the staff car to the side of the complex, he stepped outside and lit a cigarette from the pocket of the borrowed uniform. Once the attention of the guard had strayed he slipped away into the woods and disappeared. As he was leaving the area, the sound of an explosion ripped through the air from the location of the Rastenberg complex. A swift escape was now the key, and he had a perfect hiding-place to wait out the war.

An 800-mile journey had faced John Naylor at the outset of his trek, but concealed amongst a host of refugees a change of attire back into nondescript clothing protected him from enquiring eyes. The Russian advance on the eastern front had caused mass panic, and large numbers of Poles and Germans fled before them, heading west. Crossing a now abandoned border post three weeks after leaving Poland, he was in the Swiss town of Interlaken as night fell. Joyous arms embraced him at his grandparents' guest house as light from an open door lit up his face. He remained there for a further eighteen months as the chaos in Europe finally began to subside. It was in the summer of 1946 that he stepped once more on to the streets of Abbeville. Hitching a ride with a local man, he descended from the horse and cart at the gates to the farm belonging to Pierre Clichy. The farmer frowned and shaded his eyes from the sun as the stranger walked down the dusty track to the farm gate. He beamed in delight when he recognised the approaching figure. He turned to the farmhouse in search of his daughter; the figure racing across the farmyard had not needed any summons.

'Gaston!' she cried, burying her face in his shoulder as they met. 'You came back!'

'Didn't I promise that I would?' he smiled.

All for One

Andrew D. Malloy

6th June, 1944. Somewhere in the English Channel.

'Ten minutes, lads!' Behind me the sergeant's voice booms above the sound of the waves crashing against our bows. We were close. Very close. I hear my heart hammering dully through my head, as if someone were taking a pick to me. The lad in front of me takes off his helmet and runs his free hand over his head. His fingers shake like a drunk with a bad case of the DTs. I swallow down the bile as it threatens to escape. The man next to me isn't so considerate, a stream of vomit exploding from him, streaking down the uniform of the man in front. The recipient feels the vomit land, even smells it. He doesn't seem to care. Nobody seems to care. We all have more pressing thoughts on our minds. *Survival.*

Another wave, the biggest since we'd left the safety of England's coastline, buffets the small craft, sends it lurching to the right. I'm convinced we are going over this time ... No ... Everyone on board wobbles but stands firm. A final test from above? Four to a row, twelve rows in all, forty-eight souls sailing into ... God knows what.

We were close, but not close enough to see or hear anything but puffy blankets of grey mist dancing on the dirty green water, the lingering death of each wave as it falls to regroup, the incessant rain battering our helmets, stinging our faces. I glance to the right at my comrade next to me. A faint trail of vomit glistens on his chin. We exchange brief knowing looks before the reality of our situation hits home again, as it had every second of every minute of every hour since the order was given.

D-Day. They said it would become etched into folklore. Nobody even knew what it stood for, but everyone knew what it meant.

Top brass had stood in front of us barely two days before: there were thousands of us on the parade-ground. The main man stood head and shoulders above the others, both in stature and presence. When he spoke, it was as if he were speaking personally to each and every one of us. Afterwards, we had all said as much. I had never even seen a real life general up close before, let alone met one. Brigadier General Malcolm Wilson-Smith was a Scotsman, like me, but that's where the similarity ended. Wilson-Smith had bigger fish to fry than I did. He had to worry about the fate of 150,000 men over the next few days. I had only to look after myself. How easy would my job be compared with his? I had considered including this question in the letter to my mother. I decided it could be construed as somewhat heartless and flippant. As if my death would seem pointless and unimportant to her.

The letter ... There were tears. I cannot say any different.

The general finished off his address by advising us to get as much rest as we could in the hours leading up to the invasion. Our country needed people who were bright and alert, he had said. Early bed, early rise, and we'll catch Jerry with his pants down, he had said. Relax. Enjoy the next couple of days. Have a drink on me ... but don't overdo it, he had said, wagging a finger. Everybody laughed. And, at the end, spare half an hour or so, he had said. Write a letter to your wife, your mother, your father ... You get the idea. Then his expression changed. His speech became short and choppy, as if the words were beginning to affect him. Your loved ones will receive a letter from us ... only if you don't return, he had said. An eerie silence was then shattered by a question from someone in the rank and file asking what a man should do if he wasn't able to read or write. 'A bit late to take a course now, isn't it, son?' the general had said to enormous gales of laughter. But his smile soon dissipated. My door is always open, son, he said to the unfortunate soldier. Then his gaze swept over the parade-ground. To all of you, he had said.

That night I somehow managed to grab some shut-eye before eventually waking up around 2am. My senses were alive. I grabbed my pencil and dog-eared notebook and began to write ...

To my dear Mother,

I hope this letter finds you well. Please give my love to the family, especially my little sister Mary and to baby John. I hope Mary still brushes her teeth every day and the wee man is not disturbing your sleep too much. Please give them a big cuddle for me. Don't suppose you have heard anything from Dad? I'm sorry I didn't get a chance to tell you before I left but my Dad is not worth it. You are worth ten of him and well shot. Even my Aunty Beryl said so and she is his sister.

Anyway I hope you are not too sad that I took one. I wouldn't like you to be sad. I want you to remember the good times we had as a family. You, me and the weans. Not Dad. Not him.

I would like it if you could ask Mrs Moffat to play Abide with me *one Sunday at the kirk. I really like that hymn. I know she is not the best of organ players. Please tell her I am sorry for saying she should take off her boxing gloves before she played. Ha ha! I hope she will forgive me.*

I have to go now, as the general says we have to rest up. He says we'd need all our strength to kick Hitler's you know what! I guess if you are reading this, I'll never know if we did or not. Kick his you know what, I mean. I hope we did. The general says that whatever happens we should feel proud of what we're about to do. That we're fighting so that our children and their children and so on can sleep safe in their beds.

I hope you are proud of me, Mother. The general says if our families are proud of us it makes everything worthwhile.

And please don't feel too sad. Tell Mary and John I will be looking in on them from time to time. I hope they both grow up to be kind and loving, just like their mother. That would do for me.

Always
Your loving son, William

Writing that letter was the hardest thing I've ever had to do. After I'd finished, I put down the pencil, wiped away tears, careful not to let anybody hear my snivelling, and settled down. After all, I *am* eighteen. Well, nearly. I'm not a kid anymore and don't need to act like one. I just wish I could give my family one last hug ... just in case ... well, you know.

I didn't get much sleep that night. Maybe even none at all. But then, I expect nobody did.

The nearer we draw to the beaches, the worse the weather gets. I cannot see a thing. I glance all around me in every direction. Then suddenly, the mist opens up in front of us like giant theatre curtains, though the wind and the rain are not in a benevolent mood, driving their punishment harder and harder into our faces. Everywhere, hundreds of small, squat, boxy vessels appear, dotting the water as far as the eye can see. I estimate each of the vessels is carrying dozens of unfortunate souls. I sense a feeling of relief and optimism at the sight – call it weight of numbers, the power of the mob. That feeling was not to last, as I get my first view of the landing site. I see that none of the boats has reached the shore yet, but there are many preparing to lower ramps. My heart lurches for the millionth time. In a few minutes my boat will be beaching on French sands.

The rain is incessant now. Another wave buffets the bows, sending freezing cold water cascading over us. The lad directly in front of me buckles at the knees. His comrade beside him catches him before he goes down. I feel scared ... terrified actually ... but also proud to be among such a fine bunch of lads.

My mind drifts back to the day a few weeks ago when we all met for the first time. Everyone got on from the off, but I grew closer to the lads nearer my own age: three in particular. Billy Thomson is a Londoner, a cockney. I had never met a cockney before, hadn't even met anybody from England. In fact the only reason I knew Billy was English and a cockney was that I went to the pictures in Glasgow – the Rio - back in February with Fiona Riddell to see *The Life and Death of Colonel Blimp*. I swear Billy could be Spud Wilson. He wasn't best pleased when I told him that, until I said Spud was a lieutenant in the film. Didn't stop him calling me 'Haggis' from then on, though. Billy likes to think of himself as a jack-the-lad, but he's a good sort, and we get on famously.

Fiona? Ah, she's just a mate. Much too pretty to be interested in a lad like me. I think she went with me to the pictures only because she felt sorry for me. Mother says it's as plain as the nose on her face that Fiona likes me, but I get so embarrassed I tell her I'm not interested in girls. But I am. In this one. Maybe after this is over I'll ask Fiona on a proper date ... that is, if I'm ...

Taffy Thomas is the tallest man I've ever seen. Billy asks him what the weather's like up there. Taffy says Billy is such a short-arse that he should stand up when he's asking someone a question. Billy says he is standing up. Taffy comes from Cardiff, in Wales. I ask him where the name comes from. He says Thomas is a common name in Wales. I say no, I mean Taffy. He says he knows what I mean. Everybody laughs. I feel like an eejit. Then he says everybody in Wales is called Taffy. I say, even the girls? It gets a bigger laugh.

'You, Jock, are definitely worth watching,' Taffy says. I point to Billy and say,

'*He* calls me Haggis and now, according to you, I'm Jock!'

Wee Geordie MacDonald is exactly that ... wee, and a Geordie. From Newcastle. My uncle Bobby once told me that Newcastle was very close to Scotland. So close, he said, that the Scots used to say people who lived there were just Scotsmen with their brains bashed in. Wee Geordie pretended to be annoyed when I mentioned this to him. But he had to laugh in the end. Everybody did!

The night before the operation, the general tells us all to enjoy a couple of shandies. We all gather in the mess area as the beer is passed round. I pretend I'm a hard-bitten, hard-drinking Scotsman, but I think the lads see through this. They certainly do when I take my first mouthful. Yeeuck! Uncle Bobby was right! English beer really is manky. We're half-jaked in no time, and everybody is hugging and slapping each other on the back. There and then we make our pact. Some posh sort mentions a line from a book this Frenchman wrote: *all for one and one for all. The Three Musketeers.* And don't forget D'Artagnan, says the posh sort!

Who? Billy holds out a hand, and first Taffy, Geordie, then me lays a hand on top. There and then we promise to look out for one another when we hit the beaches in Normandy. We make a promise to survive this and carry on our friendship forever. I'm sure I see Billy wipe away a tear. I decide not to mention this, as I know it would embarrass him, and he'd only deny it anyway.

A hundred yards in the distance, the first of the boats hits the beach. The ramp flies down, and I hear an almighty roar. I realise it is coming from the soldiers as they pile out into the water, clutching their rifles above their heads. Another hundred yards or so further up on the grassy hill overlooking the beach, I see dozens of bright flashes from four, five, six, seven, a dozen positions. The deafening chatter of German guns turns the soldiers' defiant roars to cries of agony, the dirty green water to dark red. Another boat lands, then another, and yet another. Hundreds of young warriors hit the water, but most are cut down before they can reach dry land.

I have to blank this out. I can take no more. I close my eyes as tightly as I can, but the action only intensifies the sound of their screams. My breathing is like a steam-train out of control on a plummeting gradient. The waves, the rain, the screams, the gunfire – my hands lock hard on my rifle as we close in fast. 'Steady, lads! Nearly there! God be with us!' The sergeant steadies himself as a final wave rocks us on the way in. Clutching the ramp's release lever, he waits for the bottom of the craft to hit the sand before throwing it open. The ramp crashes down into the water as a hail of bullets land all around us. The first three or four rows are pitched forward by the boat's momentum, a couple of dozen of us sent tumbling into the freezing cold water. I take a deep breath as I go under. I hear the sound of bullets zip past my head like damp squibs on bonfire night. I try to dive down deeper, deeper, but I'm close to the bottom anyway. My lungs are already aching for air as I wait there for as long as I can.

A shadow. Something heavy lands on me from above, knocking me flat on my back. I try to wrestle the thing from my chest, but it is too heavy. I'm pinned on the ocean floor. I begin to feel drowsy. My lungs are screaming for oxygen. I muster all my strength. I manage to move the object a few inches. Red coloured liquid streaks from it, dissolving into the salt water. Using up my last reserves, I heave against the thing with all my might. It moves again, and I manage to free my legs. The thing turns over as it glides away from me. The staring eyes of my dead sergeant bore into my brain as his body rises above me to the surface. I see the ghostly silhouette of the dead man framed against the sky. My body is beginning to shut down. I have to breathe, or I will be dead in seconds. I am losing consciousness ... I feel a heavy hand on my shoulder, another grabbing at the lapels of my uniform. I am pulled up, up ... up towards the light. After what seems like an age, my face breaks the surface. I splutter back to life like a new-born baby emerging from the womb, hacking the salt water from my lungs. The sound of gunfire is deafening now, only matched by the terrified screams all around me. Bullets fly past my head, plunging into nearby flesh, splintering bones, dozens of them thudding harmlessly into the water. I freeze for a split second as I fight to regain my senses.

'Get down, Jock! Stay low!' A familiar voice from behind me does the job in an instant. I turn to nod at Taffy Thomas before being pushed back down into the water. I thump my nose on something hard just below the surface. I scream out in pain, reach out to push the thing away. I feel soft, rubbery tubes at one end and something hard, something solid at the other. I recoil, my hand pulling away as I see the dismembered leg, still booted, float away. I feel for my rifle which has been strapped to me the whole time and try to get to my feet. I point the rifle aimlessly at the hills in the distance, squeezing off a few defiant rounds in the general direction of the enemy nests.

'Save your ammo, Jock!' Taffy shouts. 'You can't get near them from here!' My throat red raw from swallowing the salt water, I turn again to nod at Taffy. More boats are flying in all around us. I see one heading straight for Taffy, and I shove him off to the right into the water, just in the nick of time as the ramp crashes down on to the exact position we'd been standing in.

The man next to me reaches down to help us back to our feet when he takes one in the back of the head. The bullet rips out most of his throat as it exits, pellets of bone and brain matter showering the water's surface. He crashes face down into the icy water. I stoop to try and help him but Taffy grabs my arm. 'He's dead, Jock! He's dead! We have to get out of here ... now!' Taffy and I half-walk, half-crawl towards one of the abandoned boats about twenty feet away. A soldier – young, though not much younger than me - is bent over, staring into the water. He is straining to keep his face clear of it and he looks as if he is on holiday, calmly and meticulously searching for shells in the shallows. He is oblivious to the carnage all around him.

'What are you looking for? Can I help?' I shout to him, reaching over to pull him up by the shoulders. He doesn't answer, can't answer. I see the confusion in his eyes.

'My ... my arm,' he whispers. The young soldier straightens and swings his shredded stump in front of my face. I feel my stomach retch. Taffy reaches over to grab him before ... too late ... the bullet strikes him squarely in the back, rips a hole out of his chest six inches in diameter. I see the terrified look on the lad's face as he realises his life is slipping away from him. Taffy, shaking his head furiously, lowers the body carefully into the water.

'Right, Jock, follow me!' he shouts. 'It's time we did something about this!' I sense the fire, the fury in his eyes before he turns and prepares to face the enemy. A hail of gunfire peppers the water around me as I take off after Taffy. I follow his lead, and we stoop low, zig-zagging as we run, somehow managing to avoid instant death. We thread our way through a crimson sea, among the dead and dying, until our feet are no longer inhibited by the drag of the water. I see huge footprints in front of me: Taffy's. We are on land, and the wet sand is making it easier for us to gain momentum, to build up a head of steam. Up ahead, the ground changes colour. It is shades lighter. Dry sand. Taffy changes direction, shooting off to his left just before we reach the dry sand. A trail of deadly bullets snakes the ground at our feet as we jump together into a stray hole. Our feet hit the bottom of the hole, and we pitch forward to the front as we land, using the steep bank as cover. The bullets continue as ever, flicking the sand above us, pinging harmlessly beyond our feet.

'What kept you, boys?' My heart stops as a familiar voice beside me pipes up. I hold my chest and roll on to my back laughing as I see wee Geordie MacDonald's crooked smile shine out from under his oversized helmet. Then the three of us swing our rifles round as we hear heavy footsteps approaching from behind. My finger tightens on the trigger as I take aim. Billy Thomson trips as he reaches the hole and tumbles down into the middle of it. A hail of bullets accompanies his entrance as Taffy and I grab an arm each and haul Billy to cover. Billy rolls over on to his back, his chest heaving with the effort. As usual he has a cigarette in his mouth, although it does look a little the worse for wear. He reaches up to pull the battered fag from his lips.

'Anyone got a light?' he jokes. Geordie reaches into his uniform and pulls out a lighter. Billy props himself up on an elbow, cradling the cigarette from the breeze, and takes a deep lungful of smoke. He eases back down, closing his eyes as he exhales slowly.

'And they said this was supposed to be a surprise mission!' Billy giggles before the cigarette-smoke turns his laughter into a coughing fit. We all laugh more loudly than the joke deserves. Pure nerves, or so I assume.

Four of us, on our backs, side by side, staring at the sky. *All for one ...* Nobody speaks for a minute, maybe two. The heavens open, the rain slamming down on top of us. We laugh as the sudden downpour extinguishes Billy's fag. He rips it from his mouth, pursing his lips as he tears off a little skin from them. Swearing loudly, he flicks the butt out of the hole in disgust.

'You finished?' Taffy says. Billy nods, licking his lips.

'What you got in mind: big stuff?' Geordie asks.

'We have to take out some of their positions,' Taffy says, 'to give the lads back there a chance to get ashore. Agreed?' All three of us nod in agreement.

'All right, we have to pool our resources. Let's do an ammo check. Jock, what you got?' I wipe water and sand from my brow with the back of a hand and begin to rummage around in a little knapsack I'd forgotten I was carrying. The others do the same, laying their wares on the sand. I do a count.

'Ten magazines and ... five grenades,' I say brightly. Taffy's face breaks into a smile.

'That's 100 rounds,' he says. 'You're the best shot, right, Jock?' I look at Billy and Geordie. They nod. I turn back to face Taffy:

'I suppose so,' I say, shrugging.

'You know fine well you are, Jock. I'm as blind as a bat, Geordie couldn't hit a donkey on the backside with a banjo, and Billy ... well, let's not go there!'

'Hey-!' Billy protests.

'But that's not to say you don't have your uses,' Taffy says, drawing a sarcastic smile from Billy. 'You're a cricket man, yes? Can you bowl?' Billy nods.

'I could knock your block off from twenty-two yards, Taffy. Big as you are.' He laughs.

There is a slight pause in the gunfire. Nodding towards the enemy, Taffy picks up a grenade.

'How far do you think you can throw one of these?'

Billy slithers up the bank on his belly and sneaks a quick peek. He scurries back down to safety, takes the grenade from Taffy and tosses it up repeatedly. His eyes narrow.

'Hmmm ... fifty yards?'

'You don't sound convinced,' Taffy says. Billy tosses up the grenade a final time, nods.

'Yep, I reckon I could chuck this at least fifty yards.'

'See that tree on the hill, in the distance?' Taffy asks.

'I see it.'

'That's your line. You think you can get the direction right?' Billy makes a face.

'Watch and learn,' he says. 'Fire in the hold!' Billy pulls the pin and grunts with the effort as he hurls the grenade into the distance, dead on the line of the tree. A few seconds later they hear the explosion. Taffy shimmies up to take a look as the dust settles.

'Outstanding, Billy. Now do you think you could do that again?'

'What's on your mind, Taffy?' I ask.

'The hole in the sand up there isn't big enough to take all of us.' Taffy turned to Billy. 'We need you to throw another one into the same spot, to make the hole bigger. You think you can do it?'

'I can do it, no problem,' Billy says as he stoops to pick up a second grenade.

'All right, now hold your horses,' Taffy says. 'This time we're following the grenade. By the time the dust settles we'll be in the hole, right?' No response. 'Right?'

'Right,' Geordie says, fixing his bayonet. I've never seen the wee man look so serious, so determined. Billy makes a face at me. I roll my eyes.

'Everybody ready?' Taffy says as we stuff our ammo back in our knapsacks. The three of us nod in unison.

Billy winds up like a Yankee baseball pitcher and number two spears into the distance, following the same line as the first, like a guided missile. Seconds later, hearts pounding, we are piling out of the hole, heading for that tree in the distance. A hail of bullets thuds into the sand as we again zig-zag for our lives before the second explosion rocks the ground in front of us. A huge blanket of sand flies into the air, thick enough to cover all four of us as we reach the hole in the nick of time, just as everything is settling back down. I lie still for a few seconds, wondering whether I am dead or alive. I realise I am still alive as I begin to spit mouthfuls of sand.

'Everybody all right?' Taffy's male-voice choir voice is easily heard above the gunfire. We are fifty yards closer, and the noise is now deafening. Geordie and Billy give the thumbs up, and I turn over to face the sky, nodding. 'Ok, Jock. Now it's your turn. Here, take a look.' Taffy hands me his binoculars. I clear the sand from my mouth and nose and crawl to the top of our man-made crater. I sweep the binoculars back and forth across the hill, taking mental notes of the positions of the enemy nests. I turn back over and slide down the bank. 'Well, what do you see?' Taffy asks.

'Each nest has a sniper with a 'scoped Gewehr 43 and a man on a machine-gun, probably an MG 131,' I say. 'The MG 131 is a heavy gun, deadly. No wonder everybody's being cut to - ' I stop. I don't want to dwell on this.

'You know your guns,' Billy says, smiling. I nod.

'That I do. There is one good thing.'

'What's that?' Taffy asks.

'Their mortars can't harm us. We're too close.' Geordie shakes his head and asks:

'What about their snipers?' I shrug.

'That's why this man's here,' Taffy says, putting his hand on my shoulder. 'It's time to earn your corn, Jock. The snipers. If you can take them out?' he says, sounding to me more hopeful than convinced. The notion makes me even more determined. I lick my thumb and flick it across the end of the barrel of my Enfield No. 5, Mk 1. A whole 2 lbs lighter than the Enfield No. 4, the No. 5 also has a rubber butt-pad which cushions the recoil better. Self-doubts creep into my brain until I remember heading the class at the rifle-range. Nobody could get near me. My mother always said everybody was good at something. The problem is most people never get the chance to find out just what they could do better than anything else. I was good at this.

I remove my helmet and slide up the bank. I pray that the 'scope isn't damaged or has been bumped out of kilter. I would soon know. A couple of final checks before I snuggle the scope around my right eye, sink the butt-pad into my shoulder. I lower the barrel, slide up until only my eyes and above are visible. Basic sniper training. Basic common sense. I sweep the rifle from left to right, my sights landing on a helmet. I aim high, just above the helmet, take in a deep breath and squeeze. The butt-pad slams into my shoulder, but I don't feel a thing. The Jerry throws his hands up in shock when my bullet pierces his helmet. He pitches forward, face down into the sand. Taffy sees the shot through the binoculars and throws both arms up as if he'd just scored the winning goal in a cup-final. Geordie and Billy both slap me on the back. I should be elated, but I'm not. I suddenly want to puke. Bizarre thoughts are invading my mind: I've just killed some mother's son, some poor kid's brother. I've decimated a whole family. I drop the rifle and fall to my knees, heaving as I hit the sand. I draw the back of my hand over my mouth. I turn and stare out to sea. Boats are still landing, mortar-shells are flying everywhere, and our side is still suffering heavy casualties. Taffy puts a comforting hand on my shoulder.

'I understand, Jock,' he says. 'I really do, but it's us or them.' I feel tears close in but manage to abate them. I nod at Taffy, glance at the others. I can see from their expressions they feel my pain. I take a deep breath and return to my post, grabbing the rifle. Again, I am careful not to show too much as I sweep slowly back and forth over the foxholes. My sniper training kicks in again, the instructor's words burning into my brain: be like the cat sitting in the tree for hours upon hours upon hours, waiting for the bravest of birds to stray too close; be patient ... Long slow breaths ... wait ... wait ... I am concentrating so hard I am almost completely unaware of the carnage all around us. I see a movement to the right. I concentrate my cross-hairs on the exact spot. I begin to count: one, two, three, four, five ... The soldier's head bobs up. He fires off a couple of rounds, and then ducks back down. I begin counting again: one, two, three, four ... As I reach five, I pick out a position slightly high and squeeze off a round. Again I am oblivious to the impact from the gun's butt-pad. I watch the soldier's head appear in my sights just as the bullet reaches him. The force of the impact tears off his helmet and, with it, part of the top of his head. A glistening spray of blood arcs into the air as the limp body disappears out of sight. This time there is no celebration from Taffy, barely a tap on the arm.

'Another one, Jock,' he says. 'And then we'll move. We'll head for the Jerry position at the edge, on the far left. Stay here and cover us until we get there, and then we'll cover you, all right?' I shake my head.

'God help me!' I say.

'Just make sure you don't hit any of us, Haggis,' Billy pipes up.

'Any more from you, cockney, and I'll shoot *you* now,' I say. A big smile spreads over Billy's face. I try to smile back but can't. Thing is, I know he's right. I was just about to see my comrades disappear into the devil's parlour. How can I absolutely guarantee that one of my bullets wouldn't hit at least one of my friends? Quickly, I banish the thought as I slide up the bank into position. I close my eyes, say a quick prayer, tell myself it's us or them and get ready. My hands are shaking. I take four or five deep breaths. I feel my heart slow, the tremors going through my body begin to subside. I take a final look at my comrades and feel pride coursing through me. *My comrades ... my dear friends ...*

Taffy assumes a sprint position, the flat of his left hand resting on the sand. Geordie is holding his rifle so tightly I swear his knuckles are glowing white. His bayonet is pointed straight ahead in readiness. I look into Geordie's eyes and instantly thank God he is on my side. Billy pockets two of our remaining three grenades. He throws his rifle over his shoulder and holds the remaining grenade in front of him at chest height, preparing to rip the pin from it. He turns to me, says,

'Come on then Haggis, we haven't got all day!' This time I match his smile. I return to the job in hand, my finger floating over the trigger ... I see a head appear in my 'scope. Bang! My first shot takes him out in a heartbeat.

'Go!' I shout. Billy tosses another grenade into the distance, and all three of them pile out into no-man's-land. My heart leaps as I sense a heavy footfall behind me, close to my position. I swing the rifle round. A soldier, one of ours, gives me the thumbs up as he runs past, then another, and another. I hear their roars as they head for the hill. I am exhilarated. I feel the overwhelming urge to follow them, but I remember I have a job to do first. I snuggle back down as I hear Billy's grenade go off in the distance. I peer through my sights, but all I can see is dust and sand. The soldiers that had just passed me also disappear into the cloud. I have to get ready. It would only be a few seconds ... Bang! I identify an enemy soldier through a break in the clouds. His contribution to his country's war effort was now over.

I sweep the rifle left to right, right to left. I blink a couple of times to clear my eyes. My finger tenses ... and releases as I realise I am almost about to shoot Billy as I'd earlier promised! I sense movement to his right. Bang! Another enemy soldier falls. The cloud disperses and, just for a moment, I catch the wonderful sight of a dozen soldiers, rifles at the ready and bayonets drawn, charging the enemy positions. Again, I fight the urge to leap out of the foxhole and join them. Again I tell myself I have an important job to do here. I fire a volley of shots into the mayhem, careful not to hit any of our lads. I manage to take out another couple of the enemy before I see Taffy in the distance waving at me to join them. I reach in my bag and rummage around for my bayonet, expertly clicking it home. I take a few more deep breaths and jump into oblivion, zig-zagging up the hill as I run.

I see Billy in the distance, throwing another grenade into a neighbouring foxhole. Another enormous plume of sand fills the sky. I see Geordie thrust his bayonet into an unfortunate victim, then another as they go hand-to-hand. Taffy is crouched down, firing off round after round. I pray he is hitting the right targets as I remember how bad his eyesight is.

More footsteps close in on me as I turn around and see another forty or fifty brave souls follow me up that hill. The sight gives me added momentum, almost allowing me to float to safety. Taffy grabs me as I reach the hole, pulls me down to cover. I thump into something solid as I fall. A body. I draw a sharp breath when I survey the scene around me. Six dead enemy soldiers, their blood staining the sand, their bodies twisted on the ground like discarded marionettes. Billy and Geordie, their chests heaving with the effort of trying to breathe, are sitting side by side, like bookends. Billy is drawing on a fag, and Geordie's face is bright red. It looks as if it's ready to explode.

'What kept you, Haggis?' Billy spouts between drags. 'There's a war on, y'know.' Geordie begins to giggle.

'So I see, Billy, so I see.' I reach out my hand, palms down, in front of my friends. Geordie, then Billy, and finally Taffy do the same. *All for one*. I make a mental note to visit the library when I get back home. I am not normally one for reading. I can read but not very well. There is a name for my condition, but, for the life of me, I cannot recall it. No matter, if I get stuck with a word there's always mother. *The Three Musketeers*: sounds like a good read. Not forgetting D'Artagnan. I smile. I feel a movement to my left, close to us. I turn round. One of the 'dead' soldiers is sitting up, his hand fumbling inside his tunic. He has been gut-shot or bayoneted, as all I can see is a huge red stain. Blood is pouring from the wound. He is struggling to breathe and, I think, close to death. He is staring into my eyes, almost apologetically. He stops fumbling because he has found what he has been looking for. A grenade. Taffy reacts first, swinging his rifle towards the soldier ...

***

In the quiet moments before the mind is fully awake, when the subconscious is in control, I am aware of an overwhelming sense of well-being, of contentment. I feel no pain. I hear ... silence. No guns. No sickening screams. I am aware of a smell, not of death, but of freshly cut grass, of the most brilliant summer's day and everything it brings. I feel the heat of the sun on my back, the gentle breeze caressing my face. I open my eyes. I can hardly contain myself! I am standing on the little bridge at the top of the hill above my home town. The sun is indeed high in the sky. It is the most beautiful day. I am home! I see my house in the distance. I run down the hill as fast as I can. I don't know why, but suddenly I am at the front door in seconds. I realise I feel no pain at all from the ankle I broke when I was five, the one that the doctor said I'd have to be careful with. I reach for the door, pause when I hear singing in the distance. It is coming from the little church in the middle of the village. I hear the strains of the organ. I smile. I can picture Mrs. Moffat there, peering into her sheet-music, doing her best, a cheery smile on her face. The music grows louder, and the congregation joins in. Right away I recognise the hymn. *Abide with me*. I close my eyes, listen intently. It is the most beautiful thing I have ever heard: the organ, note perfect; the voices, like angels in heaven. Then I am in the church, standing in front of my weeping mother.

'Please don't cry, mother,' I say. 'I love you, and I will be with you always ... in here.' I put my hand on my heart. Just for a second my mother looks straight at me. I see a faint smile behind the sadness. I reach out to stroke her cheek. Another faint smile. Then I am back at the top of the hill. Taffy, Geordie and Billy are standing on the bridge, all in battle uniform. I realise I am also in uniform. They are smiling, beckoning me to them.

'Time to go, Jock,' says Taffy.

All for one.

Darkness and Light
Steve Morris

This story is based on a true account of an escape from Auschwitz

Hell.

Is that a straight enough answer for you?

There is no other word for it. It was hell.

People ask me how it felt to escape and assume it was a wonderful feeling. I can tell you that I've spent every single day of my life since then thinking about *the place* and the prisoners in there. For that reason, in many ways, I'm not sure I ever really escaped from it.

19 June 1942

We talked secretly. Saturday morning would soon come around (although the fact that it was Saturday rather than any other day meant absolutely nothing in there). Saturday was a work day. Saturday was a cold day, like the rest. Stanislaw, Jozef and Eugeniusz were with me. Together we would make the four. It would take all four of us and a whole lot of luck. We had decided that Saturday was to be the day because there was always a change of routine. At noon. There was a tiny window of opportunity. We had been watching our captors carefully in our fear and our hatred. On Saturdays some SS men always left the camp to go to spend time with their families until Monday. That left gaps. The camp had grown and merged with a neighbouring camp. By then there were thousands of SS guards there. There were many more of us, but we never seemed to be around for long. The camp ran like clockwork. The clock, however was a cold ticking killing machine.

Although I had long lost track of calendar dates and lived in a time when weekends and holidays were a long-distant dream in a living nightmare, I seemed to have lasted longer than many others. My survival for the length of time was largely due to 'luck' after having being given relatively light work by one of the Kapos[1]. I kept out of the way of trouble by means of my 'cleaning' job of dragging the dead to the crematorium. I worked as part of a pair. My partner carried legs, I carried the arms. That didn't mean I escaped the constant kicking, however. Nothing was ever done quickly enough for *them.* In ultimate irony, work indoors often meant a better chance of survival, especially during winter where there was some warmth to be found. Seasons never seemed to change. Time meant nothing. The weather was bitter. It was always bitter. We barely felt glad to be alive. No one escaped, we were told. We also knew that a punishment for escape attempts was death by starvation. They wouldn't have shot us. That would have been easier for us. I'd seen it. They liked to reduce us to food-craving animals. Some lost their faith. 'There is no God,' they said. 'How can he let this happen?'

Despite everything we knew, we planned to escape nonetheless. *What was the alternative?* We had been in *there* long enough to know that we were all living on borrowed time. The only thing that was keeping us alive was that we were still useful to *them.* We knew that wouldn't last long, however. We could become lame at any time or ill owing to the cruel shortage of rations. I went to work hungrier and slightly weaker each and every day. This could not continue indefinitely. We knew where things were heading.

'You're mad to even think of it,' some said. We had to be careful whom we told. *Perhaps we are mad not to.* We planned the event meticulously. All four of us were under no illusions. We knew that any one of a number of things could go wrong, resulting in failure.

The first part of our plan meant we had to step out of line. We had to pretend to be a mock haulage detail so as fraudulently to gain access to the motor-pool area of the camp. It was the only way we could get into the area. This area was where there was a vehicle stored in which we planned to escape. My role in the four was essential due to my ability to speak German like a native. My friend Eugeniusz, a Ukrainian, was a motor mechanic and a good one too. His role was to sort out the vehicle. *They* respected him in a way. They actually *needed* his skills and that was keeping him alive; so much so that he was allowed to drive the cars he was working on around the camp. The sight of him driving a car would not stand out, but the sight of other men in striped uniforms heading for the perimeter area would do. This was his job in our quartet. That was until Eugeniusz saw his own name on a list of those to be shot. There were a lot of lists in that place.

Another part of the plan depended on our getting disguised. Dirty striped uniforms stood out to the trigger-happy SS men in the gun-towers if they were remotely near anywhere they shouldn't be. By complete chance I had stumbled on the uniform store while on an errand to collect some empty boxes from the upstairs of the storehouse. Through a half-open door I had chanced on a guard sorting shelves of SS uniforms and equipment. After he spotted me peering in through the partly open door I paid with another beating but I had learned some valuable information that would prove crucial to our plans.

The storehouse was in a part of the camp strictly out of bounds to prisoners. The above-mentioned guards in the towers often randomly 'picked out' inmates who strayed too close to the fences and sometimes those who did not. Even when this happened right in front of you, you carried on working unless you wanted to be the next. It was best to step over the body and carry on where you were going. I had noticed, however, that there were very few of *them* in the storehouse at weekends.

We were to get in though the coke-bunker. Earlier in the day, when shovelling coke from a delivery, I had deliberately left the hatch of the bunker unbolted. That was effectively the first move of the operation. On the Friday night, the four of us secretly met in an attic to discuss the plan. We shared a precious cigarette and rehearsed the plan over and over. We all had to be up to the job. The life of each one of us was entirely dependent on all the other three. There was another difficulty we had to face from the start. When we first arrived at the camp, *they* had warned us that if any attempt were made to escape from our specific work detail, ten others in the work-detail would be immediately shot dead as a result. Every escape would cost ten lives.

None of us could live with this guilt if we made it against the odds. Therefore we decided that the best way around this would be to make our attempt while we were not part of our detail. If we returned from work with our specific work-detail, then attempted our escape by later going back out to work in the guise of a completely fictitious work-detail, we could hope that *they* couldn't take out their revenge on a party that effectively didn't exist. The other thing we had to realise was that if this (perhaps mad) attempt did succeed, *they* would track down our families and bring them to Auschwitz, where they would at some point inevitably kill them. We solemnly agreed to take our own lives if our attempt failed. For the rest of our time in the secret meeting in the attic, we spent time in silent prayers for our families.

'We will make it,' we agreed.

20 June 1942 Noon

Our journey started with the four of us taking a wagon from outside the kitchen. In ordinary life before the war, outside *that place*, this was the sort of cart that would be pulled by horses. The handles were long and, depending on the weight of the contents of the wagon, it could need anything up to twelve prisoners to push it. That day there were only potato-peelings on the wagon. Before we even began, we were weak, tired and sore from the morning's labours, and we were hungry, having been given only a small amount of thin soup again. Any other animal would be seeking refuge and rest. We immediately faced a major hurdle. The rest of the plan depended entirely on whether the sentry at this first gate checked out the number of our fake work-detail or not. We took off our striped caps and as usual obediently stood to attention while we waited in front of the gate. We wanted everything to look as normal as possible. We waited. Little did he know the extent of the fear in our minds. He didn't check. We knew he was in the habit of doing this. It was part of our plan. If he had checked our work-detail number in the book and then saw that it didn't exist, we would have been shot on the spot. It was as simple as that. Instead he just opened the gate.

Together we lifted the wagon handles and pushed the cart into the next area of the camp. After a few minutes of the four of us pushing the cart with our heads down, daring not to look if we were being followed, Eugeniusz turned us in the direction of one of the garages. He managed to open the lock with a fake key he'd made to show us the car he had been working on. It was a Steyr 220, a fast type of SS staff car. So the next step was to get into the storehouse. The route we had planned was by crawling through the coke-bunker and then into the boiler-room before heading upstairs.

Straightaway we had a problem. My heart sank. The coke-bunker was supposed to open easily by lifting up the hatch. The others kept a lookout while it was my job to lift the hatch. When I came to try, it wouldn't move. It wouldn't budge. I had let everyone down and probably any moment we would be seen. The hatch was always bolted from the inside but I had managed to remove the bolt itself out of the lock at the end of the day before. First Josef came to help, and then Stanislaw before all four of us were crouching yanking at the door. It was a miracle than no one saw four inmates kneeling on the floor in the middle of the yard. The door was very heavy, and it took the efforts of all four of us in the end. None of us was looking out. If we had been spotted, how would we have explained this? We had got away with another high-risk tactic, and, as we finally all climbed in turn into the pitch-black filth below, we wondered what else could go wrong. There was little talking, though. We were quiet. Thoughts were still going through my head faster and faster all the time, and I suspect that they were similar thoughts to those of my fellow conspirators.

Are we crazy to even attempt this?

Would we be more crazy not to? We know what will happen to us soon.

At least one other inmate had refused to join us, purely for fear of repercussions for his own family.

From the damp darkness of the coke-bunker, we proceeded, dirtier than usual, coughing, into the boiler room and ran upstairs to the store where I'd learned that the staff uniforms were kept. Our soft pathetic shoes made little noise on the wooden staircase. The door was locked, but, even in our weakened states, we combined to prise the poor open. There was treasure indeed, and I looked behind us half expecting to see a troop of guards surrounding us. There was more than uniforms in the room, though. There were also guns, ammunition and grenades. This gave us a glimmer of confidence. I saw lips on the others curl into a slight smile, something I had not seen for a very long time.

I'm going for the full works. I'm getting tooled up. Rifle, pistol, everything.

By then we were running on adrenaline alone. Having no energy other than that generated by fear and perverse excitement, we went for high-rank uniforms. Because of my German language I was given the uniform of SS Untersturmführer[2].

We quickly checked each other's appearance making sure that the hats completely disguised our shaven heads, and that collars covered any visible cuts or bruises.

Suddenly we were disturbed to hear an SS car pull up outside the storehouse. We kept back from the window. For some reason three officers had got out and were taking a quick look around.

Are they looking for us? Had someone told?

Josef loaded a rifle. Yet, as quickly as they had arrived, the SS men simply tapped ash from their cigarettes, looked at their watches and got back in the car before driving away. Things could have been different.

In full SS uniforms, complete with loaded rifles and two of us dressed in senior rank, we walked downstairs and out of the storehouse. Our jackboots made much more noise this time on the wooden staircase. Briskly we walked across the yard to the garage where the car was. So as not to give ourselves away, we needed to become the people whose uniforms we were wearing and to appear confident, with our heads held upright. Things were moving quickly. I felt sick with nerves and adrenaline as we went into that garage. We boarded the car in our rehearsed positions, all four of us. I sat in the front seat next to Eugeniusz who drove. One 'officer' in the front, one in the back.

This thing had better run.

The car started noisily in the garage but without any trouble. The exhaust fumes and petroleum filled my nostrils. Sitting back, we drove out of the garage and then the yard but not until we had closed the doors and gates behind us. We wanted everything to seem as routine as possible. As we turned the corner, I saw the watchtower looming. I saw the thing day and night whether I was awake or asleep. It was always there, but on that particular day it seemed more menacing than ever. A guard was positioned with his hands on the machine-gun as we headed towards the main gate.

Were they waiting for us?

This notorious main gate lives long in the memory of many people even now. That was where we were heading. A few moments later reality began to hit me unexpectedly. Remarkably while on the road we received two 'Heil Hitler' salutes. I'd known that there were literally thousands of SS staff in total in the place. Nobody could obviously recognise everyone.

My God! Have we become SS guards?

We turned the corner to head on the final straight road towards the gate. The others began to return salutes from pedestrian guards and those on bicycles as we drove past them. We were the only car on that road. I felt like saying, 'Don't! You might give us away.' As the main gate finally came into view, we slowed down. Our hearts sank. Things were not as planned. They must have seen us coming. The gate was closed. Normally it was raised when officers' vehicles came into view.

Why wasn't the gate open? The gate should be open!

The SS guard had seen us but for some reason made no effort to open the gate. With my heart in my mouth at that moment I thought, 'It is all over for us.' And I began to say my goodbyes to my family, perhaps even audibly. Suddenly I was punched painfully in the shoulder blade. It was Josef.

'Do something!' he screamed quietly between his teeth into my ear. Everything was now entirely down to me. I was the only one who could get away with using German language. Nothing was happening. None of use dared look behind us. I had to make a decision. Either I spoke or I waited to be spoken to. To wait was to invite questions. If I spoke first I could give commands and direct the conversation. I had to speak first and my mouth was as dry as dust.

Glancing again at the gun-tower from beneath the beck of my cap, I opened the car door slightly and leaned out shoulder first so that the guard could see my shiny rank badges. I shouted something sarcastic like 'Open up, or I'll open *you* up!' at the guard, but it was the sight of my rank that woke him up. He jumped to raise the barrier, saluting as we drove through. To this day I don't know how I ever came out with it. The barrier was raised, and we continued to be saluted. The world outside was there in front of us. We all kept looking straight ahead. I don't know to this day if the others returned the salute. We were through! We were through and they had saluted us! We were outside!

As we drove away, we knew the gate behind us bore the inscription *Arbeit Macht Frei*[3]. We drove on. We drove on for thirty-seven miles before the car broke down and we went our separate ways. The life that followed was not easy for any of us. But we had left that place.

On 20 June 1942. Kazimierz Piechowski, a political prisoner and two other Polish prisoners, scout Stanislaw Gustaw Jaster and priest Józef Lempart together with Ukrainian mechanic Eugeniusz Bendera all effectively condemned to death, had audaciously escaped from the notorious concentration camp Auschwitz disguised as Nazi officers in a SS Commander's car. They were saluted by guards as they exited the death-camp through the main gate. The camp had to answer to Berlin as to how this had been allowed to happen. The procedure of tattooing prisoners was allegedly bought in by the Nazis as a result of this escape. It is estimated that around 1.1 million prisoners died in Auschwitz concentration camp.

[1]Kapo - A German criminal prisoner also imprisoned in concentration camps, given special powers to keep prisoners in order in an assigned bloc.

[2] SS Untersturmführer –Second Lieutenant.

[3]*Arbeit Macht Frei* — Work Sets You Free.

Granddad's Armchair

Neil J Morton

I had never seen our mother weeping. Not all through the war and even after her husband, my step-father, left us in the summer of 1946. Mother remained strong and confident in the work she did at a radio-parts factory and in caring for me. In '43 a bomb fell close by the flats we lived in, and a huge crack appeared in the wall of our small home. The bomb also blew out the windows, and forever thereafter not one single door would close properly. Through this entire period mother remained calm and cheerful. Blissfully unaware of any strangeness in the absence of a father, uncles, aunts, cousins and any other assorted relatives, I grew up happily playing in the two lovely parks nearby and with the neighbourhood children.

All throughout the war years, as evening fell, all of us small children were carried and dragged, complaining and uselessly resisting, down into a huge underground air-raid shelter. Bunks ranged along the inner wall in which we were supposed to stay until early morning. Of course in summer, with the sun shining brightly, even after we'd had our tea, going down this dingy hole was a torture beyond all measure. The smell of damp and malodorous children lingers in my memory today. After dark, the menfolk - those not away on active duty - would gather at the entrance, smoking and gazing up into the night sky. Although our address gave our location as Surrey, the huge cul-de-sac in which we all dwelt was very adjacent to London and some factory estates. As a result, it was not uncommon to see search-lights weaving silver cobwebs across the starry heavens. The men would mutter softly so as not to wake us children, 'Gerry is busy tonight,' and 'Croydon is copping it again.' Croydon aerodrome often came in for the attention of the Luftwaffe.

The day mother wept and heaved great heart-wrenching sobs occurred shortly before WWII ended. On a bright sun-filled late-autumn day, mother and I had journeyed by train - a great adventure in those days - to visit an unknown personage called Granddad. At the age of five, the first view of the parents of one's owns parent is daunting, and herein I have attempted to capture the moment in time. Within two years of meeting Cornelius Hawkins, my grandfather, he passed away aged 73. The year we met for the first time was 1944. By Christmas 1946 our family had lost a great soldier.

***

The journey deep into the county of Surrey, on two buses and a train, took around one and a half tedious hours. The station was full of servicemen, in uniform, and the sight, together with the crunch of highly polished boots, filled my senses and imagination with glory. As the train rattled along following the Thames Valley, the scene from the window slowly changed from sooty backyards, rickety garden sheds and tall weeds to lovely green fields and the glorious amber and yellow tones of autumn. I soon became bored and fidgety; the pictures above the seats advertising seaside destinations soon palled, as did the tattered much-thumbed book I had read 100 times. I showered my poor mother with innumerable questions as to our destination.

'Quiet, you'll see when we get there,' was all I received by way of answer.

On arrival we walked from the tiny railway-station along a narrow road that paralleled the railway-track for about ten minutes and knocked on the door of a neat terrace house. The small front garden was paved with ornate tiles, in the middle of which a lonely rose-bush thrived in glorious pink splendour. At our knock on a highly polished brass lion's head, a thin pale women sniffed a welcome and ushered us into a narrow, gloomy, and rather frightening hall. Above us, in the shadows, high on the walls, the heads and horns of large animals glowered down.

'Your grandfather was a soldier in Africa,' was the answer to my whispered question concerning this daunting décor. We were shown into a back room that overlooked a narrow garden. The mysterious personage we had travelled so far to see sat in a huge over-stuffed bright-blue brocaded armchair. He sat, waistcoat open, the collar of his shirt flying out on either side having escaped from the gold stud that drooped from the neck of his shirt. His head and upper lip bristled with thick iron-grey hair, the drooping whiskers stained with nicotine. We stood silently just within the threshold.

'Don't dither there, Josie' - the voice gruff - 'come you in'. He beckoned with a large nicotine-stained hand. I clung sheepishly to my mother and gazed about in fascination. Behind grandfather and slightly to the right there hung on the wall a wondrous great clock; the ornamented face, with Roman numerals and gold leaf, shone brightly. Below the face sat a nest of brass chains and weights that lengthened as the day wore on, the whole encased in a highly polished glass-fronted wooden cabinet. I dragged my eyes away from the wonderful clock and noted further to the right, in a tiled alcove, a huge black range on which a black kettle boiled and a large silver saucepan steamed. The small room, filled with a delicious aroma, opened into what appeared to be a lean-to addition, which contained a large sink and wash-boards and several cupboards. I later learned that this was called a scullery. Plumb in the centre of the small square room in which we stood, a large often-scrubbed wooden table, with a few seats surrounding it, occupied most of the space. This was the only place, other than the huge armchair, to sit, which we did on enormous straight-backed chairs. In the silence the loud tick of the clock was the only sound.

At the range, the slender pale women who had admitted us lifted the lid on the silver pot and gave the contents a stir. Mother introduced her as Aunt Min. I sat as still as a mouse, overwhelmed by my surroundings. Aunt Min offered a cup of tea, which mother gratefully accepted. Tea things clattered into the silence, and a cloth of white cotton was thrown over the table. Min poured grandfather a black foaming liquid into a pewter mug. I knew this to be milk stout: mum drank a bottle now and again for her nerves, and his blue-eyed gaze never wavered from my nervous countenance as he deftly rolled a cigarette.

'Now then, Josie,' he rumbled from the huge armchair, 'so this is the boy?' The boy in question said,

'Hello, sir.'

'What age are you, son?'

'Neil is five years old, father, and his birthday is New Year's Day.' Aunt Min quickly chimed in:

'Would he like to play in the parlour?' Mum, taking me gently by one hand, led me into another room at the front of the narrow house wherein an upright piano took pride of place. On the walls, stern faced people stared down at me as I sidled into the bay-window which was the only source of light. My mother disappeared, leaving me alone in the silence. In the forthcoming summers I would notice that everything was spick and span as though dust was afraid to settle. As time went by, I would sit before the highly polished piano laboriously tapping out *Golden Slumbers* with one finger. In the window's embrasure, a small round table displayed a plain but highly polished wooden box through the glass top of which I could see a row of silver and bronze medals with colourful ribbons attached. Above the piano one of the pictures showed a lady in old-fashioned clothes sitting on a huge crescent moon; she was the only one smiling. I was to learn at a later time that this was my grandmother from whose DNA we received our dark hair, brown eyes and dark complexion. My mother, who was a small dark vivacious brunette, had received wolf whistles from the troops at the rail-station. Presently Aunt Min came in carrying a cardboard box full of little tin animals and fence partitions. Placing it on the floor, she left without a word. I tipped the contents out and erected the fences to make two paddocks and placed sheep in one and cows in another. There were a farmer in a smock, his rosy-cheeked wife in an apron and a herdsman with a crook. By this time I was hungry: it was well past lunchtime, and I wondered whether these mysterious strangers would provide a meal. When mother eventually came to fetch me, she was stern of face.

'We shall have some soup and then must get started home: it is a long way,' she said. Once again at table all was quiet, the soup delicious and the homemade bread rolls crunchy on top and soft and warm inside. There was home-made jam to spread on the rolls after I had devoured every drop of soup. The clock ticked majestically on the wall. Outside, rain clouds gathered, and the room dimmed. Aunt Min took a taper from the stove and lit a lamp suspended above us that popped and glowed. At my amazed and enquiring glance mother explained:

'That is a gas lamp, son: there are very few houses with electricity down here.'

The short stocky figure of Cornelius, my imposing grandfather, sat immediately in front and below the clock at the head of the table. He pulled a large silver pocket-watch on a chain from his waistcoat pocket and checking it against the time on the clock declared:

'You will have to get a move on, Josie, if you want to catch the 3.20.' I looked at the clock: it read 2.30. We scrambled into our raincoats; the farewells were stiff. I was relieved and happy to get away from the place. At the door, the stranger who had become my grandfather offered me his hand: it was hard and powerful.

'Well, Neil, now we have met you, you must come and stay with us some time soon.' His eyes had softened, and the voice seemed sort of cracked and wheezy. Oh, no, I thought, mum wouldn't do that to me, would she? As we walked quickly up the road, getting thoroughly soaked, I peered over my shoulder: grandfather stood at the gate, rain running down his face. He nodded once and turned back inside.

On the train, my mother explained that she had left home to work in London several years prior to this visit and had not been home since. Communication had been difficult after her mother had died, and Aunt Min had arrived at granddad's house. Suddenly the general air of mystery and stilted conversation penetrated my skull and piqued my latent curiosity.

'Did grandfather know my father?' I innocently enquired. Mum sighed and stared sadly down at me whilst the train rattled homeward.

'No,' she replied, 'your father came from up north and was killed in a motor-bike accident shortly after you were born.' No more was said, as I could read a great sorrow in her beautiful brown eyes. Gazing from the rocking carriage window I visualized my dad as a dispatch rider seated on a Triumph motorcycle roaring through enemy lines with vital information.

One day, the overstuffed armchair that Cornelius Hawkins had occupied on my first visit appeared mysteriously at our small abode. The huge blue brocaded armchair, bequeathed to mum in her father's will, took up a great deal of space in our tiny home. The shade of the old man seemed to hover accusingly from the corner beneath the small window. The box of medals from the Boer War and WW1 gleamed from the crystal cabinet.

However, before this occurrence, I spent two glorious summer holidays in grandfather's house before his demise. The tiny house in Queen's Parade opened like a tropical flower, to reveal all its mysteries. Between the Boer War and WWI and WWII, four girls and one boy had been born to Cornelius and his first wife, whom I believe to be Clara Harris, a lady from the Midlands. Another girl, my Aunty Bessie, was born to his second wife whom mother called Aunt Min. Bessie became a nurse. Aunt Bessie was very kind to me, and I recall the bicycle she rode on her rounds as a District Nurse.

In the summer holidays of 1945, I again journeyed down to grandfather's home. On this occasion, my mother left me in his care with strong words on behaviour and minding my manners. Cornelius spent the majority of his teenage years and adult life in the army. His father, my great-granddad Isaac, had placed Neil, as he was known within the family circle, and his brother John in a military school at the age of twelve. He eventually became a colour sergeant-major and, on retirement, a proud member of the Royal Corps of Commissionaires and was employed at an aircraft factory in Weybridge, where his only son John rose from office-boy to director. In later years I learned that Cornelius aged from twelve to sixteen had developed an ear for music. The musical training he received led him to be a member of the regimental band which doubled on the battlefield as first-aid and rescue personnel.

During those long summer weeks, I would sit on the wide and comfortable arm of the stately armchair, whilst my beery and tobacco-redolent hero regaled me with yarns of derring-do. None of the tales he told concerned him personally. The medals and where and how they were won remained a mystery. Grandfather spoke of India and South Africa, of barrack-room humour, spit and polish and what he called 'hoochie-coochie' girls. He could draw magnificent pictures in my mind of rank after rank of crimson-clad soldiers marching in time to his bandsmen as he marched proudly at their head. The Boer War, soldiers of the Queen, red uniforms and white helmets marched through my dreams at night as I lay in a candle-lit room that I shared with a huge painting of a kilted Scottish soldier.

Then WWI, the war to end all wars, loomed on the world stage. His face would sadden. Aged thirty-eight by this time, although still serving in the regimental band, he was too old to fight. However, with his chest full of medals and sergeant-major status, Cornelius became a recruiting officer.

'It was not a happy time, young Neil,' he would say softly, 'sending young men to dig trenches and fight in mud and filth.' My place on the arm of his chair was now a sombre theatre. The scenes he conjured filled me with sorrow.

In the evening, he would wind the clock as soon as the BBC announced the six o'clock news, checking to make sure both clock and turnip-silver watch were both in accord. As he wound the key, he would chant as the weights and chains climbed back up toward the clock-face:

'Hickory Dickory dock, watch out for the mouse, young Neil.' The mouse, of course, was never seen. At around this time, as soon as the meal was over, he would fasten his waistcoat, put on a shiny black jacket and walk up to the village-hall where he played the euphonium in the village band. On the way home, a pint of ale at the Queen's Arms was in order. In my young mind, grandfather changed from being a looming, somewhat frightening presence to be a person of awe, and, once I began to understand his life, a figure of pride. Mother informed me that he had been a drummer-boy at age fourteen: the medals stood in mute testimony of his contribution to our island heritage.

On those holidays, lying on a narrow bed in the small candle-lit bedroom that I shared with the bear-skinned Highlander, I would listen to the old house creak and imagine that the train that rattled along the line at the foot of the garden was carrying me off to fight for king and country. Flickering and dancing shadows from the candle's flame gave the bonnie Scotsman a somewhat eerie lifelike presence. The old house still had no electricity, even as late as 1951, the year of the Festival of Britain. Even in 1953, when I rode my new bicycle down to visit Aunt Min, the gas-lights still daubed great shadows on the walls and lent a frightening aspect to the souvenirs from Africa. By this time the stuffed heads with glassy eyes and the pointed horns of the poor slaughtered beasts appeared to soften and no longer shafted my innards with fear.

In musty cupboards there were piles of fascinating books that the Hawkins children had shared over the years. I had two favourites: one in which all the pictures stood up as one opened the pages - in particular, a large pelican with an enormous beak tickled my fancy - and a beautifully illustrated copy of the *Water Babies* by Charles Kingsley, within whose covers Mrs Do-As-You-Would-Be-Done-By left an indelible impression: a mantra that served me well in years to come. To the rear of this wonderful old house - for such it had become - a small garden opened on to a lane and the railway-line to London. There was an outside lavatory that was a challenge on chilly nights, so we used chamber-pots and scoured them each morning. Beside the privy, a gooseberry-bush flourished, and a huge wooden barrel stood adjacent to the outhouse wall to gather rain from the roof. Our ablutions were made in a big tin tub placed before the large black kitchen range or at the scullery sink.

The lane, entered by a creaky gate, was alive with weeds and tall grasses and ran its dusty length between the street and the railway, eventually leading to the river Mole, a rather insignificant waterway which, although constrained between concrete banks as it passed beneath the rail-line, offered pleasant walks. My long school holidays were always in summer and some evenings were spent with a stick, a length of string and a hook, fishing vainly in the shallow waters. That marvellous armchair graced our little home for many years. If the stories and secrets it held could only be told, it would have pride of place in the British War Museum.

Voices and Faces from the Past

Ronald Ooms

The following short story is a work of fiction, but some parts of it are based on true historical events and persons during WWII.

Brooklyn, New York, 10 September, 1984. There's knocking on a door. The door of an apartment on the second floor of an old five-storey building. Again there's a sound of knocking on a door. It's a young man around his thirties who's doing the knocking. He's standing six foot tall, brown eyes, black hair combed to the back with grease. He wears a black leather jacket, a pair of denim trousers and crocodile-leather boots. He gets a bit annoyed because nobody is opening the door. He reaches into his inside pocket and takes out a pack of cigarettes and an old golden lighter. He lights up a smoke and puts the pack back into his pocket. He plays with his lighter for a bit and puts it back in his pocket as well.

'Hey, open up, will ya? It's me!' the young man shouts while knocking furiously on the door again, but there's no answer. On the other side of the corridor another door opens.

'Can you keep it down?' an old grey-haired guy in his eighties yells. The man with the leather jacket turns round and looks at the man standing half-behind his door. 'Oh, it's you, Salvator! Didn't recognise you,' the elderly man says. 'Joe not in?'

'He should be. He called me to get over here at once. You seen him, Billy?'

'Can't help you with that, Sal. Haven't seen the Swiss in a while now, but I'm sure he will be back if he called ya. And this time of the year he always acts a bit funny,' old man Bill replies. 'Got to go now or else the ol' lady's gonna kick my ass. You know how she is, eh?' And he closes and locks his door.

Salvator turns round and tries his luck again at Joe's door as he turns the door-knob. Click. It's open. Sal looks surprised as the door is normally always locked. He opens the door partially and takes a peek inside. It's dark inside, so he reaches for the light-switch which is to his right, next to the open door. But it doesn't work. He tries a couple of times flipping the switch up and down, but to no avail. He throws his cigarette on the floor and stamps it out as he pushes the door wide open so the light from the outside hallway shines into the apartment. He creeps gently through the inner hallway as he takes out a pistol and calls out:

'Hey, Swiss, it's me - Sal! You in here?' But still no answer. 'C'mon, man. I'm here, as you asked me to be. What gives?' he continues. With his sidearm leading the way through the apartment's corridor, the first room he enters is the kitchen. He tries to put on the light there as well, but nothing happens. He sees an ashtray on the counter filled with cigar-butts, and one of them is still burning. There's also an open bottle next to it which has no label. It's almost empty. The greasy-haired man picks it up and smells from it. 'Schnapps,' he whispers. He puts the bottle down and shouts again: 'You here?' But still no-one answers. He walks back towards the front door in search of the fuse-box. He finds it, opens it and looks inside. The light coming from the outside helps him find the fuses which are down. He puts them up again, and all the lights turn on. He closes the box and walks towards the front door and closes it. He then turns round and wanders back to the kitchen as he looks around. He opens the bathroom door: nobody there. No one in the bedroom or small living area either. He walks back to the kitchen, takes the ashtray off the sink and puts it on the round wooden table in the middle of the room, which has four chairs around it. He puts his gun down on the table, picks up the schnapps bottle and a glass and places them next to the ashtray. He pulls up a chair and sits down as he reaches inside his pocket. He takes out his pack of cigarettes, lights up another smoke and pours some of the left-over schnapps in the glass. As he takes a nip from the glass he sees a rat crawling on the table. 'What the ... !' he shouts and in a panic throws the table on its side, and the glass and bottle shatter in millions of pieces. 'Bastard,' he shouts. 'Filthy vermin!' He looks round for the rat but doesn't see it anywhere. He suddenly notices a thick white envelope sitting on a stack of old newspapers on one of the other chairs. He picks it up and looks at the envelope. The young man looks at it closely and can't contain his curiosity so he opens it. There are audio-tapes inside, three of them. And they are numbered from 1 to 3. He looks round the room and sees a cassette-player on a side-table. He inserts cassette number 1 in the player and presses play while his eyes scan the room for any other sudden surprises. He doesn't see anything out of the ordinary and starts the tape.

> *Test, test, testing, one, two three ... Ahem. Well ... I've decided to make this recording for posterity. And to get rid of the weight that is resting on my shoulders for many decades now. You who are listening to this tape have probably known me for many years or maybe you haven't ... But the life I was leading was probably a bit misleading. It's not easy to tell about my past to anyone. Not even my beloved Charlotte, who was so dear to me for such a long time ... And especially to some friends of ours who wouldn't be happy about this. But I can't keep it inside any more. And now when it's all out it doesn't matter anymore. Let me tell you about myself first, the real me. My actual name is Johannes Löwenhard, and I was born in the Austrian city of Klagenfurt in 1921. My mother was Austrian, but my father was German, he was from Munich. We moved from Austria to Germany when I was about two years old. I'm not from Switzerland, as most of the people think. For most* - Click.

Salvatore had pressed the stop button. And he says: 'Ouf, marone! What the heck is this?' He pulls up a chair, sits down and presses the play button again.

> *- of his working life until the 1930s, my father was a mechanic for a German car-maker, but in the early '30s he managed to become a car salesman and owner of his own garage. He was also a member of the NSDAP, the German National Socialist Workers' Party. And I became a part of the Hitler Youth in 1933, when all the other youth organisations were banned. First I felt sad that I had to leave my former scouting group, but most of my friends joined*

the Hitler Youth too, so actually it wasn't all that bad. Also I was in my father's workshop almost every day and did some minor work for him, like mopping the floor, cleaning up bits and pieces. Just little stuff like that. And as time went by, I couldn't get my eyes off those beautiful cars and those engines my father was working on. I got more interested in how these machines worked, and in no time I learned a lot of stuff.

It was when I was about fourteen years old that I got permission to take the cars out for a test drive. And as time went by I became more and more comfortable with the vehicles I was driving. I went faster and faster all the time, and I think my father did not like the way I was conducting myself. He gave me hell a lot of times when I went too fast. I was lucky I did not get hurt in an accident, as I was always trying to push my limits. My father would have killed me if I'd crash one of those cars. And of course, if I'd survived it, he would have dealt with me too.

Back in the '30s, there was already some organised automobile-racing going on. I was able to attend the 1938 German Grand Prix on the now infamous Nürburgring. My father was invited by the Auto Union team, which had Hans Stuck and Hermann Lang in their team, two great German racers back in that day. It was a great experience, and who would have known that a year later I would be sitting in a racing-car myself, as a substitute at the start of a Grand Prix event, also at the Nürburgring?

With the help of my father's friends, I became one of two test-drivers for a southern German racing-team. They saw potential in me while I was shaking down some of my father's cars, and they signed me up. The team raced with Italian-built Maserati MC4 Grand Prix cars. Edward McGrath, a Scottish bloke, was the other test-driver in the team, and, because we worked closely together, we became quite good friends. We enjoyed each other's company and the mutual passion we had for speed. His sister, called Charlotte, attended some of the tests and races during the 1939 season. When we were first introduced to each other ... well, let me tell you this. It was love at first sight. I first thought Edward would be opposed to it, but he actually embraced the affair I was having with his younger sibling. Sometimes he just – Click.

And the tape stops again as Sal presses the stop button. He looks at the player and sees the fast forward button. He presses it for a few seconds and presses on play again.

- broke out, and I decided I would join the airforce, the Luftwaffe. As I aspired to be the best myself, I made sure I wanted to fight side by side with the best too. Click.

He presses the fast forward button again, for quite some seconds. Then starts listening to the tape again.

I shot those Italian boys, although they weren't armed. I had to. I was ordered to by the Wehrmacht officer. Although not part of my outfit, he outranked me. I had no choice. They were partisans, they said. What could I have done? If I did not do it, someone else would have, and they would have shot me ... But those kids ... they were just kids. That was a horrible month of September. Click.

'Oh mio!' he shouts. 'What's this, for heaven's sake?' The young man takes the tape out of the player and tosses it to the side. He then looks at the other two tapes on the counter and lets out a sigh. He rubs his face and eyes and pinches his nose with his left hand. And he sighs yet again. He picks up all the tapes and puts them inside his jacket pocket, stands up and, before he leaves the apartment, puts the table back in its place and picks up his gun from the floor. As he exits the apartment, he shuts the door and takes the stairs down. He goes outside and walks towards his car - a new black Ford Capri - and gets in. He turns on the radio-cassette player after he starts his engine. He takes the second cassette and inserts it into his car-radio and turns the volume up.

I was in Belgium in early September of 1944 in the province of Antwerp, in the Kempen region. It's been a hard few months already for our boys at the front because of the Allied invasion of France. I just recovered from my wound sustained during the battle of Carentan where I got shot in the chest close to the heart by an American soldier. I was lucky to have survived that ordeal. Not sure if he did because of the bayonet wound I inflicted on him. And there I was, rejoining my company, and we knew the Allies were coming here too. At the moment all was quiet until, that evening, I heard a lot of shouting coming out of a local bar and saw a lot of people running out of the place. I was in the store across of the pub buying some stuff, and then I thought I should go and have a look for myself to check what was going on. It was about twenty or fifteen minutes before the curfew.

When I entered, I saw a soldier aiming his pistol towards the head of a young civilian. The soldier was from the Waffen SS. The Flemish civilian was on his knees next to a pool-table and still holding on to a cue.

'What is going on in here, sergeant?' I asked the black-uniformed military man.

'It's none of your business!' was his reply in a quite arrogant tone.

'This is no way to talk to an officer. Tell me what is going on in here!' I ordered. In the meantime I took my own pistol out of its holster, ready to use it if necessary.

'This man doesn't respect the curfew ... sir,' he said with a smirk on his face. I looked at the young man on his knees on the ground and asked him:

'What's going on here?' The Belgian replied:

'I was minding my own business and shooting some pool, lieutenant.'

'Yes,' I nodded. 'And?'

'And this guy came in here and started making a fuss,' the civilian continued. The Waffen SS-man shouted:

'You are in violation of the curfew, you peasant!'

'Silence!' I shouted. I walked towards the SS man and ordered him to put his gun down.

'You cannot order me, you fly-boy,' he taunted. While we were

ranting back and forth, the civilian stood up and fled through the back door. The now-furious soldier turned round and wanted to go in pursuit, but I deliberately tripped him up, and he smacked his face right on the side of the pool-table, knocking himself out. At that moment, two Feldgendarmerie men came inside and asked me what happened. I told them what they needed to know, and they arrested him and took him away.

Just a few days before the Allies would ride into this town, I went back to the local liquor-store to pick up my tab from the day before. I saw the civilian of last night again. It seemed he was the son of the store-owner. He got startled when he saw me, but I told him not to worry. I was just there to pay my bill. Click.

Sal arrives at his destination and turns off the ignition. He presses eject on the radio and takes out the tape and puts it back into his pocket. He looks in his rear-view mirror as if he's making sure no one has followed him. He gets out of the car which he had parked in front of a diner. He walks towards the diner and goes inside. He takes a place in a booth which has a clear view of the front door. Sal always wants to sit in a strategic position while in public places. Therefore he can see who gets in and out. It gives him a safer feeling. A red-haired waitress around her mid-forties comes towards him.

'What would it be, love? The usual?' she asks while she pours him a hot cup of coffee.

'Yes, Eveline, please,' he answers. 'And tell Vinny I'm here, will ya?'

'Sure. Right away, hon,' she says and walks off to the bar. Sal lights up a cigarette as he waits for his order to arrive. About ten minutes later, Eveline returns with a plate of hot food: a medium-rare steak with fries and two eggs.

'Here you go, dear. Enjoy,' she says. Sal replies:

'Thanks, dear. You told Vinny I'm here?' Then suddenly a loud baritone voice cries out:

'Wow, here he is!' It's Fat Vincent Clemente, Salvatore's half-brother from his mother's first marriage. Vince is a large fellow, also standing six foot tall and weighing over 320 pounds. About fifty years old and half-bald. Sal stands up as Clemente comes towards him. He gives him a big hug and a kiss on the cheek.

'How've you been, Sal?' the robust man asks.

'Can't really complain, I guess,' Salvatore answers. With a frown on his face the big guy replies questioningly:

'You guess? What's goin' on, Sal?'

'Well, I got a phone-call from the Swiss telling me to get my ass over there.'

'So what are you doing here?' Clemente asks.

'I already went to his vermin-infested pigsty of a place, but no-one was there. His door wasn't locked, the fuses were down, and I found some strange tapes,' Sal says while he takes out the tapes from his jacket pocket. Vincent takes the tapes and looks at them and asks:

'What's on them?'

'It's Joe talking on the tapes ... Well, not really his name, Joe. His name is Joachim whatever, and he ain't no Swiss either. He says on there that he was a Nazi soldier or something.'

'Seriously? You kidding, right?' Vince says in amazement. 'The skipper ain't gonna like that, Sal. You know what he thinks of those guys 'cause of what they've done to his family in Italy.'

'I know, Vinny,' Sal says. 'But maybe some of them did not have a choice.' Fat Vincent looks Salvatore in the eye and tells him:

'Listen, kid, the skip don't see no difference. After that tragedy all krauts are monsters to him. Maybe you should get rid of those.' And he points his fingers towards the cassettes. Sal sighs and nods his head.

The next morning, Salvatore leaves his flat in lower Manhattan early and takes his Capri out for a spin. While driving through Little Italy, he puts in the second cassette again but flips it to side B. It starts playing.

We were under heavy fire from the Sherwood Rangers. Mortars hitting close by as I was looking for cover behind the church. Bullets flying everywhere. On the ground lots of debris, broken glass, bullet shells, blood and dead soldiers. We were falling back towards the station. Actually moving to the north towards the Albert Canal. Suddenly I heard squeaky noises combined with engine noises. I heard that before. I took a peek from behind my cover and saw a Sherman tank approaching. I turned round and saw Café Het Schild. Schild means shield, so I gathered that would be a safe place for me to take cover from the advancing tank. While I ran the short distance to the café, bullets were flying around my head. And then suddenly I got a hot feeling, a very hot feeling, and then pain in my ankle. As I got hit, I fell and smashed into the front door of the café. I opened it and crawled inside. I had got shot in the right foot, and the bullet had shattered my ankle. It looked as if I was going nowhere soon. I shut the door with my other foot and tried to get up, using my rifle as a crutch. As I turned round towards the bar, I saw the bar-keeper standing there holding a bottle of schnapps in his hand, and he himself was shaking like a leaf. In front of the bar, with his back towards me, I saw a German officer. Couldn't really see who it was until he turned his head towards the window and I recognised him. It was my old buddy Heinz, the commanding officer of the 5th Company, which was part of the 2nd Battalion of the 6th Falmschirmjäger Regiment. As he looked outside, he noticed the tank getting closer and closer. In his right hand he was holding a shot glass filled with schnapps. He put it up against his lips and drank it in one go. He put the glass back down and turned round. He then walked past me towards the window, which was near the front door. He opened up the window, picked up a panzerfaust which was resting on a table next to him. He aimed it at the tank which was now across the street from us, only a few metres from the café, and he took the shot. 'Bam!' That took out the tank, and, as fire was coming out from it, he closed the window, turned round and walked back towards the bar. He asked for another drink. I couldn't believe my eyes! He drank it and then went in his pocket and took out some change. He asked the scared bar-tender how much he owed him, and he paid the man! He then turned around to me and said: 'You staying or going?' Click.

Sal stops the tape and takes it out of the car-stereo. Then he inserts the third and final one.

He stood there right in front of me. I was lying on the ground between a whole bunch of rubble, bleeding like a pig. I ran out of bullets, and there was nothing I could do ... At that point I wasn't sure that I hit him, but when he dropped his Thompson machine-gun at his feet, I instantly knew something was up. He took a few steps closer and came out of the shadow he was standing in ... I couldn't believe it ... It was ... It was ... Dammit! I still can't ... (Sigh ...) It was Char ... Charlotte's brother. Dammit all to hell! It was my best friend. It was Edward. My team-mate. My buddy ... Gosh ... After all those years ... It's hard, you know. I remember that suddenly there was blood pouring out of the corners of his mouth, and he fell down on his knees. His eyes were staring directly at me ... as if he were looking directly into my soul. I saw the fear in his eyes, and I'm sure he knew now whom he shot and who shot him ... I couldn't get up. My legs were torn up, so I dragged myself closer to him, pulling myself further with the help of all the debris, stones and wood that was scattered all over the place. I got next to him and took hold of him with both hands. I pulled him closer to me and gave him a hug telling him that I was sorry ... His eyes were closing, but he did raise his head towards me, looked at me and mumbled something I couldn't comprehend. I felt his hand pinching my neck very hard that it almost hurt and then it suddenly stopped ... He then said something I did understand. He whispered: 'Don't tell her ...' Then I felt his last breath - and he was gone. It was 11 September 1944 - The day I lost part of my soul ...

A long pause follows, and one can hear sobbing on the tape. Salvatore sighs and opens up his car window to get some fresh air. The tape continues:

This feeling of ... of guilt has been a burden during my whole life. I killed innocents and ... I murdered my best friend - my future brother-in-law. She never knew. My beloved Charlotte ... never knew. Click.

Sal turns off the engine and thinks about the date that he heard on the cassette. 'That's forty years ago today,' he tells himself. He gets out of the car which he had parked back in front of Joe's apartment. He goes back into the building and climbs the stairs. He walks towards the door, which was unlocked the night before. Very gently he tries the door-knob again, but this time it's locked, so he knocks on the door. No one answers. He knocks again, but to no avail. Nobody's home. He goes back downstairs, and, as he exits the building, he bumps into old man Billy.

'G'morning, Sal. You looking for the Swiss? I saw him go out about ten minutes ago,' the old-timer says. 'Going that direction,' and he points towards the Brooklyn Bridge. Sal asks:

'You know where he was going?' Billy shakes his head:

'Nah, not sure. He did not say anything. He looked a bit off, you know. But he went that way.'

'Okay, Billy, thanks,' Sal says as he jumps back into his car and drives off in the direction of the Brooklyn Bridge. The cassette, now turned to side B, starts to play again.

After my capture and when I was healed from my wounds, the British brought me to a POW camp in Featherstone Park near the Tyne river. When I arrived, there were still Italians there, but they were being moved to another camp in a few days because more German officers were coming to this one. At any given time about 4000 officers were there and about 600 orderlies. I believe it was one of the largest camps in Britain. It was a mixed camp with officers from the Wehrmacht, the Kriegsmarine, the Luftwaffe of course and even diplomats, bureaucrats and whatever. The most senior officer there was General Ferdinand Heim.

I was released in the summer of 1948. I decided to put myself off the radar and stayed in England. After a year or so, I finally met Charlotte again ... It wasn't easy ... feeling the guilt, but I kept strong, and, after almost a decade, we picked up our relationship again. She had not married anyone all this time ... After a long illness took away my love in the early 60s, there was nothing left for me there. I had nothing, so I decided to go to the States with the money I had in my pocket and the clothes I was wearing. And that's when I decided one day to call myself Joe or 'the Swiss'. So I took a new identity, a new life. It would be much easier if people thought I was something other than German. I had nothing else left back at home. And now New York City became my home. Click.

Sal stops his Capri and shuts off its engine. He has arrived somewhere in the middle of the Brooklyn Bridge and sees Joe. He gets out of the car, runs towards the old man who's standing on the ledge. Almost getting run over himself by oncoming traffic. As he is now only a few feet from him, he shouts:

'Don't do it, Joe!' Joachim turns his head round and looks right towards Salvatore. Still ready to jump to his certain demise, there are tears coming out of the old-timer's blue eyes. The beleaguered war-veteran shouts:

'My tapes are gone! They took it! They know too soon!' Sal answers him with:

'No, Joe. I know. I know. I took them. You wanted me to come yesterday, you weren't home! I found them!' The man on the ledge doesn't listen to what Sal says as he turns round again, facing the drop.

'Nobody has to know, Joe!' Sal yells.

'Those voices ... those faces of the past are haunting me. Es tut mir leid. I'm sorry. I lived a lie,' the old Fallschirmjäger cries.

G.I. Gerry's Gifts

Chris R. Pownall

At the outbreak of WWII, Betty Simpson and Robert Jones were fondly in love with each other. Robert had just turned eighteen, and Betty was heading for her sixteenth birthday. They had known one another since their schooldays, and, by this time, they had been courting steadily for over a year. They spent a lot of time together when visiting each other's homes, and, although they had not experienced carnal intimacy, they had come very close to it. Whilst Betty found Robert physically attractive, she wished to maintain her sexual innocence, at least until she reached the age of consent, and beyond if possible. They both came from good English families and had been taught right from wrong, but they experienced tantalising temptation whenever they embraced each other and engaged in passionate caressing.

It was the morning of 3 September 1939, and Robert was visiting Betty's home as a guest for Sunday lunch. He had arrived early with the intention of taking Betty for a stroll around the park nearby in order to work up a healthy appetite for a hearty midday meal. When Robert arrived, Betty's parents were in the sitting-room listening to the wireless, and Robert noticed that her father had a very stern expression on his face as he invited Robert and Betty to take a seat. As the clock on the mantel-piece was showing nearly 11.15, broadcaster Alvar Lidell announced that the Prime Minister would be addressing the nation in two minutes' time. They all listened intently, while Prime Minister Neville Chamberlain announced over the airwaves that, following the Nazi invasion of Poland, Great Britain had now declared war on Germany.

Shortly after the outbreak of WW2, Robert received his call up papers and was recruited into the army. The night before Robert was leaving home to join a training-camp in Yorkshire, he and Betty arranged to meet, and, after taking a stroll along the river bank, they returned to Betty's home, where her mother and father had gone out visiting their local pub for a few drinks. The couple were feeling the pressure from their forthcoming separation, and they both sensed a kind of awkwardness between them. Betty was having second thoughts about maintaining their celibate relationship and whether it would be best if they were to make proper love before Robert's departure the following day.

The opportunity could not have been better, with the family home empty apart from those two highly charged individuals. They cuddled up on the sofa and began kissing as never before. Betty whispered in Robert's ear,

'How about us visiting my bed?' Robert was shocked with this suggestion, and, although nothing would have given him more pleasure, he wasn't sure it was the right thing to do. His mother had often suggested to him that sex was for married couples only and that he should respect his girlfriend's purity and not take advantage of her innocent knowledge. He held her firm in his arms and said,

'You know we should not do this, because who knows what might happen if I make you pregnant, and me going off to fight in the war?'

'But I love you so much,' said Betty, 'I don't know how I shall manage without you, and maybe I shall never see you again.'

'Don't be silly,' replied Robert, 'It may only be a short war and then we can think about marriage and starting a family.' Betty began sobbing, and she held Robert so tightly in her arms, kissing him with intense ardour, such that he could hardly breathe. After a while Betty stood up, held out her hand and having pulled Robert to his feet, she guided him to the doorway leading to the staircase, and at the top of the stairs, she opened her bedroom door, and they stepped inside before sitting on the side of Betty's bed.

'Let's make love,' said Betty, 'I think it's the right thing to do.' Robert's hands were trembling as he explored her beautiful body. He was wrestling with his fervent desire to satisfy their physical passion, but his conscience was telling him it was not right and shouldn't happen. They were now in a state of partial undress, and Betty was encouraging Robert to go all the way, when they heard Betty's parents enter the house via the front door. This was a dreadful shock, and panic set in. They hurried to make themselves decent, and Robert told Betty it would be best if he was to leave the house by means of a bedroom window. He was a very fit young man, and he managed to lower himself from the window-sill and drop down on to the pavement below.

That was the last time they saw each other before Robert's departure, as next morning he had to catch the early train to commence his military training. He was soon involved in the war, when he became part of the expedition forces in Europe and saw much action very early on. When the invading forces faced impossible resistance from the ferocious German troops, evacuation and retreat seemed the only option. 'Operation Dynamo' was launched to bring home as many as was possible of the retreating British soldiers and Allied forces. The operation began on 26 May 1940, when a flotilla of small ships set sail from England to rescue the soldiers from numerous locations on the other side of the English Channel.

Robert was one of many who had arrived at Dunkirk and was rescued by a small steamship, which had been owned by the 'Caledonian Steam Packet Company'. The escape from the beach was hell on earth, with constant German gunfire and aerial bombardment. Robert unlike many others was extremely fortunate being pulled from sea on to a shallow-draft vessel, ideally suited for an inshore rescue. This little ship, named 'King George V', made numerous Channel crossings, rescuing more than 3,000 British troops in total.

The months and years passed by, and Betty was now recruited into the Women's Land Army and playing her part in the war effort by serving on a farm in Leicestershire. She was billeted along with twenty other girls in a hostel, and each morning after breakfast she would walk the two miles to Johnson's Farm where she and three other girls worked on the land. At first it was very hard work, but Betty appreciated toiling in the fresh air and looking after the animals. It was something she enjoyed doing and, in return, her wages amounted to 22/6 per week. She disciplined herself to send the majority of her wages home to mum and dad, and the rest she saved for a later day. Her physical attractiveness was always receiving considerable attention from the young men in the village where she was billeted. There wasn't much social life, except that every now and again there would be a dance held in the local village hall. Betty loved the excitement of these occasions, which only lasted a few hours on the last Friday in the month, but she enjoyed dressing up as best she was able from the limited clothes in her wardrobe. She had a couple of tidy frocks and one pair of nice shoes that she kept just for best. Like most of the other girls in her hostel, she had no stockings owing to the lack of silk, following the outbreak of war. She adopted a common practice that caught on, whereby she would wipe her bare legs with gravy-browning before setting off to the dance, and she would ask her closest friend to complete her leg dressing by painting an imitation seam down the calves of her legs, using a fine eyebrow pencil. One particular friend was very artistic and was able to paint on very impressive Cuban heels. Betty's painted legs were always admired by the youth's attending these dances and she spent little time resting between requests for her to dance. Although she had not seen Robert for over three years, she remained loyal to their relationship and wrote to him on a regular basis. She was always on the receiving end of invitations to walk out with those seeking female companionship, but she resisted their approaches, despite her increasing sexuality, as her hormones reached the height of their stimulating activity.

News soon got around that a disused Air Force camp just a few miles from Johnson's Farm was to be occupied by incoming American soldiers. The first dance after the G.I.s arrived was swamped by these Americans, and many had to be turned away. Fights broke out between the local lads and the smart looking butch military servicemen, who received instant attraction from the regular girls.

Betty was in much demand, and she was instantly spotted by one particular G.I. who took little time in telling her how pretty she was. They had several dances together, and, at the end of the last waltz, he asked whether he could escort her home. Betty explained that she had a serious boyfriend who was now serving in North Africa fighting in the war. He told her his name was Gerry Bonazoli, and he was from Boston MA, USA. He also told her he was twenty-four years of age, and he had no wife or serious girlfriend back home in the USA. He was very persistent, and Betty fell for his charming manner and handsome looks. He had a bicycle and he rode her back to the hostel, whilst she sat side-saddle over the cross-bar.

When they arrived at the hostel, he told Betty he would like to see her again if she was interested in a bit of fun.

'You have a gorgeous smile Betty and an amazing figure,' he said. 'Please forgive me if I kiss you on the lips.' At that, he placed his arms around Betty's waist and pulled her into a close embrace. They kissed for several minutes before Betty said she would need to go. She agreed to meet him on Sunday evening, when they could take a walk around the village and get to know much more about each other. They kissed long and hard, and again, Betty repeated she would need to go. Gerry removed his arms from around her and handed her a couple of packets that he said was a little gift in appreciation of her company. They said good night and Betty returned to her sleeping quarters. She was excited about the attention this American had bestowed on her and wasted no time in opening the packets that Gerry had given to her. She was in disbelief when she saw they were nylon stockings with striking seams, and she couldn't resist showing them to her dormitory mates. They were astonished, and one girl asked Betty to try them on. She sat on the side of her bed and carefully placed a stocking over one of her feet, before stretching it to the top of her leg. She did the same to her other leg and then stood up to show her mates. One said she looked very sexy and wished that she too could be on the receiving end of such a great gift.

Sunday evening arrived, and Betty decided to wear her nylon stockings before meeting Gerry for their walk. She borrowed a suspender-belt from another girl, and by the time she was finally dressed she told her mates that she felt a million dollars. She had agreed to meet Gerry by the canal bridge, and they set off down the lane holding hands and smiling at each other with gleeful anticipation of what might happen next. Betty had not received a letter from Robert for several months, and she was wondering about his safety, as she knew he was involved in bitter fighting. She was also having doubts whether their relationship would survive the traumas of war, and now the temptations going through her mind were something she considered to be somewhat out of control. She and Gerry chatted about anything and everything, and they were both enchanted by the other's presence. As it was approaching the time for Betty to return to the hostel, she felt a stirring passion within her whole body that she was unable to suppress. Her sexy nylon stockings were a contributor to how she was feeling, and her appetite for intimate pleasure with Gerry was influencing her conscious mind. They arrived back at the canal bridge, where Betty took control of the situation and on the embankment behind the canal towpath she encouraged Gerry to make love to her, and this he did to her complete satisfaction.

The following day, Betty received a long awaited letter from Robert, and that put her head into a complete spin. In the letter, as always, he expressed his fond love for Betty. He apologised for not writing sooner but explained that his unit had been involved in almost continued battles with the powerful German enemy.

Over the forthcoming days, Betty struggled to cope with feelings of guilt that were ever-present in her head. Deep in her heart, she still loved Robert. However, her passion resulting from the physical contact with Gerry was such a strong emotion that it was overpowering the feeling of regret at what she had done. She needed to reply to Robert, and she spent an entire evening constructing a letter that she considered appropriate. It wasn't going to be easy, as she was not good at hiding the truth. She began by thanking Robert for his lovely letter and told him she had been worried about his ongoing safety. She didn't refer to the

Americans and concentrated on news from home and what she had been doing at work. She said she had heard on the wireless that the war was going well and our troops in North Africa, led by Lieutenant-General Bernard Montgomery, had secured an incredible victory. She described how her hands were sore from the singling work she was doing in the turnip fields. Having written that, she went on to explain what the term meant. She described how singling involved using a long handled hoe to thin out the many rows of seedling turnips, to leave a single tiny turnip, enough space to mature. She finished her letter by wishing Robert continued safe passage with her usual expression of her continued love and then a long row of kisses.

She now felt tormented in her mind and lay awake at night deliberating whether to see Gerry again. The next time they met, she confided in Gerry, explaining that her real boyfriend was serving overseas, and she felt very guilty about giving her body to an almost unknown American soldier. Gerry held both her hands and gently whispered in her ear:

'You really are a sweet girl, Betty, and I can truly understand your feelings of guilt. On the other hand, there is a conflict taking place, and that has created situations, which are unreal outside a state of war. Separations are unnatural, and loneliness can bring about pressures that are difficult to control.' They kissed each other, and then Betty broke into tears as Gerry held her close to his chest. They made love whenever they could before the news came through that Gerry was being relocated.

Their last opportunity to make love was an immensely passionate occasion, when they both finished up naked in a disused barn on Johnson's farm. Afterwards, they relaxed over a cigarette and then, as they were replacing their clothes, Betty noticed Gerry's cigarette case was lying on the ground. She placed her foot over it, and, when Gerry wasn't looking, she picked it up and placed it in her pocket. She wished to keep it as a reminder of the wonderful time she had spent with Gerry, during their brief but unforgettable times together. Betty was saddened by Gerry's departure, and she cried herself to sleep for many nights after his unit moved on. On one occasion she took Gerry's cigarette case from her bedside locker, and, when she opened it, she was amazed to discover that it contained a hand-written letter from Gerry's mother. She sobbed uncontrollably as she read the letter, which contained news from home in the USA. In the letter she wrote about visiting the 1942 PGA championship at the 'Seaview Country Club' in Galloway Township, New Jersey. She expressed their delight when Sam Sneyd beat Jim Turnesa 2-1 in the final. Gerry had already told Betty about his parents' love of golf, and he too played off a handicap of four strokes.

Betty and Gerry had not taken any precautions when making love, and she was soon to discover that she was expecting a baby. She was able to conceal this situation for six months, but then she had no choice but to announce her condition to her boss. There was no alternative but for Betty to leave the service and return home to her parents. They were very upset initially, but they soon decided to house her and offered their ongoing support.

Another letter arrived from Robert, and now she was totally unsure how to respond. She discussed the matter with her mother, who suggested she should do what her conscience told her. Betty felt she would be unable to inform Robert about her pregnancy and decided to keep the matter secret until, God willing, he returned from the war, and then she would have no option but to confess all, in a face-to-face situation. She was devastated that she had not heard from Gerry, even though she sent several letters to his unit. In desperation, she decided to write to Gerry's parents in Boston, informing them of her plight. She described how she had fallen in love with their son, and now she was expecting his child. For weeks, she waited for a reply, but nothing arrived, and she soon realised they didn't wish to communicate with her.

Betty gave birth to a little girl, whom she and her parents smothered with love. She had the baby christened Geraldine, and, when finally VE day was declared, Geraldine was almost three years old. Betty continued to receive letters from Robert who had no idea what had been taking place in her life. She explained that leaving the Women's Land Girl movement was down to poor health by making reference to a fictitious heart disorder. She received a letter from Robert saying he was returning home soon and hoped to be demobbed from the army before the end of 1945. Betty was dreading the day when Robert knocked on her door. She still had the same feelings for him despite their long separation, but she feared that, once Robert found out about little Geraldine, he would ditch her, and quite rightly so. Both Robert's parents had moved away from the area, and they had no knowledge of Betty's plight, which they might have passed on to Robert.

Robert paid a visit to meet Betty at her home, and, when he arrived, her parents made their excuses and went off to the pub, thereby leaving Betty alone with Robert, apart from Geraldine, who by this time was fast asleep in her bed. Betty had felt strange as she answered the front door, and there stood her boyfriend of many years, who looked much older than when went away to war in 1939. She leapt into his arms before he had chance to step inside the house. They kissed each other with such passion that they had not experienced in many a year.

Betty made Robert a cup of tea and then asked him to listen carefully to something very serious that she had to say. By this time the colour had drained from her cheeks and she started to weep.

'Whatever is the matter, Betty?' Robert asked.

'I've been very silly whilst you were away, and I'm certain you will never forgive me for what I have done,' she replied.

'Please explain,' said Robert. Betty could hardly speak as she stumbled over her words trying desperately hard to find a way of breaking her news in the best possible way.

'I've been unfaithful, Robert. I'm totally ashamed of myself, and I know that you will never forgive me for what I have done.'

'Tell me, Betty, tell me now, as I need to know!'

'Oh, dear,' said Betty, 'I don't know how to begin.' Robert clenched her hands in his, whilst saying:

'Betty, I love you: please explain why you are so upset.'

'I've been unfaithful to you, and it's not easy for me to tell you the truth. I have kept a major secret from you for the past three years, as I didn't wish to hurt you, and I lacked the courage to admit what I've done.'

'Oh, my darling Betty,' said Robert, 'I can't begin to understand what you are trying to tell me.'

'I saw an American soldier who was stationed near to the hostel, and we had sex on several occasions,' said Betty. Robert's face was also pale and contorted as he fought hard not to break down and cry.

'Are you telling me you are finishing our relationship?' asked Robert.

'I don't know,' replied Betty. 'Whilst I still love you with all my heart, I don't see how you will ever forgive me for the things I've done.'

'Where is this American guy now, and are you still seeing him?' asked Robert.

'I haven't seen him in years,' said Betty. 'He moved away, and we have not had any contact since.'

'I don't understand how you can say that you still love me and at the same time you are telling me that you have been unfaithful with someone else,' said Robert.

'I was lonely at the time,' said Betty, 'but I know it's no excuse and I can never expect you to forgive me.'

'The war has been very cruel, and we have all done things we regret,' said Robert. 'If you have no feelings for the American guy and you still love me, then of course I can forgive you,' said Robert.

'But there is more,' said Betty, as she burst into uncontrollable sobbing.

'Please tell me, Betty,' said Robert. 'Whatever you are trying to say?'

'I have a baby daughter,' said Betty. Robert went completely quiet, and there was nothing but silence apart from the repeat inhalations of breath as Betty sat breaking her heart. The silence broke with Robert saying,

'Where is the child now?'

'She is fast asleep in bed,' replied Betty.

'Can I see her?' asked Robert. Betty stood up and asked Robert to follow behind, whilst she led him to the bedroom, where little Geraldine was lying in her cot. There was just enough light shining in from the landing for Robert to see Geraldine's pretty face.

'She's lovely,' said Robert.

'She is very precious to me, and I shall always look after her as best I can,' said Betty. Robert left the room and told Betty he needed time to think.

He had to return to his base the next day, and it was about a week later when he wrote to Betty with the following words:

My Dear Betty

Having taken a few days to think about my visit last Saturday, I have searched my soul and now find it easier to express my feelings in writing as it was so painful for us both when you were informing me about Geraldine and your brief relationship with her father. My love for you is as strong now as it ever was. Naturally, I was saddened and shocked to hear that you have made love with another man, and I understand if you wish our relationship to end.

Before I give up on you I wish you to know that I can see it in my heart to forgive you and I would dearly like us to continue where we left off when the war started.

I know you will always be my true love and I would love to spend the remainder of my life with you and of course your beautiful daughter Geraldine. You are so important in my life that I don't know how I can face the future without you. The thoughts of you and seeing you again after the war were the only things that have kept me going, particularly so, when things got really tough.

Possibly this is not the best way to do this but I am asking you to marry me and I will do my very best to forgive you for what has happened. Let's marry as soon as we can after I am demobbed and find work in the area.

Please write to me soon, and here's hoping you will be my bride and we can love each other forever.

Your ever loving friend

Robert xxxxxxxxxx

When Betty read the letter, she cried endlessly, but now these were tears of joy. She sent Robert a letter by return, accepting his offer of marriage and confirming her devoted love for him.

Everything in Betty's life was now going smoothly and she was counting the months until her true love Robert would be returning home for good. It was a Monday morning, and Betty was out doing her part-time cleaning job, whilst her mother was looking after Geraldine and doing the weekly washing. There came a loud knock at the front door, and, when Mrs Simpson answered, there stood a middle-aged couple who appeared very smartly dressed. The gentleman, who was wearing a trilby hat, said they were hoping to meet a Miss Betty Simpson.

'I am Betty's mother, and Betty is at work this morning,' said Mrs Simpson, 'but can I help?'

'Not really,' replied the lady at the door, 'it's Betty we need to see.'

'May we return later?' asked the man.

'She will be home at dinner-time,' said Mrs Simpson, 'and you can see her then.' The couple left, and Mrs Simpson couldn't wait for Betty to arrive home. As soon as she came through the door, her mother explained that a man and women with a strange accent had called, asking to a see a Miss Betty Simpson.

'Who can they be?' asked Betty.

'I don't know,' replied Mrs Simpson. 'I hope you are not in any kind of trouble.'

Soon after dinnertime, there came a knock at the door and Betty went to answer it.

'Are you Betty Simpson?' asked the gentleman.

'Yes, I am Betty. Is something wrong?' she replied.

'We are Mr and Mrs Bonazoli from Boston, USA, and we'd like to discuss something with you.' Betty went weak at the knees, when she heard the name Bonazoli, and her mother, who was standing behind Betty, had to support her, otherwise she would have collapsed on the doorstep.

'Please come inside,' said Betty, and she led them into the sitting-room.

'Is everything all right, Betty?' asked Mrs Simpson.

'I don't know, mother,' replied Betty. 'Will you please leave me alone with Mr and Mrs Bonazoli for a little while?' Mrs Simpson left the room, and Betty invited her visitors to be seated on the sofa. Mrs Bonazoli spoke in a gentle voice saying,

'Betty, we have some news for you which will come as a shock. I received your letter a couple of years ago, informing me of your relationship with our son Gerry and that you were expecting his child. I'm sorry I didn't reply: I thought it better if I handed Gerry the letter when he returned from the war.' At that point, Mrs Bonazoli broke down, and her husband took over the conversation.

'You see, Betty, Gerry was killed last year in the Normandy Landings, and we are still coming to terms with our tragic loss. We only had the one child, so you will see we are now facing a huge gap in our lives. We sat at home recently wondering about Gerry's time in England, and we read your letter once again. I suggested to my wife that we should go over to England and try to meet Betty and, if possible, Gerry's child.' Betty sat listening but not believing what she was hearing. It all seemed too much to bear, and the thoughts about her passionate times with Gerry all came flooding back to her. Then came the moment when Betty decided it was time for Mr and Mrs Bonazoli to meet their granddaughter. She excused herself and disappeared upstairs where Geraldine was having her afternoon sleep. A few minutes later, Betty returned to the sitting-room holding Geraldine in her arms. Mr and Mrs Bonazoli both cried openly when they saw little Geraldine, and they soon decided to leave after inviting Betty to dine with them that same evening at the local village inn.

Over the meal, they surprised Betty beyond belief when they invited her and Geraldine to go and live with them in America. They explained that they were very wealthy, and Betty and Geraldine would have the opportunity of a new life, living in considerable comfort. It was all too much for Betty to take in, but, after another couple of meetings with Mr and Mrs Bonazoli, she was seriously considering her options and trying to make an impossible decision, as, no matter what she decided, people were going to be hurt. She kept lying awake at night thinking about Robert and wondering whether he would be the same person after the war. She also wondered whether making love with Robert would measure up to those unforgettable times when she and Gerry gave each other such intimate pleasure.

Mr and Mrs Bonazoli returned to the USA, leaving Betty with an open offer that she needed time to consider. Betty discussed the situation with her parents, and they were surprisingly supportive about Betty going to America to begin a new life. After all, they said, if you marry Robert you will remain a working-class girl for the rest of your life. Betty wrestled with her dilemma and finally decided she and Geraldine would go to live in America, but she now had the problem of how best to inform Robert. She decided it would be better to give him the news by letter, because that way, it would be less painful and emotional all round. She set about writing a letter to Robert, which she constructed with great care. It read like this:

My Dearest Robert

It is with deep and heartfelt sadness that I write this letter to you, and I'm sure you will realize what pain it brings to my personal feelings from what I am about to explain. I recently received a visit from an American couple who turned out to be the parents of Geraldine's father. They brought sad news that he had been killed during the Normandy landings and having received an earlier letter from me, when I told them I was expecting a child fathered by their son, they had made the decision to make contact with Geraldine and me. They have no other family and the sad loss of their son has left a cavernous hole in their lives, which is increasing as time goes by.

They are wealthy people and they have offered to provide a new home for me and Geraldine over in the USA. I have laboured long and hard what this will mean to my mum and dad and of course to you, if I decide to take up their offer.

Although my love for you will always remain strong, my feelings for Geraldine's father were something special that I shall probably never find again with another partner. I shall inevitably make comparisons and this will be unfair to you if we go ahead with our marriage. I don't expect you to take this decision easily or ever to understand the logic of what I am doing. I'm certain that you will meet someone else very soon and I pray to God that they will love you in a way you deserve.

I am not leaving a forwarding address, as I wish you to sever all contact with me and focus on finding a true love in your life.

I'm deeply sorry to bring you this news but in the end I believe you will find the will to forgive me.

Good luck in the future and God bless

Your dearest Betty

After finishing the letter, Betty cried all night, yet deep in her heart she believed she was making the right decision.

The next morning, she read the letter once again, and then sealed it in an envelope, before attaching a postage-stamp. She left home to go and post the letter, thinking she would feel a sigh of relief, once the letter was on its way. She arrived at the post-box and went to place the letter through the slot, and, as her hand reached out, she could see her arm trembling, and for a brief moment her entire body froze. She felt she was out of control, and something had taken over her actions. There was a sense of a presence, and Gerry came into her thoughts once again. She then thought of Robert and wondered what was making her reconsider whether or not she was doing the right thing. She thought she heard Gerry's voice in her head telling her not to post the letter, and this made her think very clearly about what she was doing. She placed the letter in her pocket and ran all the way home, in floods of tears. As she entered the house, she hurried into the living-room and threw the letter on to the fire.

Robert came home after being demobbed and soon found work, having being discharged with an exemplary testimonial regarding his conduct and impeccable army service record. They were married in June 1946, and ten months later they had a baby who was baptised Christopher Robert. Betty would never be unfaithful again, as it wasn't her nature. She was a victim of the war and fell into a trap set by a charming guy who was seeking nothing more than a good time. It wasn't only those fighting overseas who were affected by the ravages of war, and there were many more like Betty whose lives changed as a result of the unfortunate circumstances they had to endure. It seems G.I. Gerry Bonazoli played his role in the war, in more ways than one, by giving his all.

The Enemy (no, not that one)

Derek Rosser

I was born on St Valentine's Day just a few years after the armistice which signalled the end of the great 'war to end all wars'. My mother was one of a family of eight children, five girls and three boys. The two eldest boys were of military age and joined the rush to volunteer in August 1914. Both of my uncles survived the rigours of the western front and, during the mid-'30s, I listened in awe to their tales of the horrors of Ypres and Passchendaele. By the time I was eight years old I could recite the casualty numbers of most of the major battles of that four-year-long carnage.

My father was not called on until just three months before the armistice, and he was training as an air-gunner with the RFC when the end came. Fortunately he was a driver on the Great Western Railway in 1939, a reserved occupation which kept him out of the armed forces. He married my mother in 1925, and I appeared on the scene some three years later, doomed to be an only child owing to the hard time experienced by my mother at my birth. My father spent my early years complaining that, when my mouth was open, he could not see the rest of my face. It was my mother's habit to walk the length of the High Street every Saturday afternoon looking for bargains in the shops. How clearly I recall the sight of ex-soldiers, some with missing limbs and ugly scars, trying to make a living by playing popular songs to the passers-by! Not for them the compensation now being paid for the war-shattered lives of today's military personnel.

Throughout 1938 my parents and those of my friends wore worried looks as they discussed the international situation and the possibility of another war on the horizon. However, the sword of Damocles was lifted in September when Mr Chamberlain returned from Munich to tell us that that nice Mr Hitler had promised that there would be 'Peace in our time'. The cinema newsreels showed him waving his piece of paper in the air, and there were sighs of relief all round. My dad got free tickets on the railway, and we went for a week's holiday in Blackpool, where I remember seeing Jack Warner and Gert 'n' Daisy in the Tower Theatre.

This was my final year in junior school. I had taken the scholarship exam in the summer, and we had been notified that I had been allocated a place in a secondary school about six miles away and would be starting this month. At the last school Christmas party, the headmaster, dressed in red robes and with a long white beard, gave me a present which turned out to be the parallelogram shape of a western front tank. Perhaps it was an omen of things to come.

Dad had been spending a lot of time overhauling my bike in readiness for the daily commute to school. Mum came with me on my first day, and we were arranged into forms in the lower hall. We bought our first-year text books from the previous year's third form which was being promoted (with some exceptions) to the fourth. My uniform had been purchased from a school outfitter, and it was considered a privilege to wear it. The new routine was familiar in a couple of weeks, and I soon got used to leaving home at eight o'clock each morning to cycle the six miles. The traffic was much lighter then, and there was no sign of the Chelsea chariots which block the roads during today's school run.

In 1939, the worried looks returned, and the rumours started all over again. In the late summer, two men turned up with a lorry-load of curved steel sheets and dug a huge hole in our back garden. They poured concrete into the bottom of the hole and then enclosed the whole thing with the curved steel sheets. I found out later that it was called an Anderson shelter. My father did not appreciate the destruction of his vegetable patch, but the time was to come when we were glad that the shelter was there. My gran did not have a back garden, so they installed what looked like a tiger's cage under the kitchen table. It was known as a Morrison shelter, and my gran was supposed to crawl into it in the event of an air-raid. Not much use; my gran could barely crawl into bed, let alone the tiger cage.

Shortly after that, our school was visited by a group of uniformed men, and we had a frightening but, at the same time, exciting afternoon being fitted with gas-masks. We were also provided with a cardboard case and told never to go anywhere without the mask. There were little holes in the side of the box through which one could thread a piece of string to carry the box over one's shoulder. My mother (who had also been provided with a mask) treated it as a fashion item and purchased a canvas case with a leather strap to match her handbag and gloves.

My father (I have mentioned that he was a driver on the Great Western) worked very unsociable shifts and spent much of some days in bed, causing me to be shushed whenever I made too much noise. As an only child, I was obliged to make my own amusements without the benefit of the high-tech gadgets with which many of today's children waste their time. My heroes were the cowboys of the day, Tom Mix, Ken Maynard and Hopalong Cassidy. I spent a lot of my time killing imaginary Red Indians with the six-shot cap revolver which lived in a proper leather holster and had been obtained in Woolworths for about a shilling (5p in today's monopoly money). Sometimes our garden was knee-deep in fallen braves, and I had to stow them in the air-raid shelter to hide them from my mum.

Cycling home from school one day, I spotted a bill-board carrying the message, 'German troops enter Danzig'. I had never heard of Danzig but realized this was news of some importance, and I hurried home to tell my parents. I was too late. They were having tea and listening to the wireless which, between the screeches and static whistles, was spreading the news around the country. This news was very shortly followed by even more sombre news. The German army had launched an armoured assault across the Polish border and was rapidly advancing with very little opposition from the Polish cavalry. Meanwhile Luftwaffe dive-bombers had attacked the city of Rotterdam and virtually razed it. According to my father, it was not totally unexpected but was still a shocking insight into what we could expect in the future.

A couple of days after this, Mr Chamberlain made an announcement on the wireless to tell us that, unless the Germans withdrew from Poland, we should be at war. We got the news second-hand because our wireless-battery was round at the garage being charged up. We got a bit more news about a week later to tell us that the German army was mopping up the last resistance and Poland was completely occupied.

Mr Hitler took little notice of Mr Chamberlain's announcement, and we waited anxiously for the next chapter to begin. Christmas was a somewhat sombre affair but, owing to my success in the exam, I got a No. 4 Meccano set which had cost my dad 7/6 (37½p). It was about a sixth of my dad's weekly pay - which showed how pleased he was with me.

The army had been sent to France as soon as war was declared, and my dad reckoned they'd send those upstarts back to Germany with a flea in their ear. This was the period later referred to as the 'phoney war' while the combatants sized one another up. Little happened until May, when the Germans launched an assault on Belgium and France. Instead of going via the French border-defence known as the Maginot Line, they sneakily bypassed it and went through Belgium instead. I was settling down nicely at my new school by now, and we put up a large map of Europe in the lower hall, which was also the dining-room. The intention was to use little flags to record the advance of the British forces.

However, it was not to be. The German progress across France was even more impressive than their gobbling up of Poland, and, before the end of May, the French had surrendered, and what was left of the British army was crowded on the beaches at the French port of Dunkirk under continuous attack by the Luftwaffe. It looked very much as if all was lost, but over 300,000 soldiers were brought back across the channel through the miracle of the little boats. Our neighbour's husband was one of those rescued, and his wife read us the letter he wrote to her to let her know that he was safely back in England.

Our future now looked even more uncertain, and my dad suggested that it might be a good idea to learn German. He was joking, of course, but things looked decidedly dodgy even to this twelve-year-old. The country needed a new leader, and they found one in Winston Churchill, who became Prime Minister just before the army was rescued.

Every Saturday morning I was given a penny, which was the entry price to the 'Saturday rush' at the local cinema. There was always a cowboy film and a serial titled 'The Skull', which was very creepy. One Saturday in late May we were on our way to the cinema when we came across three men hiding in a corner. They had a tripod made of wood and another piece of wood tied with string to the top of the tripod. They all wore arm bands with the letters LDV embroidered on them. We asked what they were doing, but they told us to go away or they'd turn the machine gun on us. I later discovered that they were founder members of the 'Local Defence Volunteers', a force hastily mustered to resist the invasion which was expected now that the Germans were only just over twenty miles away on the French coast.

It was at about this time that a German commander called Rommel began his armoured advance across North Africa with the objective of capturing the Suez Canal, an essential route for British shipping. Rommel's troops were called 'The Afrika Korps', and the British troops of the eighth army (the 'Desert Rats') were trying to stop them.

We changed our map on the lower hall wall to the new battlefields of Tunisia, Libya and Egypt. There were strange sounding names on the news these days, like Sidi Baranni, Tobruk and Benghazi, and our little flags moved this way and that but mostly in an easterly direction. Usually the wireless news and that in the cinema was pretty depressing, but I'm sure that Mr Churchill's speeches did much for our morale. Even after seventy-five years they still send a shiver down my spine.

There was an influx of lady teachers, because many of the male ones had been called up for the forces. We discovered that we could get away with a lot more with the ladies. It reduced the risk of an invitation to visit the headmaster's study. Such a visit guaranteed the receipt of a sore behind. Our headmaster was an artist and could lay six strokes along the same groove ... Yes, it did sting a bit.

Not all of our new masters were mistresses, if you'll pardon the expression. One of them was an elderly man - must have been at least fifty. He was about five feet tall, had a long wispy moustache and an unpleasant expression. It was our custom and practice to 'rag' new members of staff, and we looked forward to the opportunity. His subject was maths, and we were due for a maths period on Wednesday morning in room 10. There was a gangway from the door to the raised platform containing the teacher's table, and the desks were arranged in rows either side of the gangway. We had practised his welcome. As he entered the room, the rear row would set up a low hum, and, as he proceeded to his table, the hum would be taken up by each row as he passed it. He entered the room at precisely 10.00 and, with gown flowing wildly behind him, made his way to his table accompanied by the hum. Halfway to his station, and without slowing his gait, he waved his arm and swiped Elliot's ear with a large book. The blow knocked its recipient out of his seat, and he landed, spread-eagled, in the gangway. Our new maths master continued his passage to the table, stood behind it and leaned forward with his palms laid flat on the table.

'Now then, gentlemen, my name is Mr Guido. Do we understand one another?' There was a deathly silence as we contemplated his remark. The silence was followed by a grudging,

'Yes, sir,' and the class continued without further interruption. First round to Mr Guido - but we shall see. Of course, if he had behaved in the same manner today, he would probably have been prosecuted for child abuse and spent the rest of the war in the slammer.

The following day Mr Guido made himself even more unpopular. We were gathered round the map in the lower hall at lunchtime checking the flag positions. Without invitation, he moved several of the flags further to the east and explained that Rommel had advanced at least ten miles since we last set the flags. He accompanied his explanation with the information that he was himself Spanish, so had no interest in the war other than the principle of accuracy.

The Luftwaffe was bombing the RAF airfields in the south and east of England. My dad reckoned they were softening us up in preparation for the invasion. I didn't see my dad very often those days. He would leave home one day and not come back for four or five days, having spent time in some siding waiting for track repairs or avoiding enemy attacks. One day he came home and gave me four cannon shell-cases. They had dropped into his cab from an aircraft that had been strafing his train. It seemed that they liked to follow the railway-line at dusk and shoot at the glow from the furnace when the fireman opened the door to throw in more coal. It got so bad that they put an armoured sheet at the back of the cab to protect the crew. Those shell cases were made of brass, and my mum polished them up and stood them on the mantelpiece clock. They lived there for many years after the war, but I have no idea what happened to them after I left home to get married.

The news on the wireless was full of the numbers of German aircraft that were being shot down each day. The numbers sometimes ran into the hundreds, and a famous phrase crept into the English language: 'One of our aircraft is missing'. At the time we believed it like gospel but, no doubt, some of the numbers were inflated as morale-boosting propaganda. The battle in the skies over south-eastern England continued for about three months, but, by September, the numbers were dwindling, and what was to become known as 'The Battle of Britain' was over. Mr Churchill made a speech on the wireless that stirred our spirits: 'Never in the field of human conflict was so much owed by so many to so few'.

So far we had seen no sign of enemy aircraft in our area, although the siren had been sounded for test purposes, and the local ARP wardens shouted, 'Put that light out!' if we dared to show a chink through a door or blackout curtain. We still took our gas-masks with us wherever we went but had, so far, not seen the inside of the air-raid shelter. My dad had been quite busy in there and had rigged up a couple of bunk-beds from scrap timber and stored dozens of tins of food under the bottom bunk. Good job he had been so industrious, because my mum and I were due to spend a lot of time in there during the coming months.

With the Battle of Britain finished and the threat of invasion receding, the enemy turned his attention to the bombing of British cities, and, in early September, we had what I believe was the first raid in our area. The target was obviously the aeroplane factory at Filton. The factory was severely damaged, and there were many casualties because it was a daytime raid and some of the bombs fell on the air-raid shelters containing the factory workers. We could see the bombers from our school-yard, and the sky seemed to be full of them.

When we went to school the following day, it was to find that many of the lessons would, in future, be conducted in the school basement where there were no windows and less risk from flying glass if the bombers came our way. Mr Guido was put in charge of one area of the basement and did his best to make school life as intolerable as possible. My friend Jim was told to await the headmaster's pleasure just because he had forgotten to bring his gas-mask down from the classroom. The basement was damp and claustrophobic, hardly an ideal place to be struggling with mathematics. Mr Guido made sure that we had more than enough homework to keep us busy until the next time we came under his jurisdiction. His unpopularity was gaining momentum with every day that passed, and we decided that something must be done in revenge.

Then things at school improved. We gained another new teacher (Mrs W–) whose subject was botany. She was very pretty, and, although the subject interested me not at all, her lessons were a pleasure, and we all behaved like the gentlemen we were supposed to be. She taught us about silk-worms and gave each pupil about a dozen of the creatures to look after until we could harvest the silk which they would eventually produce. She even provided some old biscuit-tins in which we could house them. She told us about their life-cycle, their habits and their dietary requirements. Fortunately there was a mulberry-tree growing in the school grounds which provided the leaves necessary for the survival of our new pets. Some weeks later, the worms wrapped themselves in a chrysalis, and it was time to reap the reward of pure silk from the chrysalises (or would you prefer chrysalides or chrysalids?!).

I had been intending to make a scarf for my mother from my share but, after I had unwound the whole lot from my personal herd, I discovered that you'd need about a million worms to knit a pullover for an ant. I lost interest after that and cast around for some other interest.

Wednesday was sports day, and, in the afternoon, we gathered at the school ground to play games. The school played rugby in the winter and cricket in the summer. It was a great privilege to be picked for a school team, and there was great rivalry in games against other secondary schools in the area. I did manage to get into the rugby seconds, being pretty quick on my feet: just what is needed for a wing three-quarter. On my first outing I was slammed bodily against a static water tank at the side of the pitch by one of the opposing forwards (Reg D–). At twelve years old, he was nearly six feet tall and would have made two of me.

Yet again Mr Guido spoiled the game for me. He told me to stand up, get on with it and stop being a cissy. The field was going round and round, and I couldn't straighten my leg, so I declined his kind offer and hobbled off back to the pavilion to nurse my wounds. When I was examined later, they discovered that I had a displaced cartilage, and it took three days before I could walk properly again.

In early November the air-raid siren sounded at about 6pm. My dad was away on his engine, but my Mum and I made our way into our shelter. It had been arranged that our next door neighbour and her fourteen-year-old daughter would join us because her husband was away in the western desert fighting Rommel's crowd. My dad had had the foresight to include a paraffin-stove in his furnishings, and mum had just made a cup of tea when we heard, again, the resonating drone that was to become so familiar.

Not long afterwards came the crump-crump as the first bombs started falling. We knew that there was an anti-aircraft battery on Purdown about a mile away from us, and, soon after the start of the raid, Purdown Percy, as it was known, added its own almighty bang to the cacophony all around us. I had heard that Percy was a 16-inch naval gun. Even if it didn't shoot them down, it must surely frighten them a bit.

My dad finished his shift at about 10pm, but he did not get home until almost twelve hours later. Several times he was stopped by wardens because his route took him through some of the heavily bombed areas. Park Street, one of the major thoroughfares of the old city, was a scene of devastation with rubble strewn everywhere. Dad had been roped in to help shift some of the stuff so that the ambulances could get through. He was also demoralised because he heard that the Regent cinema had been put out of action. It was my dad's favourite picture-house where an organ came out of the ground and was played to the audience during the intermission. Dad was a lover of 'Gainsborough' films and refused to attend any other. He transferred his allegiance to the New Palace in Baldwin Street but never really got over the destruction of the Regent.

Christmas was fast approaching, and my financial situation was, to say the least, hazardous. Dad was obliged to contribute two guineas (£2.10p) a term towards my education, and I was allowed 3d (about 1¼p) a week pocket money. This sum was gobbled up by my visit to the Saturday rush and the 2oz of gob-stoppers which lasted for about fifteen minutes each. I took 4d a day to school to pay for the mid-day meal provided on the premises.

To supplement my income, I stopped buying school dinners and went each day to a local bakery where I could purchase a Vienna loaf for 2½d which staved off the pangs of hunger and showed a net profit of 7½d a week. In the three weeks to Christmas, this would grow to about 2s, which was still not enough. Our baker's rounds-man delivered every day, driving an electric van, and I offered to help him at weekends and during school holidays. I gave up the Saturday rush and met Len (the rounds-man) at 7am at the start of his round half a mile from home. He reckoned that my assistance knocked at least an hour off his shift, and he gave me a shilling at 2pm when we were finished. Our relationship blossomed, and, on quiet roads, he allowed me to drive his electric van between stops. There was little danger of accident, since the side-streets were devoid of traffic but full of children playing games in the middle of the road. They watched me enviously as I manoeuvred the van between their goal posts or tennis nets delineated by jackets and cardigans.

By Christmas I had accumulated enough to buy my father a packet of Craven A (his taste in cigarettes) and a new tea towel for my mother. I even had enough left over to keep me in gob-stoppers for some time.

Just after the holidays, we had an all-night visit from the bombers. My mother had insisted that I go to bed in the shelter just in case there was a raid. To keep me company, our neighbour's daughter got the bottom bunk, and I was in the top one. I was a bit too young and unsophisticated to take advantage of the romantic opportunity thus presented. Our parents hurried in as the raid developed, and we could not hear ourselves speak with the combined noises of the guns and the bombs. I was conscious of a screaming whine, and my mother leaned over me as a bomb fell not very far away.

When things quietened down, I went outside and stayed behind the blast wall to see what was going on. I felt perfectly safe because mum had bought me a sixpenny tin hat from Woolworths at the weekend. The sky over the city was bright orange, the reflection of the huge fires that were burning. As I stood there, I heard a thud by my side and looked down to see a hot chunk of metal half buried in the garden. Whether it was a bomb fragment or shrapnel falling from a shell I still don't know. I dug it out in the morning when it had cooled down and it joined the rest of my shrapnel collection in an old biscuit tin.

The search lights were weaving across the sky, and, suddenly, one of the bombers was illuminated in its glare. Other lights focused their beam in the same place, and I could see the anti-aircraft shells exploding around the plane. It weaved about trying to evade the lights and eventually disappeared from view without being hit.

In the morning, after the 'All Clear', I put on my tin hat, got dad's spade from the shed and went out to dig for survivors. The bomb had fallen at the top of our road and demolished the front of my friend's house. Luckily there were no casualties, the family having been in their shelter at the critical time. I replaced the spade in dad's recently tidied shed. He'd said that, if I ever tidied his shed again, he'd take one of his kidney-bean canes to me. (Just doesn't appreciate tidiness, my dad.)

Much of our food was being sent to feed the fish in the Atlantic due to the terrible toll inflicted on our merchant shipping by U-boats. There were posters around telling us to 'dig for victory' and grow our own food. Dad was doing his bit by working an allotment when he had time. Some food items were already rationed, and the list grew longer as the war progressed right up to that terrible day in 1942 when sweets were put on the list. How would *you* like to survive on 12oz a *month*?

In the following summer there was an announcement at school. Volunteers were required to go camping for a week and help bring in the potato harvest. It sounded like a good way of dodging lessons for a week, so I badgered my parents to be allowed to volunteer. They got about thirty volunteers, and then came the news that the party would be accompanied by our enemy Mr Guido and Mr Brown (the French master). It was also understood that the potato gathering would be done during the day and two hours each evening would be dedicated to improving our knowledge of maths and French. It was too late to back out now, and we duly set off on Monday morning in a motor-coach. It took us to a cricket ground in a small village about twenty miles away and our first task was to pitch the tents under instruction from our two guards. During this operation Elliot hit my hand with a peg mallet. I'm not going to say it was deliberate, but my instant reaction was to land a haymaker in his eye. Naturally this assault was witnessed by Mr Guido who, in the absence of the headmaster, considered it his duty to administer justice by attacking my rear end with a gym shoe. He claimed not to have seen the original incident, but I think it was just his nasty temperament showing again.

We had yet to get our revenge on him, and this was just another thing to add to our list of grievances. We inflicted retribution on Elliot later in the tent after lights out. My mother had insisted that I take a tin of black boot polish with me, and it was about to come in useful. We hauled Elliot from his comfy sleeping bag and held him fast with his back against the pole in the middle of the tent. Martin Preston, who had also suffered humiliation due to the activities of Elliot, took the top off my tin of polish and proceeded to spread its contents all over the personal appendages of our victim. The resulting pandemonium was heard by the masters bedded down in the comfort of the pavilion changing-room. They entered the tent with a torch and demanded to know what was going on. It was a rhetorical question since the boot polish was shining in the reflected light from the torch. I'm sure I saw the glimmer of a smile on Mr Brown's face but, naturally, Mr Guido saw another opportunity. He sentenced us to one hour's detention every evening for a week when we returned to school. Then they both returned to the pavilion while we climbed back into our pits and listened to Elliot's snivelling.

The following morning dawned bright and clear and, after breakfast, we were marched to a farm half a mile away and left in the hands of the farmer and his boy. They left with the promise to return at 4pm to conduct us back to the billet.

The farmer (I can't remember his name) showed us a field and instructed us in the nature of the task ahead. His boy was going to drive the tractor, which was towing a potato-spinner, around the field in ever decreasing circles fetching out the potatoes. We, each armed with a basket and allocated a specific position in the circle, would pick up the potatoes before the next visit of the tractor. It sounded easy, and we set to with a will. We soon discovered that it was back-breaking work and, with the decreasing circuit, the visits of the tractor became more and more frequent. The farmer marched up and down the field shouting instructions: 'Now don't 'ee let tractor run over they tatties or 'e'll squash 'em.' Even I, with my limited knowledge of physics, could have worked it out for myself. At mid-day a horse and trap arrived containing what we took to be the farmer's wife, a large barrel and a selection of earthenware mugs. Bliss ... it was rough cider, and we recovered enough to keep working until the masters turned up. They skipped the evening tuition and informed us that, if we kept it up we should each earn 4s (20p) by the end of the week. It was good news, and we sang 'Roll out the barrel' to celebrate. In the late evening we could see the familiar glow in the sky and hoped that our parents were under cover.

By the end of the week we were exhausted but wealthy and were ferried back home in the motor-coach. We never did do those detentions. It was considered dangerous to delay our home going into the evening with the threat of further air-raids.

It was only a few days before Christmas that we heard about the Japanese attacking the American naval base at Pearl Harbour in the Hawaiian Islands and sinking most of their warships. Mr Roosevelt said the day would 'live in infamy'. Dad said that would make them join us in the fight and the tide of war would turn in our favour. But the news got worse. The Japanese did not limit their hostility to America. Around about my birthday in 1942 they overran Malaya and took the British base of Singapore. Mr Guido said it was all America's fault. The poor Japanese had no alternative. They were being starved of essential supplies because the Americans were sending it all to help us in Europe. Dad said he should be hanged for a remark like that, but I explained that, although Mr Guido was no friend of mine, he was Spanish, and they were neutral so he had a right to his own opinion. Dad said: 'Not while he's living here, he hasn't.'

***

Spring was turning into summer one day when I was taking a stroll in the sunshine and eating fish and chips during the lunch-hour. A column of khaki coloured lorries with white stars painted on them passed by. Men in unfamiliar uniforms were hanging over the sides and whistling at the girls. The Yanks had arrived. Unfortunately I saw Mr Guido watching the cavalcade on the other side of the road and, what's more, he saw me too. He had me bang to rights: wearing school uniform and consuming fish and chips in a public place. It was a hanging offence, and there was no feasible excuse. Mr Guido wrote something in a little note-book and walked away. I returned to school wondering how long before I was expelled.

I was beginning to hope that Señor Guido had taken pity on me; but no. After the last period of the day, I was summoned to the head's study and lectured for a good ten minutes. 'Privilege to wear it ... pride in appearance ... honour of the school' and similar phrases were drummed into me. I expected them to be followed by the whack, but the old man must have been in a good mood because he ushered me out without fetching his stick. Guido saw me emerge, and I fancied he was grinning. Another black mark to add to his score.

We had discovered that the Yanks were always good for chewing-gum and sweets, and the girls had discovered that they were also good for nylon stockings and lipstick. My dad subscribed to the general opinion that they were 'overpaid, oversexed and over here'. He also said 'late last time and late again this time', but didn't explain what he meant.

The U-boats were still sinking a lot of ships, and mum was trying out all sorts of outlandish recipes to keep us fed. On the green down in town by the cathedral was a tent with a notice outside, 'British Restaurant.' You could get a reasonable meal in there for about a shilling, and you didn't need your ration book. All very well for the wealthy, of course, but a shilling was a lot of money to my mum.

***

A cinema called the Olympia was showing a film, *Old Mother Riley and Kitty,* and I, with a couple of mates, spent the afternoon laughing at the on-screen antics. Today the film would be called unfunny and stupid, but, in the atmosphere of war, we would laugh at almost anything. On emerging, we witnessed a bit of an international crisis. An American soldier was walking along the pavement with a girl on his arm. He came face to face with a group of other American soldiers. The latter were apparently insisting that the one with the girl should step off the pavement to pass them. Yes, you've guessed it: the one with the girl was black, and the others were white. It was our first experience of racism, and we watched in disbelief. I had seen our soldiers fighting with our sailors, but that was an entirely different thing, just friendly rivalry. The black man was not going to obey and whipped out a knife to defend himself. In no time at all more soldiers of both colours arrived on the scene, and the war was being carried on in the middle of the road. Someone called the military police, and they soon sorted things out.

On Monday, when we went back to school, it was to discover that Mr Guido was no longer in evidence. We found out that someone had reported him for making anti-British remarks in a pub. He was arrested as an 'undesirable alien' and probably spent the rest of the war in an internment camp.

Well, how the mighty had fallen! The enemy had been soundly defeated, and, while his downfall was not of our making, the taste of victory was nonetheless sweet. His duties were taken over by Mr Brown, an altogether more reasonable character, and school life became more bearable. Later in the year, Rommel got a trouncing at El Alamein, and the tide of war seemed to have turned.

In the final year of the war, I joined the Air Training Corps and was lucky enough to get several flights from RAF stations as part of our training. I particularly remember one of my flights and the nightmare it brought me. It was in an 'Oxford', a twin-engined machine where the cadet sat on the step between the pilot and co-pilot and was plugged into the intercom. The pilot (Flight Lt M–) was an ex-fighter pilot and was what we used to call 'bomb happy'. He took me out across the English Channel and boosted, then cut the engine. Through his conversation with his colleague, he implied that the aircraft was in trouble and we should have to abandon it. Although cadets were issued with chest mounted parachutes, we had never been instructed in their use. The flight-lieutenant told me to open the trapdoor to the rear of the fuselage and be prepared to drop out when he told me. I sat on the edge of the trap and watched in horror as the water below went by. Then he snickered, told me to close up and come back because it was a joke that they both enjoyed. If I had repeated this story, he would probably have spent some time in the glasshouse, but, once I was sat between them again, I began to see the joke too.

***

I wish I could tell you about the rest of my schooldays, but the limitations of time and space will not permit it. Anyway, now that the enemy had been vanquished, there seems little point. Suffice it to say that the old adage claiming that schooldays are the best days of your life must have been written by someone who went to a different school at a different time ...

Honest Deceit

Avril Dalziel Saunders

3 September 1939. 11.15am. Meg Barnes was seven years old. She and her younger brother (Robert Barnes), mother (Mary Barnes), father (John Barnes), grandfather (Ronnie Sawyers), grandmother (Ethel Sawyers), auntie Kathy and uncle Reg, all sat grimly by the big Bakelite radio. Their hearts sank as the prime minister, Neville Chamberlain, announced that the British deadline for the withdrawal of German troops from Poland had expired and that Britain and France were now at war with Germany following the invasion of Poland two days previously.

John Barnes' parents had been good friends with Mary's mother and father. His father was killed in an accident at work in the docks when John was fourteen; very sadly his mother died six months later after a short illness. John had no other relations, so Mary's parents took him in to live with them. John and Mary were the same age, and romance blossomed between them; they got married when they were seventeen in 1932 and stayed on with Mary's parents. Mary's younger sister Kathy and brother Reg still lived at home, so with the arrival of Meg a year later in 1933, followed by her baby brother Robert eighteen months after that, this took the total number of occupants to eight, making it rather cramped in the neat little rented three-bedroom terrace house off Roman Road, Bethnal Green, east London. The front door opened directly on to the pavement, and the toilet was in a shed in the back garden. In the living-room, two brown leather armchairs with wooden arms flanked the fireplace; a matching two-seater settee sat opposite the fire; behind the settee was a big solid wood dining-table; four chairs with brown leather seats sat around it; two more matching chairs were against the wall. Bath-time for the kids was in the kitchen-sink. Every Friday night the big tin bath was brought in from the garden-shed and placed in front of the fire. Mary, Kathy and their mother filled the big pans with water and boiled them on the stove to pour into the bath. The men went first: they took it in turns to climb into the bath and scrub themselves clean. Then the men went to the pub while the ladies each had a bath.

John Barnes was a cheery man, 5ft 8ins tall, with short light-brown hair, of stocky build, with big masculine hands, and a real Cockney at heart. He grafted hard, as a labourer in the London docks, five days a week and took what overtime he could to help pay the bills and keep the family fed. Mary was a quiet homely girl, small, slim, with piercing blue eyes and long dark wavy hair, pulled back at the sides and falling down in teasing curls over her forehead. She thought the world of her parents and enjoyed being a wife and mother, helping her mother with the housework and cooking. Mary's mother, Ethel, was a typical proud East End woman. She was small and slim. She put curlers in her greying ginger hair every morning, then tied a turban round her head to hide them, but she always had two showing at the front. She kept her house and front step shining like a new pin. If she was not cooking or doing the weekly wash, she had a duster or cleaning cloth in her hand. Her nylons were permanently rolled down to her ankles ('to protect them', she would say), and she was never seen without her overall on to keep her clothes clean. Mary's father, Ronnie, worked nightshift at the docks, checking goods in and out. He was a good-looking man, of medium build, with dark wavy hair greying at the temples, balding on the crown, and a small dark moustache. He took a pride in his appearance and always wore a sports jacket or suit jacket over a tie with a white shirt. He never left the house without his soft hat. He enjoyed pottering about in the garden in the afternoons and popping down to his local for a pint with his old cronies on his nights off. Kathy looked like Mary. In fact, although she was two years younger, they were often mistaken for twins. She worked in a docklands café. Reg was nineteen and the youngest of the family. He inherited his father's good looks and was seldom seen without a girl on his arm. He was a likable lad, very obliging, although he had a cheeky sense of humour. His brother-in-law John (whom Reg idolised) got him a job as labourer alongside him at the docks.

The family were concerned for their homes and livelihood, because, even before the start of hostilities, the government realised that the Port of London would be a major target for enemy attack. The riverside areas of the lower Thames were densely packed with housing and commercial or industrial premises. It was therefore inevitable that bombs dropped by enemy aircraft would affect both the port and the people of the docklands' communities. With the threat of air attack, ships carrying foodstuffs were redirected to other safer ports. The huge warehouses in London's docks, which had previously been used for stockpiling vast supplies of imported meat, dairy produce, grain, sugar, were emptied of much of their stores. Only those required for London and the south east of England were kept – still a vast amount - and most of the provisions unloaded in the docks were quickly carried away by road or rail.

Rationing was introduced in January 1940. Food became expensive and scarce, so many Britons turned their gardens into vegetable patches. Mary's father Ronnie loved his little garden but realised that there were more important things he could be growing. He dug up his lawn, along with the roses, daffodil- and tulip-bulbs, irises, lupins, hydrangeas, sweet peas and rhododendrons and planted potatoes, carrots, peas, onions and rhubarb. He also made some hutches and a hen-house. He bred rabbits and chickens for food and eggs. Meg and Robert loved the little farm in the back garden. They were too young to realise that it was serious business and helped to keep the family fed.

February 1940. A brown envelope popped through the letter-box addressed to John. Mary's heart sank. She had a good idea what it might be. She took it through to John, who was sitting in the kitchen having a cup of tea before dashing off to work. He opened it and then stared at Mary. He did not have to say anything. Mary hugged him close as her tears welled up: she did not want her man to leave them and go away to fight in strange lands; she wished Hitler had never been born! Within a few weeks, John was sent to a British army-camp up north for training. After six weeks he came home on a short leave before being sent abroad to fight.

Everyone knew it was only a matter of time before Hitler started bombing London, so, while John was home on leave, he spoke to Mary about the dangers that could lie ahead for the children living in such a vulnerable area. He was very worried and reluctantly, with an aching heart, they agreed that it would make sense for Meg and Robert to be evacuated to safer areas in the UK countryside. A few days later and with a heavy heart, Mary waved goodbye to John. She did not know where he was going. That same week, she took her two children to Paddington railway-station and joined all the other evacuees. Hundreds of children stood on the platform with their little cases, gas-masks and labels tied to their clothing with their details written on them. Some were clinging to their mothers in fear; others were excited, thinking they were going on an adventure. Meg was bewildered: her mummy had told her she was going to a much safer place for a long holiday. She was scared, but she had a streak of independence in her and was very sensible for her seven years. Her mummy had tied her long dark hair back neatly in two plaits with a big red bow on each. She looked immaculate in her double-breasted red woolly coat with velvet collar, red beret and brown buckle shoes. Robert looked smart in his short grey trousers, long grey socks, black lace-up shoes and grey blazer. The freckles on his nose, along with the fringe of his red hair, stood out under his grey cap. Mary held her children close to her: she did not want to let them go, but they were being told to get on board the train. Mary sat Meg and Robert in a compartment with other children. Her stomach was churning. Hating to leaving them there on their own, she was very tempted to change her mind and snatch them back, but a voice inside her told her that they had to go for their own safety. Meg held Robert's hand tightly and said,

'Don't worry, mummy, I'll look after Robert, we'll be fine!' Mary felt the tears welling up as she hugged and kissed her children goodbye. She tried to put on a brave face for her children, but as the train pulled out of the platform, she wept uncontrollably along with all the other mothers. The realisation then hit her that she was alone, with no husband or children, and she did not know when, or whether, she would ever see any of them again.

Reg was called up three months later and joined the RAF. There were only Mary, her parents and her sister Kathy living at home now, but life was not easy in the East End. Kathy left her job in the café and started working with the emergency services driving ambulances. This worried the family, as she would be in the midst of the danger-spots, but Kathy was a plucky girl and wanted to do her bit for the war effort. Mary got a job in a factory making uniforms for the troops: this helped to keep her mind occupied, but she sorely missed her husband and children.

The first German raids on British cities took place at the end of August 1940, when Birmingham and Liverpool were attacked, but on 7 September the Blitz intensified when around 950 German aircraft attacked London. It was the first and last mass daylight raid on London, but it heralded the first of fifty-seven consecutive nights of bombing. The daylight raid alone caused some 300 civilian deaths and a further 1,300 serious injuries; by the end of the Blitz, around 30,000 Londoners would be left dead, with another 50,000 injured. For those who were left in London, a rigorous policy of blackout began. An air-raid warden went round the streets in the evening to make sure that every building had extinguished or covered its lights. Car-owners had to reduce their headlights to a thin horizontal slit, with rear lamps also dimmed severely. The number of road accidents shot up, exacerbated by the lack of street lighting and the dimmed traffic-lights. Sirens went off as German bombers were approaching, warning everyone to take cover in an air-raid shelter. Mary's parents had a tin shelter in the garden and often questioned what good it would do if a bomb dropped on them. By late summer 1941, because Mary missed her children so much and did not want them forgetting her or developing a new way of life with a different accent, she decided it was time for her kids to come home, even though London was taking a bashing from German bombers: she wanted her family to be together, no matter what the outcome.

It was a cold misty Saturday morning when Mary set off and travelled to Anglesey to pick up Meg and Robert. They were living at a farmhouse with Mr and Mrs Pickles, a cheery couple in their late fifties. There were four other children there, all seemingly healthy and happy. Meg and Robert were overjoyed when they saw their mother. Mary was very emotional and relieved that they still remembered her. Mrs Pickles was a big round country woman. She wore a hair net and a cross-over flowery apron, while Mr Pickles had a ruddy complexion, smoked a pipe and wore a gamekeeper's hat and tweed jacket. They insisted that Mary stay for lunch. When Mrs Pickles told the children to go and gather some eggs, they all raced out to the hen-house and came back with four big brown freshly-laid eggs.

'Ah, that should be enough,' said Mrs Pickles, her big chubby hands reaching out and taking the eggs off the children. Mary gathered Meg's and Robert's belongings together and packed them into their little bags. She was so happy to be with them again.

'Take your ma out to see the animals while I prepare lunch,' said Mrs Pickles. Meg and Robert held on to their mother's hand and skipped and jumped their way round the farm, looking at the sheep, cows and hens, plucking apples and pears from the trees and eating blackberries from the bushes as they made their way to the fields where corn, potatoes, cabbages, carrots, peas and turnips were growing. Mary felt a bit guilty because she could see how much they loved this way of life and the fresh air: there was no way they could have anything like this living in the city, but she had to have her children back where they belonged.

When they returned to the farmhouse, the table was set. Mrs Pickles said:

'Ah, you timed it nicely, take a seat, lunch is almost ready'. Ten minutes later she produced a beautiful home-made steak pie, with boiled potatoes, carrots and cabbage. 'Tuck in, it's all home-grown,' said Mrs Pickles. This was followed by home-made apple pie and cream. Mary savoured every mouthful; she had not had a meal like that since before rationing. Afterwards they could hardly move, their bellies were so full, but they had a train to catch, so Mary thanked Mrs Pickles very much for the delicious meal, before leaving and making her way to the railway-station with her precious children by her side. Soon they would all be back in the East End of London, and their house would feel like home again.

September 1942. Mary was at work, Ethel was cleaning the doorstep, when a young lad handed her a telegram addressed to Mary. Her heart sank as she walked through to the back garden and showed it to Ronnie. Everyone dreaded receiving a telegram when one of the family was away fighting. Mary's father rushed round to her work.

'Hello, what are you doing here, dad?' enquired Mary. She was suspicious of the look on his face; she took a deep breath, and her eyes tightened with worry. 'Dad, what is it? is mum ok?' she asked with concern. Her father bit his bottom lip as he took the telegram from his inside pocket. He took her hand and placed the telegram in it. Mary stared at it, then screamed,

'Nooo!!!!' She did not want to read the words; her instinct told her they would not be good. Slowly she tried to absorb the message; she was shaking and sobbing as she pushed the telegram into her father's hand. He read the words.

We regret to inform you that Pte John Barnes has been reported missing in action and is presumed dead.

He wrapped his arms around his daughter and said,

'C'mon, Mary, I'm taking you home.' She replied:

'How am I going to tell the kids that their daddy is dead? They miss him so much; they keep asking when he's coming home!' Mary sat in silence with her head in her hands at the old wooden dining-table in her parents' house along with her mother and father; there were no words that could ease the situation. Just after 3pm, she heard the noise of kids running along the road, giggling and shouting, Meg and Robert would be home from school any minute, and Mary knew she had to break this news to them. Robert barged in the door laughing and shouting excitedly.

'Quick, don't tell Meg I'm home, I have to hide from her!' A few minutes later Meg ran in the door and shouted:

'Gran, is Robert home? He ran away from me, I'll kill him when I get my hands on him!' Then she looked at Mary and said, 'Mummy, what are you doing home at this time of the day? why aren't you at work? Mary replied:

'Take a seat, Meg, get Robert: I have something to tell you both!' Ronnie got Robert out from his hiding-place under the bed and told him to go through to the living-room to see his mother. Mary then quietly broke the news to the children. They both threw their arms around Mary, crying.

'Does that mean we'll never see daddy again?' asked Robert.

'He'll be looking down on you both, and we'll meet him again one day in heaven,' replied Mary.

'But why, mummy, where is he now?' asked Meg. Mary could not answer that. She told them that they were to be very proud of their father: he was an extremely brave man who had risked his life to keep them all safe.

As the weeks went by, Mary threw herself into her work. Her heart was breaking: she could not comprehend that she would never see her John again, but she put on a brave face and tried to stay strong for her children.

Mid-December 1942. Mary was at work, and Ethel had popped out to get her weekly rations. Ronnie brought an old case down from the loft and placed it on the table to wait for the children arriving back from school. Meg and Robert got home just after 3.30pm. Robert went straight into the kitchen to pour himself a glass of water, while Meg flopped down on the arm of the armchair beside her grandfather to cuddle him.

'What's that, granddad?' she asked, pointing to the case.

'Ah, as soon as Robert comes in here, you'll find out,' replied Ronnie. Meg shouted:

'Quick, Robert, come here, granddad's got a surprise!' Robert raced into the room and slid to a halt in front of the table. The children looked on in anticipation as Ronnie smiled with an excited grin and said,

'Now let's see what we've got here.' His eyes lit up as he unlocked the case to reveal all the old decorations from Christmases past. The children yelled with glee, and, together with their granddad, they hung them up around the living-room. 'Ah, that's brightened the place up! Wait until your gran and mummy see them: I'm sure they will be pleased with our efforts', encouraged Ronnie.

Mary worked various shifts. On this particular day she finished at 4 pm and met Ethel on the way home. She carried the shopping-bag for her mother. They made their way past streets of rubble where houses had once stood; kids were laughing and playing on the bomb-sites, oblivious to the fact that families had once occupied houses there. Some would never be seen again: they were the unfortunate ones who never made it to the air-raid shelters. Ethel looked deep in thought, her eyes seeming to be imagining how things were before the Germans came. Then she stopped and said to Mary:

'I wonder whether we'll be next: it seems it's only a matter of time until they clear the place entirely!' Mary hugged her mother and replied:

'Let's just live for the day, mum, that's all we can do!' Ethel took a deep breath as if a shiver were running down her spine. As they walked in the front door, their anguish lifted: Meg and Robert were in the hallway, excited and giggling.

'What are you two so happy about?' asked Ethel.

'We have a surprise for you and mummy!' exclaimed the kids: they could hardly contain themselves.

'A surprise?' asked Mary with a bewildered look.

'C'mon, then, show us this surprise,' laughed Ethel. The children made them stand outside the living-room door. Then they flung the door open and shouted:

'De rah!' Ronnie was sitting on his armchair with a big satisfied smile as if to say, Didn't we do well? Mary and Ethel were amazed.

'Oh, I remember that lantern and that Merry Christmas sign from when I was little,' reminisced Mary with a happy sigh. 'Wait until Kathy gets back from work and sees our colourful room.' That evening was the first time for a while that joy and laughter returned to the house.

January 1943. The East End was a place of deprivation and hardship. Fortunately Mary's parents' row of houses was still standing. For many people, the home they had in 1939 was now a pile of rubble. Families and friends moved in together, some houses had approximately fifteen people under one roof, sharing two bedrooms and one outside toilet. The home they lived in during the day was entirely different from the place they went to sleep at night. A hall was built over the tracks of Bethnal Green tube-station; theatricals were staged there, and even the odd wedding party . The Central Line track was still being laid, and the tunnels had no trains, so it was converted into its own subterranean town. The council built a hospital and even a library down there. Chemical loos and a canteen were installed, and, eventually, the tunnels were lined with thousands of bunk beds. The people of the East End of London spent years sleeping down there away from the hell of the German bombers that plagued London, killing people and reducing buildings to piles of rubble almost every night. The air above ground level permanently smelled of smoke and fire. At the first sign of an air-raid, each family sent someone to the 'bundle shop': this was a left-luggage depot where everyone stored their bedding. They picked up the bundle of bedding and then got down to the platform to grab a decent place, while the rest of the family were rounded up. Once everyone was safely down below, some of the fathers would then go back up to get on with their work. East End folk would not be beaten: they stuck together and kept their spirits up, even though they never knew what they were going to face, or whether their house would still be there every time they surfaced from their safe haven in the bowels of the earth.

Mary became friendly with a girl from work called Annie. Annie was a giggly girl, full of fun, 5ft 3ins, with a perfect hour-glass figure. She had blond curly hair which she wore pinned up, with all the curls bouncing on top of her head. Her husband was in the navy. She got the occasional letter from him but had not seen him for two years. She did not have any children and lived with her mother two streets away from Mary. In a bid to try and cheer Mary up, Annie suggested that they go to the pictures one evening. Mary was reluctant, but Annie persuaded her that it would be good for her to get out and socialise a little. They went along to the local picture-house and saw *We'll Meet Again,* starring Vera Lynn. Annie's intentions had been good, but this film made Mary very tearful, as it brought back memories of John and reminded her how this cruel war had torn them apart forever. Annie wanted to make it up to Mary, so the next day at work she asked Mary,

'When was the last time you went dancing?' Mary replied,

'Oh, I've never really been dancing. John and I were both young when we met and were married at seventeen.'

'You've never been dancing?' questioned Annie, shocked. 'In that case, how do you fancy we go on Saturday night?' Mary was a bit taken aback at Annie's suggestion, and answered,

'But Annie, you're a married woman!' Annie laughed and told her not to be so silly, it was harmless fun, adding,

'Our men are not expecting us to sit at home like wall-flowers. Nothing wrong in enjoying music and dancing!' Mary was unsure about this; she still looked on herself as a respectable wife and mother.

Later that evening, she mentioned Annie's idea for them to go dancing to her mother. Ethel looked at Mary for a minute. Then she said:

'Well, I think you should go: it would do you the world of good; you owe it to yourself. All you do is work: you need a social life too. You know that dad and I are here for the kids.' Then Ethel's voice became more serious as she said, 'Mary, John wouldn't want you sitting moping about here night after night, you're only twenty-eight!' Mary was amazed at her mother's straightforward answer but was coming to terms with the idea that she needed to kick-start her life and start living again!

Saturday night came. Meg was excited to see her mother making the effort to look glamorous instead of wearing working overalls and a turban. Mary's sister Kathy was preparing to go on duty, but, before she left, she helped Mary tan her legs with gravy browning, and then she carefully drew a line up the back of each leg with black eye pencil to look like stocking-seams: stockings were unavailable owing to shortages, so many women used this trick instead.

'Mummy, you are gorgeous!' enthused Meg as Mary floated into the room in a pink taffeta dress with matching gloves that she had borrowed from Annie. Her sister Kathy loaned her silver sandals and a matching bag. She had butterflies in her stomach at the thought of going out into the socialising world, but her family's blessing helped to boost her confidence. Mary put on her brown shoes with thick soles, rounded toes and three-inch chunky heels, then she picked up her silver sandals for dancing, before hugging everyone.

'Wish me luck!' she said as she walked towards the door.

''Bye, have a great time!' they all echoed. Mary met Annie at the corner of their street, and they walked towards the bus-stop near Bethnal Green station. They were heading for the Paramount dance hall in Tottenham Court Road. Mary was amazed at the nightlife in bars and restaurants: she had not ventured up to town in the evening for years. You would never have believed there was a war on! They got to the dance-hall, handed their coats and outdoor shoes into the cloakroom, then made for the powder-room to freshen their make-up. All the other young women had the same idea and were struggling to grab a corner of the mirror to renew their lipstick. Annie said to Mary,

'We're never going to get near that mirror. Hang on, we'll use my compact.' As she opened her bag to take out her compact mirror, her toothbrush fell out. Mary laughed and said,

'Why have you brought your toothbrush with you, Annie?' Annie replied seriously,

'Because you don't know for sure that we will definitely get home tonight: we might end up sleeping down a tube-station. I like to come prepared. Some of my other friends even bring their night dresses out with them.' Mary's eyes nearly popped out of her head with Annie's explanation: she had never thought about the prospect of not getting home or sleeping overnight in a strange tube-station in the centre of London!

Annie was very popular: she knew a lot of people, and Mary could not help noticing how flirty she was. She introduced Mary to a few of her friends. One of them was a sailor called Eddie. Annie disappeared on to the dance-floor with Eddie's friend Sam. Eddie seemed very forward, which made Mary feel very awkward. He talked a lot and boasted about himself. He moved nearer and slipped his arm round Mary. His pushy behaviour made Mary feel uncomfortable. She shuddered but did not say anything. His breath smelt of alcohol, and his skin was greasy and sweaty. As the music stopped, she caught sight of Annie on the dance-floor. Mary was horrified when Sam grabbed Annie and kissed her passionately. Mary could not believe what she was seeing. Annie never resisted and reciprocated by wrapping her arms round Sam's big broad shoulders. Mary was feeling very uneasy by now. Suddenly Eddie pulled her close and attempted to kiss her. Mary pushed him away, stammering with embarrassment.

'S-s-sorry, I have to go to the powder-room.'

'Don't be long, then!' he told her with a confident smirk. Mary made straight for the cloakroom and grabbed her coat and shoes. She did not even wait to change out of her silver dance-shoes: she ran out of the dance-hall, all the way down Tottenham Court Road to catch a bus home. It was just after 9pm. There were women wandering up and down the street. She noticed that they were stopping to speak to soldiers and sailors; some went off arm in arm. A couple of sailors stopped Mary and asked her for the pleasure of her company. Mary realised that these girls were prostituting themselves. She was really feeling uncomfortable now, on her own in London, and just wanted to get home to her family.

On Monday morning at work, Annie asked Mary where she had disappeared to on Saturday night. Mary told Annie what had happened. Annie just laughed. She shrugged it off and replied,

'It's only a bit of harmless fun. You didn't have to leave just because you didn't like Eddie.' Mary also mentioned that she had been approached by a couple of sailors in the street. Annie said,

'Well, you just have to keep your wits about you: that's why you should have waited for me!'

Annie talked Mary into going to the dancing again the following Saturday but told her to relax more and not take everything so seriously. They joined a few of Annie's friends who were sitting round a table by the side of the dance-floor. They gradually disappeared on to the dance-floor, except for Mary and one young man. Mary could not help noticing how immaculately and smartly dressed he was in his dark blue double-breasted suit, shirt, tie along with very shiny black lace-up shoes. His dark hair was neatly combed back in a 'London bob'.

'Hi, I'm Frank. Would you mind if I sat next to you?' he shyly asked Mary.

'Not at all. My name's Mary,' she replied, inwardly astonished with herself that she had blurted this out. Mary found Frank modest but easy to talk to; she felt relaxed in his company. He told her that he was not really a dancer but came along because his friends insisted. Mary laughed and told him that she was the exact same and was there only because she had been talked into it by Annie. Before they knew it, the last dance was announced.

'Would you like to dance?' prompted Frank, holding out his hand to Mary. She smiled and nodded. As they were waltzing round the floor, Frank asked Mary whether she would like to go to the picture-house one evening, and Mary happily agreed.

Mary and Frank travelled up to London to meet each other once or twice a week over the next few weeks. By this time he knew all about her family and children and that her husband John was 'missing presumed dead'. Mary found out that Frank was thirty-five, seven years older than herself. He was an only child and lived in his parents' house in south-west London with his elderly mother. His father had been killed in WWI. Frank worked in the design-office of an aircraft factory. This was a very responsible job during the war. Therefore his conscription to the services was deferred until war was over.

Mary was on her way home from work after a late shift on the evening of 3 March 1943 when the sirens went. She got off the bus and ran for shelter in Bethnal Green tube-station. There were hundreds of people down there already, so she had very little chance of finding her parents with Meg and Robert, but she was hoping that they were in there somewhere. Unbeknown to the people already deep down in the bowels of Bethnal Green tube-station, a tragedy was unfolding above them. There was only one entrance to the tube-station from the street: a flight of rough steps led down to a landing, then there were a further seven steps to the ticket-hall. From there, escalators led to the platforms eighty feet below ground. The first set of steps was lit by a single 25-watt bulb. An earlier rain-shower had made them slippery, and there was no central rail, but most people knew the place well. People were used to forming an orderly queue, but on this occasion an anti-aircraft unit nearby in Victoria Park fired a new rocket weapon for the first time. It made a great whoosh and sent everyone into a panic, causing chaos. People started shouting, 'It's a bomb!' They were screaming and shoving to get into the shelter of the tube-station. As a result, hundreds of men women and children were crushed: 173 lost their lives, not from German bombs, but from sheer fear in their attempts to get to safety.

Mary emerged from the tube-station in the morning along with at least 1000 other people, all totally unaware of their lucky escape the night before, as all evidence of the tragedy was cleared away. She bravely made her way home past all the depressing flattened streets, where neat rows of houses had once stood. Her heart raced as she could see her house in the distance. She ran in the door to be greeted by her father, sister Kathy and daughter Meg. They threw their arms round her.

'Oh, thank God you're safe, Mary!' Kathy blurted out through tears.

'I'm fine. Where are mum and Robert?' she asked. There was no reply. She asked again, 'Where are mum and Robert? Dad, Kathy, what's happened?' Mary's voice was raised in panic; she felt her heart pounding.

'We don't know! Your mother and Robert headed for the tube-station last night when the sirens went off. I twisted my ankle, so decided to stay in the tin shelter in the garden,' replied her father, trying to reassure himself, as well as everyone else, that the missing members of the family would walk through the door any minute. Kathy went on to tell Mary that she had been on duty the night before and what had happened in the entrance to the tube-station. She informed Mary that the newspapers would not be reporting it immediately and that she and her colleagues had been asked not to speak about it because the council didn't want to cause hysteria amongst the masses.

As the day went on, there was no sign of Mary's mother or her beloved eight-year-old son Robert. Finally they got the word to come along to identify bodies. Mary was beside herself with grief; her heart was aching: how much more could she take?

A few months passed. Mary was very glad she had met Frank when she did: he was a good listener and very understanding. He was always there when she needed to talk. He came to the house often and got on very well with Mary's father too.

Frank invited Mary to meet his mother; Mary was very nervous. They got off the tube at Richmond, then proceeded to walk up a hill behind the station. Mary noticed some lovely big houses.

'Do we have much further to walk?' she asked.

'No, we're here now.' Mary looked both ways up and down the street and said

'Where?'

'Right in front of you,' laughed Frank. Mary gasped in awe at the beautiful large Victorian house with its grand bay windows.

'Do you and your mum have rooms here, then?' asked Mary. Frank smiled nervously: he was concerned that Mary would feel uncomfortable.

'Come inside and see for yourself,' he replied.

They were met at the door by a small, slim lady in her mid-seventies with sparking eyes. She welcomed them with a warm smile. Her grey hair was neatly tied back in a bun. Mary admired the cameo brooch that held the collar of her neat white blouse in place. Frank was worried that Mary would find this overwhelming: it was for this reason that he had not told Mary that he lived in a large house with five bedrooms. Both his parents came from wealthy families, so he had never wanted for anything whilst growing up as an only child, but he was never spoiled. He had had a good education and now held down a very responsible job.

'She's a lovely girl, Frank,' whispered Frank's mum as he helped her get the china out for afternoon tea. Mary got on very well with her; she respectfully called her 'Mrs Osborne'.

Mary told her father all about the different world that Frank lived in. He was amazed, as Frank had never cracked a light and seemed to fit in so well with their way of life in the East End.

A few weeks passed. Life was hell for the residents in the East End of London: there were few houses still standing, people were aware that they were lucky to survive, but no-one knew what the future held or whether they would end up homeless like thousands of others. Mary was pouring her heart and fears out to Frank when he took her hand and said:

'Mary, come and live in the safety of our house with myself and my mother.' Mary drew back and looked at him confused.

'Frank, I can't do that, I couldn't leave my Meg, dad and sister here alone. Then there's my job!' Frank held her hand tightly, got down on one knee, then looked up very nervously into her eyes and said,

'Marry me, Mary ... please.' Mary was overcome with emotion; she was not expecting this.

'But how'? she blurted out. Frank replied,

'I have told my mother about your family. She has suggested you all come to live in the safety of our house: there's only four of you, and we have plenty of room. OK, bombs have dropped in Richmond too, but not to the great extent that the East End has suffered!' Mary felt excitement creep into her chest and warm her heart. She threw her arms around Frank's neck and agreed to marry him. At last she felt her world was changing, and happiness was round the corner.

'Of course, you will have to ask my dad if you can marry me: we're a family with traditional values!' she giggled.

They made their way back to Mary's house, where Frank nervously asked Ronnie for his daughter's hand in marriage. Ronnie smiled and shook Frank's hand. He congratulated the couple. He was relieved Mary had found happiness as well as security and told Frank that he would be delighted to have him as a son-in-law. Then the couple put the idea to Ronnie about moving to Richmond, but Ronnie's mood turned serious: he was not too sure about leaving his house. Before the war, he had had many happy years there with his beloved Ethel; they had brought their children up in this house; the walls echoed with memories for him. He wished Mary and Frank well and told them they deserved happiness but that he would be staying where he was: to him this was home. When Mary's sister Kathy heard their good news, she was overjoyed for them. She was very grateful to the offer of moving to Richmond but decided she could not leave her father on his own, and there was also her important job for the war effort to consider.

Mary and Frank had a quiet wedding in Frank's mother's church in June 1943, with only the close family in attendance. She and Meg settled into the big house in Richmond. Meg loved Mrs Osborne: she was like a grandmother to her.

Six months passed, and Mary announced to Frank that she was pregnant. He was ecstatic at the thought of becoming a father. Mrs Osborne hugged Mary with glee and said,

'At last, I'm going to be a grandma.' Meg was excited to know she was going to have a baby brother or sister but was worried that Mrs Osborne would care more about this new baby than she did her, so she plucked up the courage and asked her,

'Can I call you grandma?' Mrs Osborne was walking on air by this time. She hugged Meg tightly and was so happy.

'Of course, I should be very honoured to be your grandma!' she told Meg.

In June 1944, Germany starting bombarding the UK with buzz-bombs (also known as doodle-bugs). They were terrifying self-propelled pilotless aircraft and made a rasping sound like a two-stroke motor-cycle. When they reached their maximum range, the motor cut out, and they crashed on the target below with their explosive load causing death and destruction.

September 1944. Mary gave birth to a bouncing baby boy. They called him William. Her happiness and life were complete: she had a wonderful husband, beautiful home, two gorgeous children and a lovely mother-in-law, but life was still death-defying as Hitler replaced doodle-bugs with far more frightening V2 weapons: these were proper rockets. Much larger than buzz-bombs and more destructive: unlike buzz-bombs, they gave no notice of their arrival. They continued to fall in London at intervals during the winter of 1944-45. Many people were killed as more properties were razed. Mary continuously worried about her father and sister living in Bethnal Green, but they refused to move and their house had so far been spared.

At long last, on 8 May 1945, Victory in Europe was declared. All over Britain, red white and blue bunting was strung out across roads, union flags were flying and everyone was dancing in the streets to celebrate, but the war in the Far East still raged as Japan did not surrender at the same time as Germany. The end to WWII was finally declared on 2 September 1945, when Japan formally surrendered. Everyone rejoiced, but these celebrations were more subdued than the VE-day ones. The people of Britain all hoped that WWII had been the war to end all wars, and that its ending would herald an era of world peace.

November 1945. Mary's father came to see her. He looked very serious. Mary's welcoming smile soon turned to concern as he said,

'Mary, I had a visit from army personnel: they think John's alive!' Mary froze. She tried to speak, but nothing would come out. She was overcome with emotion that he was not dead, but how was she going to tell him that she had remarried, their son had been killed and she had a baby boy by her new husband?

'He's in a soldiers' hospital near here,' said Ronnie.

Mary told Frank the news. She was beside herself. Frank was also very worried, but, in his usual caring and understanding way, he told Mary that she had to go and see John. Mrs Osborne looked after fourteen-month-old William while Mary nervously made her way to the hospital; her mind was working overtime trying to work out what she was going to say to John. When she got there, the sister took her aside.

'I just want to prepare you: your husband is in a very bad way. He was rescued from a Japanese prisoner-of-war camp. He can't tell us what happened, but his memory comes and goes. He doesn't know who he is at times and seems to be in a world of his own: it appears that he suffered years of torture.' Mary's heart dropped: she felt so guilty that she had been living a new and happy life while the love of her life was suffering so much. The sister led her into the ward and pulled the curtain round a bed.

'You have a visitor, John,' she announced. Mary looked at the scrawny little man lying in the bed, his eyes staring into nowhere; and he had fingers missing.

'They've made a mistake, sister: that's definitely not my John!' she announced to the sister.

'The authorities have checked everything out, right down to the birthmark on his right foot. I'm afraid it is John,' replied the sister with a sympathising frown. Mary pulled the cover up and looked at John's foot; she recognised the birthmark and burst into tears. Suddenly a voice said,

'Don't cry, Mary, there might not be a war. I won't need to go away and leave you!' Mary suddenly stopped crying: John was speaking to her. She was in shock and asked him,

'How are you? Where have you been all these years?' But his answer didn't make sense:

'I've been looking for you, Mary, let's get married!' Then he started shouting and swearing as if he was in a war zone. The sister rushed in to try and calm him.

'His brain is very confused!' she said. They went outside to the corridor

'Will he ever get better?' Mary sobbed.

'I'm afraid there's not much hope: he has suffered great trauma through war and torture, his heart is very weak, he is lucky to have made it back to Britain,' the sister answered.

Mary came away from the hospital; her heart was heavy thinking about what poor John had come through. Frank was waiting for her when she got home. She told him what had happened and wondered whether she deserved such happiness in life. Had it not been for this cruel war she would never have met Frank and would still be living in Bethnal Green with John, Meg, Robert and her parents, but instead she had remarried, had a son by her second marriage and was enjoying life in a lovely house in a nice neighbourhood.

'We can't help fate, Mary; no-one really knows what the future holds,' replied Frank in his usual laid-back understanding manner. Mary knew he was right. Deep down she still loved John, but the John she saw today was not the same man she had been married to, and, even if she had not married Frank, there was no way John would ever get home to continue their life together.

'I feel so deceitful, as if I've let John down,' said Mary as the tears welled up. Frank pulled her close and gave her a warm hug as he whispered caringly,

'Mary, everything you've done you did in innocence: you weren't responsible for the war, you didn't plan anything, it was an honest deceit!' Frank always explained everything in a sensible philosophical manner that made it all seem better.

Mary visited John a few more times, but his condition deteriorated, and he never was really aware of her being there. Two months later, she got a message from the hospital to say that John had passed away. Mary broke the news to Meg; she was heartbroken, as hospital rules had not allowed her to visit her father. As John had no other family, Frank and Mary arranged for a simple funeral. Mary held Meg's hand tightly as the coffin was lowered into the grave and told her daughter,

'Just remember your dad how he was, Meg: a very brave and honourable man indeed!'

Barbarossa
Derek Smith

We are in the Baltic state of Lithuania. It is an afternoon in mid-June 1941, and fifteen-year-old Otto is walking through the small town where he lives, on his way home from school. Suddenly, an arm shoots out from an alleyway, grabs Otto by the shoulder and drags him in. A hand is placed over his mouth. This was an incident that would change his life for ever and occurred at a time when things were happening that would change the face of Europe for decades to come.

In August 1939, Germany had signed a non-aggression pact with the Soviet Union. A few days later, on 1 September 1939, Hitler invaded Poland. Two weeks later, Russia invaded eastern Poland, and the following summer they annexed the Baltic States. A list was drawn up of those that the Soviets considered to be 'enemies of the people', and on the 14 June 1941, the day that Otto was walking home from school, they started to arrest and deport those on the list, together with their families.

Back in the alley a hoarse voice hissed into Otto's ear: 'Do not go home; the Russians have arrested your father and the rest of your family. If you go home, you are as good as dead.'

His father had taught English at the local college. Why he had been included on the list was not clear. His mother kept the house and looked after his younger brother and sister.

Otto still could not take in what he was being told and stood there in numbed shock. The hand was removed from his mouth, and the hoarse whisperer asked him whether he understood what he was being told. He nodded assent, still in shock. The whisperer took a pack of playing cards from his pocket and gave one to Otto.

'You must go deep into the forest and try to make contact with the partisans. When you do, show them this card. It is your passport and will explain what you are doing there. Do not lose it!' he rasped in Otto's ear. 'Do you understand?' Otto nodded dumbly. 'Do you understand?' the whisperer repeated harshly, his face right up against Otto's.

'Yes, yes,' replied Otto, still struggling to come to terms with the enormity of what he was being told.

'You have plenty of daylight left. Go now and try to reach the edge of the forest before dark. You do not want to be seen wandering about after dark. Do not tell them your name. If no one knows your name, you cannot be betrayed. What do you have in your bag?'

'Just my school books,' replied Otto meekly.

'You won't be needing those. Get rid of them. Now get going and try to keep off the main roads.' With that he slipped out into the main thoroughfare and was gone, leaving Otto in a complete state of bewilderment.

In happier times, his family had often enjoyed visits to the forest for picnics and outings, meaning that at least he knew the way, but picking parallel side-roads would not be so easy. As he walked and thought out the best way for him to go, his head became clearer, and he began to take stock of his situation. He took his books one by one from his bag, tore out the front page where he had written his name and threw the book over the fence of the house he was passing. When all the books had gone, he tore up the name pages and pushed them down a storm drain. With the few coins that remained from his pocket money he bought a loaf of black rye-bread and put it in his bag. He kept up a good pace and reached the edge of the forest just as it was getting dark. He tried to keep going for as long as he could, but eventually, completely worn out with the day's events, feeling sick with worry about his family and what may have happened to them, he cut off into the trees, lay down and fell fast asleep.

He woke feeling stiff and chilled. He knew that he had to press on to get deeper into the forest. He took a bite from his loaf and set off in what he hoped was the right direction. The day became warmer, but he was able to drink from a stream that he had to cross. He took small bites from the loaf now and again, trying to ration it out because he did not know how long he would have to make it last.

By the end of the second day he was hot, tired and thirsty. He collapsed exhausted by the side of the track that he was on and fell asleep. He was awoken by a hefty kick up his backside swiftly followed by one in the small of his back. He woke blinking against the low early morning sunlight that shone into his eyes. He could see that he was surrounded by roughly dressed men, each one carrying a weapon that was trained on him. A voice ordered him to get up. Otto rose slowly, fearful that he was going to fill his trousers or wet himself with fear.

'Don't shoot. I have something to show you,' he mumbled. 'A man gave it to me.'

'What is it?' asked the man who appeared to be the leader. Otto, aware that a sudden move to put his hand inside his coat could result in him receiving a well-aimed bullet replied,

'It's a card.'

'Let me see it,' said the man, holding out his hand. Otto slowly withdrew the card from his pocket and gave it to the man. He turned it over to see the pattern on the back. Seemingly satisfied, he asked Otto what his name was.

'The man told me not to tell you.'

'Very well,' said the man, 'you are The Kid. What have you got in your bag?

'Nothing, sir, it's my school bag,' replied Otto. 'I had my books in it. I ripped my name out and threw them all away.'

'Very good,' said the man. 'Remove all traces of where you slept last night and follow us.' Otto was now a partisan.

The partisans were ill-equipped and short of ammunition. They kept constantly on the move, destroying all signs of where they had camped at night. Their aim was to hold out and be ready to act when the time came. They had outside contacts, and it was through them that Otto heard that his family had been shot. He became consumed with hatred for the Soviet regime and was determined to avenge their deaths.

The time to act came much sooner than anyone expected. Otto had been with the partisans for only a few days when they heard distant shell-fire, and planes that were clearly German flew overhead. The partisans were completely baffled by what they were seeing and hearing. They needed to know what was happening in the outside world.

Otto was the most dispensable member of the group and probably the least conspicuous. Therefore he was sent out to find out what was going on. The group, half-suspecting what was happening, took him to the edge of the forest: otherwise he would not have been able to find them again. They gave him directions to the nearest small town. He came out of the forest and followed the road. What he saw there astounded him. People were lining the street waving encouragement to a column of German tanks and infantry. The Germans were being greeted as liberators come to save them from the communist death-threat. He pushed himself to the front to see the impressively dressed, armed and disciplined German troops marching by.

In the late spring of 1941, people in Britain noticed that the almost nightly air-raids became less frequent. What they did not know was that this was due to the fact that Hitler was grouping his forces in Poland prior to launching an invasion of Russia code-named Operation Barbarossa. It commenced on 22 of June 1941, and this was what Otto was witnessing. He knew at once what he had to do. He would lie about his age, join the German army and avenge the deaths of his family.

He found his way back to tell the group about what he had seen and was not surprised that their reaction was the same as his. They buried their weapons and made their way to the nearest town where there was a German presence. They found that they were not alone in the belief that the best way to extract revenge for the atrocities that had been inflicted on them and their families by the Soviets was to join the German army. Across the country, thousands volunteered. Many joined special Lithuanian units of the Waffen SS, the most ruthless branch of the German army. The Germans for their part had no qualms about recruiting hate-filled men hell-bent on the destruction of Russian power. The Lithuanians were trained in German weaponry, commands and disciplines and drafted into the army. Otto was now a German soldier.

He was sent by train to catch up with the leading forces. The surprise and ferocity of the Blitzkrieg had caused the Soviet army to retreat deep into Russian territory. What he saw from the train filled him with horror and disgust. At times they passed whole villages that had been razed, and the bodies of civilians lay unburied everywhere. Even though he had a deep hatred of the Soviet regime, he knew that what had happened in his own country was not the fault of these people, and he could not excuse what he was seeing.

Worse was to come, because at times he was called upon to commit his own atrocities, knowing that to refuse the orders of the SS officers would only result in his own death. It all began to weigh heavily on his mind and conscience. But what could he do? He was now part of the German army, signed up, sworn in, identified.

There was something even worse to come. It took the form of the Russian winter. The Russian army had fallen back, knowing that they could retreat almost indefinitely, such was the immensity of their territory, and they had done so. Hitler's plan was that he would capture Moscow and the Ukrainian oil-fields in the first few months. He thought that the Russian people would have no more stomach for this war than they had for the German offensive against the Tsar in the First World War - but he was wrong.

The panic of the initial retreat became a controlled withdrawal while re-grouping and re-arming was going on behind the lines. The German plan almost succeeded. They were at the gates of Moscow and towns like Stalingrad, but resistance stiffened. The war was not all over before winter set in, and the German army began to have problems. They were not equipped for the cold, and extra clothing and footwear were slow to reach them. They resorted to taking clothing from fallen comrades and binding their feet in rags against frostbite. The winter became hard and relentless. Otto was told by veterans not to gasp in air through his mouth when running or he would find himself coughing up bits of frozen lung. Aircraft flying in supplies and ammunition had to keep their engines running whilst being unloaded otherwise if they were switched off they would simply freeze up and not restart.

In the depth of this winter, Otto's company were advancing through a wood when they received orders to dig in, as there was intelligence that a large body of troops lay somewhere ahead. They raised earthen ramparts at the edge of the wood looking out over open ground and mounted their Mauser 42 machine-guns behind them. The Mauser was a monster of a machine-gun, capable of firing up to 1,500 rounds per minute. They stared out over the open ground but could not see or hear anything. They waited in this position for some time, and, just when it seemed that they should begin the advance again, the ground before them erupted.

White covers were thrown back, horses scrambled to their feet, white-coated Cossacks leapt on to the horses and, drawing their sabres, charged towards the German positions. The shocked Germans opened up with their Mausers, mowing down swathes of men and horses in the horrific crossfire, knowing that, if even a few Cossacks got through, they would all be hacked to pieces. When all that lay before them were heaps of dead and dying men and horses, there came a cease-fire order, and all became as still and silent as before. The terrified defenders were just congratulating themselves on having survived when the ground before them erupted a second time and a new wave of men and horses tore towards them. The constant rapid fire necessary to prevent the Cossacks from reaching them was causing the barrels of the Mausers to overheat, and Otto was one of the men assigned to crawl out and clamp handfuls of snow on to them to cool them down. Suddenly the guns fell silent once more, their job done.

Before them lay a scene of almost unimaginable slaughter. Otto felt sick and was soaked in cold sweat. The enormity of what they had done swept over him, making him feel dirty, terrified and ashamed in spite of all the reasons he had to be there.

The German advance began to slow down and finally came to a halt owing to the resistance before Moscow and the determination of the Russians to hold on to Stalingrad. Otto now found himself in a machine-gun emplacement dug out of the Pripet Marshes. This was a vast wetland region about 400 miles south-west of Moscow. It was impossible for the Axis forces to patrol or control it. It was wet, wild and stinking. The opposition here were not the Russian army but partisans who knew the ground well. At first many Russians felt that they were being liberated from the Stalinist tyranny, but, as the list of German atrocities lengthened, attitudes changed, and the partisan ranks grew. Life became one of continuous nerve-jangling dread. A Russian peasant, inured to cold and adversity by years of harsh winters and hardship, could remain for days hidden in a foxhole just metres away from a German machine-gun unit digging a new emplacement. He could survive, waist deep in freezing water, subsisting on just a pocketful of sunflower seeds until the emplacement was completed and all the crew were inside. Then as night fell he would toss in a few grenades and slither off into the dark knowing that no one had survived. Otto spent every second knowing that this could happen to him and that the next second could be his last. It was a time of utter terror that broke many of the men around him.

The resistance at Stalingrad and along the Volga River had given the Russian army time to reform, recruit and re-arm. When he was ready, General Zhukov ordered an offensive that broke through the weaker Romanian and Hungarian defences either side of Stalingrad, and the German 6th Army found themselves cut off. They were ordered by Hitler to hold out at all costs and were forbidden to break out. This was a disastrous decision. German forces either side of the breaks in the line had to pull back to avoid also being cut off. At first the withdrawal was orderly, but, with

Russian tanks pouring through these breaks in vast numbers, it became a rout, and Otto found himself on a long cold footslog back to the west.

The Russians took prisoners only if it was convenient and if they had time: otherwise they shot them. Waffen SS officers and soldiers were shot on sight as a matter of routine. In the eyes of the Russians, the fearful atrocities they had committed against their fellow-countrymen earned them no right to mercy. The lucky ones - if you can call them that - who did survive, were sent to camps where most died. Many of those who lived were still trying to be repatriated twenty years after the war had ended.

Otto took part in many hard-fought rearguard actions, but the outcome was always the same: his unit had to fall back.

When he found himself back on the Polish border, with the German army still in full flight, he realised that the game was up and that a German soldier was now the worst thing in the world that he could possibly be. That night he fell behind the column and broke into a deserted house. He divested himself of everything that could possibly identify him as a German soldier. He opened a wardrobe and found a dark suit, a warm three-quarter-length overcoat and a hat. In a chest he found a white shirt and the other clothes he would need. When he emerged at first light, he looked less like a German soldier than anything that could be imagined. Turning his back to the rising sun, he started his journey to the west. Otto was now a deserter.

He made his way, mainly at night, scavenging what he could to keep alive. He moved ever westward to keep ahead of the Russian advance. He knew by now that the Allies had landed in Europe and that he must reach them, as he would be wanted by both the Russians and the Germans. When he did, still a teenager and speaking the good English that his father had taught him, he charmed his way through the British and American checkpoints. He still kept moving westward and fell in with a group of Poles who had been liberated from a forced-labour camp. They took pity on the young Otto and took him under their wing. They had been made to work in a German steel works and told him that they were going to try and make their way to South Wales in Britain. They had heard that other Poles had made their way there and had found jobs in the steel works. Otto decided that he would go with them.

He had never had a job other than being a soldier; he had never even finished school. The skills that he did have he had acquired trying to survive. There was very little he could not fix, get to work or get round somehow. These skills, together with an inbuilt Teutonic inclination towards orderliness, had helped him to obtain a position as a warden at a residential caravan-site in a village just outside Swansea in South Wales.

This is where I met him. My wife and I had moved to Wales because I had been offered a job in the steel industry there, and, while we were saving for a deposit on a house, we lived in a caravan on the site that he ran. One night I called in to the village pub and, seeing Otto sitting alone in the snug, I joined him there. I knew him only casually, but over a couple of drinks he started to tell me what had happened to him during the war. I gained the impression that this was some sort of catharsis, as if, by telling someone else, he could shed some of his guilt. Telling someone British that you had been a German soldier was not the easiest thing to do.

To the people on the site he appeared to be a carefree character in a steady job enjoying his life, but below the surface there were things going on that most did not know about. When night fell and sleep beckoned, the awful things he had seen during the war and the dreadful things he had done came crawling back to haunt him. When he did succumb to sleep, his dreams were of seeing a grenade at his feet about to explode or thinking that a Cossack was about to slash him with a sabre as he lay helpless on the ground. He would wake up screaming and soaked in the sweat of fear. If it was not one of these things, then it was a memory of some unforgivable act that he had been compelled to commit, and he would lie awake for the rest of the night afraid to sleep. In time, the only way he could obtain oblivion was through the bottle.

One night he lay propped up on his bed in his caravan, drawing on a cigarette and swigging from the whiskey bottle that would eventually grant him some remission from his dreams of fear. As the drink started to do its work, the bottle slipped from his fingers and fell to the floor spilling the contents on to the carpet. Shortly afterwards, the cigarette slipped from his fingers and fell into the spilt whiskey. There then came a curious 'whoosh' sound and a sheet of flame set fire to the carpet and the bedclothes. Otto tried to rise but fell back incapable.

Very few people have seen a blazing caravan, but those that have will know that they burn with an intensity and ferocity out of all proportion to their size. When his neighbours became aware of what was happening, they tried to reach his door, but the heat radiating from the caravan was so great that it drove them back. All they could do was stand and watch. Someone ran to the phone-box in the village to call the fire services, but, by the time the fire-engine arrived, the caravan was a burnt-out shell.

Otto had joined the partisans; he had joined the German army; now he had joined his family.

Appendix

Although this a work of fiction, Otto was a real character who was hauled off the street and told to join the partisans and who did fight in the German army. The things that happened in Russia are things told to me either by him or by the German ex-soldiers who drove the fuel-tankers for the night fighter squadron I was serving with in Western Germany shortly after the end of the war.

I have no reason to believe that anyone would lie about such things.

Ghosts from my Past

Louise Wilkinson

Pip Phillips was happy with his decision. Whatever his parents thought, he was happy. He knew that he was only young in their eyes, but he thought, 'It's my decision, my life and my future.' There was trouble in the house. There always was when he came home from school. He had been lucky. His father, John, had been in the army, whilst his mother, Rita, was a housewife. Together they had decided to send him to boarding school, although, as time went on, Pip thought it was more likely to have been his father's idea: first at St Olave's School in York and then, in his senior years, to St Peter's School in York. 'It's important to get a good education,' his father had said. 'It will help you decide what to do in the future.' He remembered his mother just nodding as the decision was made. And so off he went. 'It will make a man of him,' his father said as the door closed behind him. No arguments, no crying.

Five years away from the family did things to a boy. Of course, there were holidays, which were awkward and uncomfortable. Pip felt he didn't fit in any more: his family had closed ranks in his absence, and he was an outsider looking in. He couldn't wait for holidays to end so he could go back to his friends and his studies. Rowing and rugby helped to relieve the boredom after lessons finished. He was growing taller and wider and knew that his time in school was running out as his eighteenth birthday approached. So what to do? He had no desire to go back to his family home. He couldn't bear the tension that was always there when he was around, his mother trying to make things right and his father forcing his opinions on him. He could do without all that. But what to do?

He fancied working with his hands, fixing things, making things go, or doing something that very few others could do, something new and exciting. But he knew his father had different plans for him. 'The army is the place for you,' he'd been told over and over again during his teenage years. 'It will make a man of you,' reckoned his father. Pip thought but didn't say, 'That's not the kind of man I want to be.' So what to do? He knew that the biggest obstacle in building a future was his lack of friends. He had friends, of course, but not where he lived, not in his home town, and that made things so much harder for him. But he had a passion, a passion which he knew would add to the tension at home, which would cause trouble. And he was right: it did! Pip wanted to fly. He had watched the sky in amazement as aircraft rumbled overhead, a rare sight in a small north-eastern town called Thornaby. But he had seen the posters dotted around, in the chip-shop and the Post Office and on lamp-posts, posters about a local squadron, part-timers who operated from Thornaby aerodrome.

Born in 1919, Pip had grown up living close to Thornaby aerodrome, which had been built around 1930. As a youth, he had been to the 'At Home' days, which always took place during school holidays. These days allowed him to go and look at the aeroplanes really close up, and he could see the airmen going about their work. And there was always a flying display. He watched with bated breath as formations of aircraft flew overhead, twisting and turning and diving towards the ground with great speed and then pulling out of the dive with cheers from the visitors. 'That will be me one day soon,' thought Pip at the close of each display, year after year. As he turned eighteen in November of 1937, he knew the opportunity had finally come.

So this was it, his big chance. It meant going against his father's wishes, but, as he wandered down to the aerodrome, he was filled with enthusiasm and excitement. His friend, Keith Pyman, who had been a member of a University Air Squadron, had spoken to him at great length during his last days of education. Keith was already a pilot in another part-time squadron, 609 (West Riding)

Squadron, and he had already talked to his squadron commander, Geoffrey Ambler, about him and how enthusiastic and keen he was to learn to fly. A couple of months later, Pip had received a letter to attend the aerodrome to meet the commanding Officer of 608 (North Riding) Squadron, Geoffrey Shaw, and partake in some lunch with several other potential candidates. Pip was really keen that the meeting went well: he was desperate to begin flying training. He had been watching the situation in Europe becoming more and more unsettled: civil war in Spain; the coronation of a new king, George VI, following the abdication of the king's brother, Edward VIII, over the Wallis Simpson scandal; a new prime minister, Neville Chamberlain; and most importantly the rise to power of Adolf Hitler in Germany. 'It was the right time for him to join the Squadron,' he thought, if they would have him.

Lunch went well, and he thought that he had been able to answer any questions put to him by the CO. He had held his own; he had even been taken to the commanding officer's house to meet his wife Elizabeth, and that had gone well too he felt. Now all that stood in his way was a medical. He had no worries at all, as he was physically fit. That would be it then: he could learn to fly. Telling his parents was difficult, as he had expected it to be. His announcement met with stony silence. His father stared at him, his disappointment evident. His mother just nodded. But Pip felt there was a certain admiration from his father. Maybe a part of his father felt that Pip had become a man, that he had made his own choices and that was something that perhaps his father respected. After a few days, the letter came offering Pip a commission in the Auxiliary Air Force. Flying training was to begin at Thornaby Aerodrome the following week.

Pip worked hard whilst at the aerodrome. He found the flying exhilarating and picked up very quickly the skills needed to fly an aircraft safely. He was also competent at the theory and learned to understand the different aircraft that he might fly and a bit about aircraft maintenance and tactics. As 1938 dawned, Pip's confidence was soaring, and he really believed that this was what he had been born to do. Events in 1938 were beginning to build: in February,

Adolf Hitler abolished the War Ministry and placed himself in direct control of the German military machine. In March, he announced the Anschluss with Austria and those in parliament began to realise that Hitler was becoming more of a threat to peace in Europe than they could ever have imagined. Pip knew that training was becoming much more intense as it became clear that there was a real possibility of another war, a threat that nobody would ever have dreamt of. Pip and other officers in his squadron, and in the Auxiliary Air Force as a whole, began to understand why the type of squadron that they were kept changing. Initially the government had followed the view that the most crucial aircraft in a new war would be the bomber, as it would likely be used to attack military installations across occupied Europe. As time progressed and war began to look more inevitable, there was a shift of focus to the role of the fighter. Their job would be to defeat German aircraft in the sky and prevent a possible invasion of Great Britain. There was also a focus on coastal command whose main job was to escort the convoys of ships returning to Great Britain bringing food and supplies which would be urgently needed.

Pip, like many other young officers, had dreamt of being a fighter-pilot, flying a Spitfire and engaging in aerial dogfights, becoming one of the fighter-boys who were often talked about in the press. But on 29 September, 1938, there was great excitement in Britain as the Prime Minister Neville Chamberlain had signed the Munich agreement with Hitler and a resolution with Germany, which was designed to resolve all future disputes between the two countries through peaceful means. Pip and his fellow-officers listened on the wireless the next day to Chamberlain's 'Peace for Our Time' speech in the House of Commons. There were sighs of relief and general celebration in the mess that night as the prospect of a future war was abated. The reduction in pressure was marked by increased flying training to ensure that all of the officers maintained their flying hours.

Emphasis was also placed in the training schedule to ensure that accidents were limited and infrequent. Pip was only too aware of this, having seen a fellow-pilot lose his hand, having wandered into one of the hangers to check on the progress of his aircraft and getting caught in the propeller. Accidents were quite commonplace, particularly when pilots were flying at night. Since there was no effective navigation system in the older aircraft, pilots depended on their maps to ensure that they were flying in the right direction and able to find their way back to the aerodrome. It was quite easy for pilots to lose their way, and Pip knew of one of his friends who had flown over the North Sea in error and had crashed into the water and subsequently drowned.

One of the things that Pip enjoyed was the camaraderie that existed among the officers who served in the squadron. The officers' mess was located at Thornaby Hall, a lovely old building where the officers lived, ate and slept. 'There was nothing like flying training all day and then going back to the mess for drinks with friends,' Pip thought. With so many young officers, the atmosphere in the officers' mess often resembled that of a public school common-room. The young men drank, and the more they drank the rowdier they became. It was then that the high jinks began. Circumnavigating the mess without touching the floor was very popular, as was pouring beer down each other's trousers; also piggyback races, using the local paper to whip each other. More often than not, the officers chose to stay in the mess at night. However, many of the officers had motor vehicles which enabled them to venture out further from the aerodrome and into Stockton itself. In one pub, the Vane Arms, very drunk and rather rowdy friends of Pip put him inside a very very large brass vase which was placed in the entrance of the pub. The idea then was to use anything that they could find to bang on the vase to see how long he could tolerate the vibrations. On other occasions, the young officers might pinch the brass vase and take it back to the mess until the following morning, when an irate call would be received from the landlord. Pip didn't own a motor car: he was the proud owner of a BSA motor-bike, which he enjoyed tinkering about with in any spare time that he had. He was allowed to keep it in one of the big hangers, provided that it was kept out of sight. Having the motorcycle gave Pip the chance to escape and venture further afield if the mood took him.

1939 started with a posting to 601 (County of London) Squadron at Hendon, London. Pip was very excited about moving to the capital, never having visited before. Hendon was a much bigger aerodrome than Thornaby, and Pip soon became aware of the number of women who were serving in the Women's Auxiliary Air Force. These WAAFs worked in many areas of the aerodrome, including the flight control-room, radar bases, motor transport and some as pilots flying new aircraft to the squadrons. Many of these WAAFs lived in the officers' mess. It was here for the first time that Pip became completely distracted from his work. The cause of this distraction was a WAAF named Jenny Sutherland, who worked in the control-room as a plotter responsible for aircraft movement. Pip had first noticed her in the mess bar: he had caught her eye and smiled shyly, his heart beating ten to the dozen. She was the most beautiful girl he had ever seen, but for the moment duty called, and Pip put her beautiful smile to the back of his mind, thinking that he would find her another time when his life was not so hectic. As the atmosphere in Europe became tenser, the squadron took delivery of its new aircraft, the Spitfire Vb, which had a maximum speed of 374 mph and a range of 470 miles. By the end of August, the evacuation of children from major cities had begun, and the Royal Navy and the British army had been mobilised. Within days, WWII had begun, and all of the Auxiliary Air Force squadrons were embodied into the Royal Air Force on permanent full-time duties.

War had been declared, yet events took a funny turn: Britain prepared for attack, increased her defences and waited. On 17 September 1939, the British aircraft-carrier HMS Courageous was sunk by a German U-boat with the loss of 518 crew members. On 14 October, the British battleship HMS Royal Oak was sunk with a death toll of 833 men, the work of another German U-boat. Very quickly after that, the Luftwaffe began air-raids on Britain attacking British warships in Scotland. This period of eight months became known as the Phoney War. During this time, Germany invaded Denmark and Norway, and the British government and the public were losing faith in Neville Chamberlain's leadership of the country. In May 1940, Winston Churchill formed a new coalition government and took over running the country. By May 1940, German troops had marched into Belgium, the Netherlands and Luxembourg. Following the fall of France, which had been preceded by the evacuation of Dunkirk, the real aerial battles began.

Pip had been involved in many sorties over Britain and France and had watched with despair the way in which the German army steamrolled across Europe. His time was taken up maintaining his flying hours and spending time with Jenny. It was funny how their relationship started. After a day of flying over the North Sea towards Norway, Pip had returned, and, when he had been debriefed, his thoughts came back to the girl with the beautiful smile. 'Where do I go to find her?' he thought. 'Perhaps if I hang around the entrance to the mess for long enough, she might come in on her own, and I might get a chance to talk to her,' he thought to himself, and so he waited and waited, but there was no sign of her. His friends in the mess wondered what on earth he was doing, hanging around both the outside and the inside entrance to the mess. As speculation grew, so did the teasing and the taunts. Eventually, around 6.30pm, he saw her walking towards the mess within a group of WAAF officers. Throwing caution to the wind he made eye-contact with her, and again she gave him a broad smile.

'Can I buy you a drink?' he asked, ' - but not here, maybe somewhere a little quieter?' and she nodded to him.

'Let me freshen up, and I will meet you around 8pm. The couple wandered slowly towards the nearest public house. They talked and talked, and Pip felt as though he had known her all of his life. She talked a little about her work in the control-room and the tension which all the plotters felt when pilots left on various sorties. He talked a little about his family, about his mother, about his father's plans for him, and Jenny could feel the disconnection that he felt from his family, and part of her felt sad for that. In a lot of ways, her home life had been quite similar, and her parents had been glad that she had joined the WAAF and that they wouldn't have to be responsible for her any more. The time marched on. They left the pub and wandered slowly back towards the officers' mess. They both hoped that the first steps towards a strong relationship had begun; yet they were both aware of the dangers that lay ahead for Pip as the war came closer to home.

Pip and Jenny spent as much time together as they were able to, and Pip felt a sense of security with her that he had never felt with his family. As the summer began, so did the Luftwaffe attacks on Britain. The bombing of aerodromes became commonplace, and pilots like Pip spent many an hour playing cards or football or writing letters, whilst waiting for the phone-call to get airborne. Speed was vital. If the control-room was advised that German bombers were on their way, Pip and his fellow pilots had to get the planes into the air as quickly as possible, to prevent the planes being destroyed whilst on dispersal, and secondly so that the aerial battle could begin which would show the Luftwaffe that the Royal Air Force would not roll over and allow the Germans to gain air superiority. Pip and Jenny had such a limited time together now and made the most of every minute. She worried most when British radar showed numbers of German ME 109s making their way across the Channel towards the south coast. Day after day Jenny saw Pip's name on the blackboard as being airborne, and she remained focused on her work, whilst at the back of her mind she waited for Pip's Spitfire to land safely.

The days of summer were dark and unforgiving as wave after wave of German aircraft bombed airfields across the south coast. But the RAF would not give in. Day after day, hour after hour, more often than not with very little sleep, Pip and the rest of his squadron managed to get their aircraft into the air and off to protect the British islands. Sometimes when Pip and Jenny managed to steal a moment or two together he might tell her about the kind of day that he had whilst out on sorties, but more often than not he didn't want to talk about his work; he didn't want to acknowledge the number of empty seats there were in the dining-room of the officers' mess. A number of his friends, just like him, were blown out of the sky or failed to return after their aircraft had received significant damage. The first days were the hardest, but, as the war progressed, more and more men did not return, and those that were left had to help the young lads who were arriving each day to try and plug the holes in the squadron: young boys who had maybe fourteen hours' flying a Spitfire under their belt. Full of life and excited to fly, they had no real idea about what they had let themselves in for. More often than not, they were the easiest target for the Luftwaffe, their life snuffed out in seconds. Pip had been promoted to flight-lieutenant and had a responsibility for his men. Whilst leading a section, his eyes scanned the sky looking left and right and above and below. He saw lots of his pilots killed. Jenny felt it too, seeing names of the pilots and their planes listed on the blackboard in the control-room and seeing the few that came back after yet another difficult operation.

In September 1940, Pip was lying on the grass along with many of his colleagues waiting for the phone-call to get airborne. Airmen were attending to the aircraft reloading ammunition and refuelling whilst the planes were on the ground. Suddenly the phone rang to say a large German attack force was making its way up the Thames towards London. Immediately the young men ran across the grounds towards their Spitfires, jumping on to the wing and sliding into the cockpit. One by one the planes took off from the grass airstrip and climbed through the blue sky until they reached a height of around 15,000 feet. As Pip looked round, he could see the beautiful green fields below and the cloudless blue sky above. He scanned the air above and below him looking for any sign of the German attack force. As red flight-leader, Pip spoke to his section pilots instructing them to turn, and suddenly before them was the German attack force. There were a large number of bombers, but surrounding each bomber were ME109s, whose job it was to make sure that the bombers got through to drop their bombs. In preparation for the upcoming battle, Pip flicked the catch on his machine-gun button from 'safe' to 'fire.' Within seconds, Pip's squadron-leader's voice came through his headphones giving all the individual Spitfires their tactical orders. They were told to turn in a big circle and then be prepared to attack. As each of the planes was told, down they went. Pip had his thumb next to the gun button, ready to fire. As he turned his plane into a dive he was on the tail of a Heinkel 111s. As Pip focused on the plane he would attack, he was aware that the sky was full of planes, people diving and banking and firing; the sky was no longer cloudless and blue. Pip was focused on the Heinkel he had picked out. The bigger the angle of his dive, the closer the Heinkel came, and then the plane was in front of him and completely in his gun-sight. And so he pressed the red button. Pip gave the Heinkel a two second burst from his machine-gun and then another. His shots pebble-dashed the exterior of the plane, and smoke began to pour out, telling Pip that he had made a successful shot. Flames licked the body of the Heinkel, which then went into a spin. A good hit: but Pip's job was nowhere near done. He climbed until he was above the Heinkels, and, looking around, he picked an ME 109 as his target. Again he manoeuvred his plane until the enemy aircraft was within his sights, again he fired two short bursts into the Messerschmitt. He was so close to the plane he could see the pilot's face and the horror as the plane began to dive towards the ground. Looking around again he became aware that he was above the grey skyline of London. Pip jumped and began the search for another German aircraft. His lapse in concentration meant that, as he looked into his rear-view mirror, a Messerschmitt was chasing him. He pulled straight back on the stick and the aircraft responded swiftly to his touch and climbed higher and higher. 'I've lost him,' Pip realised. A detailed recce around him suggested that the two remaining Messerschmitts had turned for home. He couldn't see any of his section and, after checking his fuel gauge, decided to head back to Hendon after what he considered to be a successful attack.

Dogfights like these were daily, indeed hourly, events throughout the months of August and September 1940. Germany had planned to destroy the majority of the British air-force on the ground. This would have meant that there were no defensive moves towards the enemy aircraft, with their loads of bombs destined for the British airfields, and later the major cities. But Hitler had made one mistake: he had not expected the tenacity and hard work put in by the Royal Air Force, and, as the Luftwaffe lost more and more aircraft, the German plans had to be changed. An invasion of Britain was no longer on the cards. New plans had to be thought of. As the summer of 1940 came to an end, Pip was called to see his commanding officer, Squadron-leader Whitney Straight, who informed him that he had been awarded a Distinguished Service Order (DSO) for his service to the Royal Air Force and the number of hits that he had made, as he bravely challenged enemy aircraft each day.

In November 1940, as Pip and Jenny continued to become closer and closer, Pip decided that she was the girl for him, and they both asked permission for a forty-eight-hour leave pass, the idea being to relax and do a bit of sigh-seeing. It was here that Pip made the decision to ask Jenny to become his wife. He planned to take her to an expensive restaurant and wine and dine her before he would get down on one knee and ask her to be his wife. Things were definitely going their way, as both he and Jenny were successful in getting the time off. Pip had booked them into a small hotel located just outside the city in an area of London called Barking. In order to save money, and because Jenny was quite partial to a ride on his motorbike, Pip and Jenny rode down to the hotel early on the Saturday morning. Ever the gentleman, Pip had booked two single rooms, but he hoped that perhaps they would use only one of them. Once the couple had checked into the hotel and Pip's bike had been safely locked, the couple wandered hand-in-hand around the capital city, taking in Buckingham Palace, Horse Guards' Parade and Westminster Abbey.

Pip's nervousness increased as the time to visit the restaurant drew ever closer. He had brought with him his grandmother's sapphire engagement ring which he hoped would shortly sit on Jenny's finger. Both Jenny and Pip had popped back to the hotel to freshen up before going out for their evening meal. As the couple ordered their meals, Pip began to look for an appropriate moment to make the proposal. As he judged an appropriate moment had arrived, he gazed at Jenny and spoke to her:

'We have been together for many months now, and I look forward to seeing you every day, I love you with all my heart.' As he got up from the table the ambience of the restaurant was ruined by the air-raid siren. Pip had no option but to take Jenny's hand and vacate the restaurant along with all of the other guests, following the instructions of the restaurant's manager who was directing them to the closest air-raid shelter. As they huddled together along with lots of other people from the surrounding area, they could hear the dull noise of bombs being dropped. The air-raid shelter was packed with people; babies cried; young children ran around the area; and adults sat chatting quietly listening to the background noise of the bombs dropping from the sky. No one had any idea how long this air-raid would last, although Pip did know that their meals would now be cold. 'Has the moment gone?' Pip thought, 'or should I take this opportunity to bring a bit of happiness into this horrible situation?' He mulled the idea over for a while, and then, whilst Jenny was sitting quietly chatting to the lady next to her, he took the ring out of his pocket and stood up. Jenny looked up at him as if to say, 'What is going on?' and then Pip knelt down and, holding the ring in his right hand, said to Jenny:

'Would you do me the honour of becoming my wife?' The air-raid shelter, Pip noticed, had suddenly gone very quiet, as people looked expectantly at Jenny. Her beautiful smile told Pip everything he wanted to know.

'Of course I will,' she said as a cheer erupted. Pip sat down and cuddled his fiancée as they waited for the all-clear siren to go, telling them that they would be able to leave the shelter. After what appeared to be an age but was in fact a couple of hours, the all-clear siren sounded, and, along with everyone else, Pip and Jenny climbed the stairs with a silent feeling of dread of what they would see when they left the shelter. They walked out into darkness, dust and rubble. Smoke filled the air, and all that they could do was to think about the lives that had been lost and the houses that had been destroyed whilst they had been safely in the shelter down below. When the couple arrived back at the hotel, they both sat in the bar, sipping a nightcap and chatting about the day's events. Taking Jenny's hand, Pip said:

'I don't want this to be a long engagement: war is here, we have no idea what can happen to us every day, I think we should begin to organise our wedding.' Pip was pleased when Jenny nodded her head in agreement.

'Life is for living,' she said.

The couple had a simple wedding three months later, in the spring of 1941. Although Pip's parents had been invited, they pointed out that it was a long distance for them to travel, so the few guests were mainly air force friends who raised many a glass to toast the happy couple. Pip and Jenny enjoyed the first few weeks of married life, Jenny knew how important a home was for Pip, given the nature of his job and the very few breaks in between flights that he got. The couple rented a small house near to the aerodrome, and Jenny soon turned it into a lovely home. As they settled into married life, Pip found that he was involved in more and more sorties which took him more and more deeply into Germany, and Jenny became much tenser as she watched the aircraft leave and return to the airfield.

Tragedy struck in 1943, when Pip was involved in a top-secret raid into the centre of Germany. The pilots had all been told that they had to fly much lower than normal to avoid the flak from the German anti-aircraft guns. Pip was leading his group as they headed towards Munich. The flak around the city was very heavy, and the searchlights made it relatively simple for the German army to fire at the aircraft. On a particularly difficult manoeuvre, Pip knew that his plane had been hit, but there was no engine damage, and he made the decision to push on to the target, rather than turning round and making for home. A second bout of flak hit the full side of his aircraft, and Pip felt a searing burning pain as one of the bullets shattered his leg. He could not control his plane, and it fell into a deep twisting dive with smoke and flames burning in the cold night air. Pip had no real option: for Jenny he needed to get out of this plane. He pulled open the hatch and managed to open the cockpit. With his parachute on his back, he managed to pull himself out of the aircraft. He drifted in and out of consciousness as he fell slowly towards the ground.

As the land came closer and closer, Pip braced himself for a difficult and painful landing. He had no idea where he was, he knew he couldn't walk far, he spoke no German, and he knew that his life now was in the lap of the gods. He quickly tried to pull in his parachute so that he was not such an obvious target. He looked around him for some cover and staggered towards some trees nearby, dragging his injured leg behind him. And there he slept, with no energy to move or to walk any further. He did not know where to go, and, as he crouched beneath the trees waiting for morning, he was aware that it would not be long before the German soldiers found him. As he expected, he was picked up in the morning by German soldiers on patrol. 'This is the end of my war,' he thought. For Jenny, things were equally bad: she had heard news that his plane had been hit, but no one had seen whether he had been able to get out of the aircraft or not. Nobody knew anything. Was he alive? was he dead? was he injured? All of these thoughts went through her mind. And she finished work in the early hours of the morning, she went home to their empty house and cried and cried, her heart breaking, not knowing what to think or believe.

Pip was one of the lucky ones. His injured leg was treated by a German doctor, and he was transferred to a prisoner-of-war camp where he lived out the rest of the war. Life in the camp wasn't easy, as his injury had left a permanent limp. He knew that he would never be in a position to try to escape from the camp and make his way back to Britain. Over time, news got back to Jenny that Pip was alive and incarcerated in a German camp. And so the young couple were separated for the remainder of the war. In 1945, when the prisoner-of-war camps were liberated, a very thin Pip was transported back to Britain. Jenny was overwhelmed at the sight of him and sobbed as she saw how fragile he had become at the hands of the enemy.

In many ways, the war had been kind to them both. They had met each other, got married and had both survived, unlike many of the British people. The pair had a happy and long marriage with three children, two sons and a daughter. Pip loved fatherhood and married life and cherished those close to him, but funnily enough he never talked about what happened to him. Many times his children would say to him,

'Dad, what was it like in the war? what did you do in the war? what was it like to be a prisoner?' Pip's answer to every question was always the same, every day, every month, and every year, always the same.

'I love my life, I love my family, I love my country, but I don't ever want to talk about the ghosts in my past.'

Meet the Authors

Karl Brockmann

Karl Brockmann was born in 1964 near the town of Mulheim, West Germany, whilst his father was serving in the British Army as a sergeant major. He works as a General Manager in the Motor industry, located in Kent. Over a decade ago he joined a WWII Living History Re-enactment Group in the south-east to live out his dreams of experiencing times gone by. He has met elderly veterans from various countries and listening to their varied experiences, combined with his own, sowed the seed for his WWII eastern front action novel, *Alles für Deutschland,* published 2012. Such was his excitement at publishing his first book, he carved out time for a follow-up title, *Panzer Storm.* His next novel *Battle of Bocage* is nearing completion.

Annie Coyle Martin

Annie Coyle Martin grew up in an Ulster village, trained as a nurse in Dublin, emigrated to Canada, attended Laurentian University and the University of Toronto, has worked in health-care management and in the Ontario civil service. She has been making up stories all her life. Her first published fiction was a short story, 'Jody', for a collection, *She's Gonna Be,* in the late nineties. Then *The Music of What Happens,* published in 2001, *To Know the Road* in 2011 and *Between Two Dusks* in 2013.

Julius Falconer

Julius Falconer, a retired translator and lecturer, is the author of several series of crime novels (eleven set in Worcestershire, eight in Yorkshire, including, most recently the 'Sherburn Trilogy', set in 1728 at Sherburn-in-Elmete and featuring the accident-prone vicar). He is widowed, with a married daughter, lives near Leeds and is full of brilliant ideas in which no one else is the least interested. His current project, nearing its end, is a translation of Immanuel Kant's famous (and infamously opaque) trilogy on the workings of the human mind.

Peter Good

Peter Good was born in Kenya and lived in Uganda, Kenya and Tanzania before moving to Rhodesia, where he joined the British South Africa Police Force. He served in the district sections, covering all aspects of policing and detective work from minor thefts to murders and taking the matter to local courts. His first book is set against this background. It was his children's continual asking about the highlights of his police career, combined with his wife's insistence, that made him write his first book: *NDLOVU The White Elephant,* published 2011. Peter and his wife Cheryl are happily settled now in Basingstoke, Hampshire - but consider Africa as 'home' and still miss the African 'bush night-noises'.

Neal James

Neal James began writing in 2007. Since then, he has released five novels and one anthology. He has appeared in the national and local press, and also at branches of Waterstone's and libraries in the East Midlands. An accountant for over thirty years, that training has given him an insight into much of the background required in the production of his writing. He lives in Derbyshire with his wife and family. Neal's books to date include *A Ticket to Tewkesbury, Short Stories Volume One, Two Little Dicky Birds, Threads of Deceit, Full Marks* and *Day of the Phoenix*.

Andrew Malloy

Stirlingshire-based author Andrew D Malloy began writing only in 2007, when he turned fifty. Since then he has had three novels published: *Frantic!* and its sequel, *Bible John – Closure,* are works of fiction, charting the lives and times of the detectives of Glasgow's Strathclyde Police Force and their struggle against deadly assassins and serial killers. Andrew's third novel is an autobiographical account of his father's life in football during the fifties and early sixties, the stunning *Memoirs of a Hard Man: The Danny Malloy Story*. Novel number four, *A Good Day to Die,* should be out soon. Malloy was delighted to be asked to contribute to this second Pneuma Springs anthology.

Steve Morris
Steve is a peripatetic teacher of maths, physics and chemistry. He lives in rural Wales close to the English border. In his spare time Steve writes stories. After they found their way into magazines and journals and resulted in an award, he had his first compilation, *In All Probability*, published in 2009. More darkly karma-themed short stories followed with *Jumble Tales*. Recently these were balanced out with *Out on Top*, upbeat stories of where things ultimately end the right way up despite the means. Steve's novel *Playing Havoc* takes an ironic look at a community's life after the world loses the use of all technology in one instant.

Neil Morton
Neil Morton took up short story writing whilst serving in the 1950s as a steward in the British Merchant Marine. Most of the vessels he served in being cargo ships, with no passengers to care for, there was plenty of time for him to record the seafarers, the sights, the sounds and the delights of faraway places, all of which appear in his first published work, *Drifting Beneath the Red Duster*. Neil lives in Melbourne with his Australian wife and family.

Ronald Ooms
Ronald Ooms is a Belgian journalist. He began writing for a local newspaper in 2007. Years later, he was signed up as a freelancer for one of Belgium's biggest newspapers. His first steps as an author came in 2009, when he started work on a book with WWII veteran Clancy Lyall, whose outfit became famous through the HBO hit TV series *Band of Brothers*. *Silver Eagle* was released in 2013. That year he was nominated for the Culture Person of the Year Award. In 2014 he released the Dutch version of *Silver Eagle*. After working for some years at a race-track, he started to report on Formula One for Belgian's *Autosport*.

Chris R. Pownall
Chris R. Pownall lives in Nottinghamshire, England. He began writing following his retirement from the James Walker Group of companies after a forty-year-long career, finishing as an industry marketing director, with responsibility for the global metallurgical

industries. Foreign travel and wide-ranging business experience provided a wealth of knowledge to draw on when his writing activities commenced. Chris has so far worked in the following genres: autobiography, social and industrial history and true life. His published books to date include *Funny How Things Work Out*, *Onwards and Upwards*, *Dane Mills Bosley* and *A Long Journey Back*. Chris also writes newspaper features and magazine articles.

Derek Rosser

Following a career as a jig and tool designer in the aircraft industry, Derek became interested in commercial computing and embarked on a second career as a systems-analyst. In 1988 he was given the option of early retirement, and this enabled him to pursue a lifelong ambition to write. He has had three books published by Pneuma Springs: *A Reluctant Recruit*, *Call Me Valentine* and *Earning a Crust*. Derek contributed to the Pneuma Springs' anthology of Christmas murders, *Terror, Tinsel and Turkey* (2014).

Avril Dalziel Saunders

Avril Dalziel Saunders released her first novel, *What's For Ye, Won't Go By Ye*, in 2006, followed by a sequel, *Chasin' That Carrot*, in 2008, the trilogy being completed with *Time Makes Changes* (2012). Avril was diagnosed with breast cancer in 2011. To raise awareness and encourage more women to have mammograms, she published her true story, *Mammograms Save Lives*, in 2012, profits from sales of which are donated to Macmillan Cancer Support and Breast Cancer Care. One of her short stories was made into a TV drama in 2012, titled *Broken Promises*. Avril worked for Thames Television/Teddington Studios. She is retired and lives in Surrey with her husband; she has one son, two daughters and four grandchildren.

Derek Smith

Derek Smith was born in Birmingham in 1931 and educated at Moseley Grammar School. He did his National Service in West

Germany serving with No. 256 night-fighter squadron, an experience that gave him the material for his first book, *No Cousin of Mine*. In 1956 he moved to South Wales and worked in the steel industry for the Steel Company of Wales. At the age of fifty he returned to university in Swansea, graduated with a degree in Integrated Sciences that gave him a teaching qualification and became a physics teacher at the Blake School in Somerset. His second book, *Wild Strawberries,* was based on the experiences of a nine-year-old war-time evacuee.

Louise Wilkinson

Louise Wilkinson is a retired history teacher who has currently written one book, *The Kipper Patrol,* about 608 Squadron Auxiliary Air Force. Her interests have always surrounded the period 1912-1957, and she is currently due to start the final year of her PhD researching into the Territorial Air Force. She has enjoyed turning her hand to fiction and is considering writing a novel in the future. In her spare time Louise enjoys exercising her two dogs and spending time with her family.

Other Anthology by PSP Authors

An Anthology of Christmas Murders - Terror, Tinsel and Turkey
Mobi eISBN: 9781782283614
ePub eISBN: 9781782283652
PDF eBook eISBN: 9781782283690
Paperback ISBN: 9781782283577

Short Description
Murder comes in all shapes and sizes. It also comes at inconvenient times. Christmas, for example. This anthology has all the classic motives: blackmail, revenge, lust, greed, anger... Murder by meat-hook, piano-wire, scarf, knife, hammer, golf-club, bullet, syringe ... It's all here, at your elbow. And there's more! Humour, intrigue, suspense...

CPSIA information can be obtained at www.ICGtesting.com
Printed in the USA
LVOW10s0719230815

451186LV00001B/5/P

9 781782 283959